Billions of people had died on the irradiated, daylight side of Earth. And, after the one-hour ...re, millions more had died from the ...stating super-hurricanes, enormous ...nd searing, continent-eating firestorms. ...rvivors of these disasters now faced ...vation and erratic, killing weather for decades to come.

John Norris, global troubleshooter, had frustrated the precise plans of a fanatic group of scientists two months ago. Now he was destined to deal with another power-seeking band of extremists. . . .

THE BURNT LANDS

Another Fawcett Gold Medal Title
by Richard Elliott:

THE SWORD OF ALLAH

THE BURNT LANDS

LANDS

Richard Elliott

FAWCETT GOLD MEDAL • NEW YORK

A Fawcett Gold Medal Book
Published by Ballantine Books
Copyright © 1985 by Richard Geis and Elton Elliott

Library of Congress Catalog Card Number: 85-90724

ISBN 0-449-12771-0

Manufactured in the United States of America

First Edition: October 1985

THE BURNT LANDS

PROLOGUE

In December 1991, the major powers of the world learned of a mysterious satellite, placed in orbit by a renegade team of brilliant Marxist scientists. Their satellite-control base was in the nation of Ubari, deep in the African desert, and they were employed by the fanatic Moslem dictator of Ubari, Abu Ben Salamat. The name of the satellite was Sword of Allah.

Aging financier Bradford Stoneman and his beautiful young wife were alarmed. The Stoneman corporations and banks had secretly loaned Salamat enormous sums of money for military adventures in exchange for exploitation rights in northern Africa. What was Salamat up to?

The United States government was alarmed. A CIA agent died when attempting to escape from the base with telemonitoring data.

The Russians were alarmed. During an attempted takeover of the satellite-control base, their helicopter fleet was wiped out.

1

President William Barr of the United States decided to send the CIA's top field agent, John Norris, to Ubari to conduct an undercover investigation of the base and the Sword of Allah.

In early January 1992, the leaders of the world, including Abu Ben Salamat, warned that the satellite possessed a super-powerful, plasma-beam weapon capable of destroying large cities. This weapon proved its capability during a test on an abandoned Israeli settlement in the Sinai, which was reduced to a cauldron of melted stone and brick by the blinding beam of fire. By means of remote-control, shielded cameras, the world's leaders were able to watch the slaughter on closed-circuit TV.

Salamat's demands were that Israel give up its occupied and annexed Arab lands, that the world assist in overthrowing the reactionary governments in Arabia, and that the Shah of New Persia be given arms and money to help forge a new Moslem empire.

It would avail the West nothing to bomb the satellite-control base. The Sword of Allah was preprogrammed to incinerate a string of the world's major cities and was itself invulnerable to space attack. Only Salamat's scientists on the base could change the satellite's deadly program.

But the renegade Marxist scientists had secretly devised different plans from Salamat's for the satellite they controlled. Their intent was to shoot the plasma beam into the sun, thereby destabilizing in a subtle, precise way, its hydrogen-combustion cycle. The result would be a short burst of solar radiation that would sear half the world—primarily the Americas. With the United States incinerated by the carefully timed solar flare, the socialist nations would then be free to develop and perfect the ideal world state that would last forever.

Bradford and Erica Stoneman were given advance warning, by their long-time mole in the CIA, of the possibility of a flare. Stoneman, after speculating heavily in precious metals and commodities during the night, flew with Erica to his well-stocked underground retreat in Maine.

Following the Salamat ultimatum, the president of the United States, William Barr, flew to Geneva to attend a gathering of world leaders.

At the base in Ubari, John Norris was captured by security forces, tortured, and finally brought, naked and bound, to the control room to witness the operation of the Sword of Allah's terrifying weapon.

At the critical moment, Norris freed himself, scrambled the final-command message, wrecked the control room, and escaped into the desert. He was subsequently flown back to the United States.

The Sword of Allah did shoot its beam at the sun, but the subsequent sequence of events was unforeseen. Huge sunspots appeared on the face of the sun, but the satellite initially failed to trigger its deadly solar flare.

Back in his apartment in Washington, D.C., John Norris learned the same night that the Sword of Allah had been overwhelmed and destroyed by missiles of another force—but not before its beam had shot a three-hour burst of plasma at the sun—the amount theoretically required to trigger the solar flare. As the first reports of the flare flashed around the world, he alerted the Director of the CIA.

Norris's interference with the satellite's program had caused a twelve-hour delay in the timing of the flare, resulting in the Eurasian half of the planet's being roasted in an intense bath of radiation. Billions of people were killed, tumultuous hurricanes swept the world, and vast firestorms engulfed Europe, Asia, and Africa. The horizon of radiation death crept toward the United States.

As reports of the catastrophe were being spread through the United States, John Norris saved Vice-President Julia Waggoner from a gang of murdering rapists.

President Barr was presumed to be dead in Geneva, a

victim of the flare, whereupon Julia Waggoner, the heretofore ignored vice-president, was sworn in as the new president, while devastating hurricanes and riots swept the nation. She named John Norris as her special assistant.

After nearly an hour, the deadly solar flare receded, and the sun returned to normal.

The North and South American continents were spared, but their governments were virtually paralyzed. Chaos gripped the nations. The United States was held together in the iron grip of Julia Waggoner's inspired leadership.

In anticipation of nuclear war, a secret underground retreat had been built by the United States government in southern Oregon. Because of the threat of nuclear strikes by the die-hard Russians who might blame the U.S. for Russia's destruction, the new President decided to move the seat of her government to this Oregon facility.

But a band of local Survivalists and anarchist libertarians had become aware of the huge, abundantly provisioned underground retreat, had captured it, intending to outlast the chaos and starvation and to emerge, years later, to build a new, libertarian country from the ruins and remaining population.

In his Maine retreat, Bradford Stoneman died, leaving his ruthless young wife, Erica, in full control of the still powerful Stoneman financial empire.

John Norris was called upon to evict by any means the fanatic Survivalists from the huge government communications and supply center in southern Oregon, as the government was almost powerless without it.

Norris succeeded in routing the Survivalists, but one of their leaders got away after a firefight with Norris.

Months later Norris barely prevented this man from arranging, with Erica Stoneman's help, the assassination of President Julia Waggoner.

Frustrated by the failure of her effort in America,

Erica Stoneman turned her attention to the depopulated, burnt lands of Europe, where a profusion of gold treasures, jewels, art, and precious machine tools remained, waiting to be looted.

CHAPTER 1

When John Norris entered the small, paneled conference room, he was surprised to find CIA Director Richard Soble in grim, low-voiced conversation with President Julia Waggoner. John's gray-green eyes darkened slightly and narrowed in anticipation.

Looking up, Soble said, "John, it's good to see you again." Gray-haired and tall, his normally thin face was puffy and slack. He looked like hell. He shook John's big hand. His grip was weak.

Julia Waggoner leaned back in her chair and smiled at Norris in welcome. She reached up to settle her blond wig more firmly on her bandaged scalp. She had been wounded during a local Survivalist assassination attempt a few days before. Now she was again 'hiding' in the huge underground emergency facility near Grants Pass, Oregon.

"John, Richard has flown in from Washington with some startling news," she said.

6

Norris sat beside Soble at the inlaid maplewood table. "All the news these days is startling."

He had noticed the red-edged folder before the president, and the videotape player and TV monitor in the corner. He knew this meeting wasn't about the food riots spreading throughout the country since rationing had been tightened. The unpredictable post-flare weather was making a hash of early food-crop farming.

"Is it about Albuquerque?" Norris asked. An Army base commander had taken over Albuquerque, declared the city a free state, and was recruiting starving Hispanics to create heavily-armed bands of "official" looters to scour neighboring areas for food and gasoline.

"No. General Tynan is handling that." President Waggoner tapped the red-edged folder. "This . . ." She sighed. "We have just received a communications package from a terrorist group in southern Germany. They may have Bill Barr. They want ten billion dollars ransom for him."

"Actually, ten billion in cash and ten billion in food and equipment and arms," Soble added.

"And," Julia Waggoner finished, "they want us to help them set up a government for the survivors in that region."

"How could he possibly be alive?" John asked. "The Swiss army in Geneva reported that his hotel took the sun's flare of radiation for the full hour of its duration. No one could have survived that. And the hotel later collapsed and burned in the hurricane winds and firestorms that swept Europe."

Richard Soble smiled wearily. "How, indeed? If he was in the hotel."

Julia Waggoner pushed the folder across the table to Norris. "Take a look. If Bill is alive, I'm honor-bound to get him back, at any cost."

Norris opened the top-secret folder. It contained front, rear, and side-view color photographs of President William T. Barr, naked, standing before a white panel marked off in feet and inches to indicate his height, and close-up views of his face and profile. There were two letters, one from Barr, signed, and one from a Hans Lauter, leader of the New German People's Alliance.

Norris studied the close-ups of President Barr's face. The face was lined, and his hair was shaggier. But he had shaved for the pictures. And there was a hint of a smile.

Still studying the photos, Norris asked Soble, "How do these check out?"

The CIA Director replied, "Probably taken with an old Rollie. Fuji film and paper. They were sold widely in West Germany. We've checked everything we can against Bill's medical records and photographs. Our analysts have tried dozens of feature overlays—nose, eyes, mouth, ears, chin, even the individual hairs that have been implanted since 1981. They're all positive."

John nodded. He read the handwritten letter from Barr. It was addressed to Julia Waggoner.

March 11, 1992

Dear Julia,

I understand you are president, now, which puts us both in an awkward position. I'm sure you're doing an excellent job and will do everything you can to resolve the problem my captivity here presents to the United States.

These people had planned my capture the moment they learned so many heads of state would gather in Geneva to deal with the Salamat threat. I foolishly decided to go out and throw a party the night we knew the satellite had been destroyed. That made their effort a lot easier. When that terrible flare of radiation from the sun hit the world, all hell broke loose.

Jimmy Flynn and I and a few Secret Service men tried to get to a deeper basement. We had to get away from that penetrating radiation. It was a horrible time.

We didn't get very far. I was the only one taken alive. My captors saved my life, with their knowledge of Geneva, and I have to thank them for that, I suppose.

I have to convince you, in this letter, that I am William Barr, and the only way to do that is to reveal knowledge about something only you and I could know.

There was no one present when I asked you to be my running mate in 1988. We were in my suite at the Imperial, on the 24th floor. We were in my bedroom, and you were wearing a green plaid skirt and coat, with a pale green blouse. Maybe it is called a shirt, since you wore a black string tie. I said, "Julia, I need you in the worst way," and you said, "Bill, I'm a married woman," and we laughed. When we sat down to talk about how to reveal your acceptance in the nomination for the vice-presidency, you took off your shoes because they were too tight, and you discovered a runner in your left stocking. You said, "Bill, you'll get every woman voter in the country if you declare a crash program to develop pantyhose that will give more than ten days of wear."

No one knows of that incident but you and I, Julia, unless you told someone. I have never before revealed it.

These people will be taking pictures of me to help convince you. I hope you won't be embarrassed to see them. On the next sheet of paper will be a full set of my fingerprints. And they're going to make a videotape of me if they can get the power generator going. We've been roughing it for two months, including some travel. I can't say anything about where we are, of course.

Hans Lauter will take care of seeing that you get this and will be the man with whom you'll negotiate. He's a very intelligent, ruthless young man, and very firm in his socialist beliefs. He'll be difficult to deal with.

I hope eventually to see you again, Julia, and to be back in Washington helping with the massive problems of our country and the world.

> Best,
> William Terrence Barr

John Norris flipped to the next page and saw a full set of fingerprints. He lifted questioning eyes to Richard Soble.

Soble nodded. "They check. Every little whorl and ridge."

Norris turned to the shorter letter written by Hans Lauter. "It was typed on an Olympia office manual, silk ribbon," Soble volunteered.

The letter said:

To now President Julia Waggoner, of the United States:

We of the New German People's Alliance hold your former president, William T. Barr, as prisoner and hostage. Enclosed are various proofs that he still lives.

We will release him to you in exchange for ten billion new American dollars in cash, to be deposited in the Zurich Credit Bank. Also, you must make available to us ten additional billions of dollars of credit so that we can buy from your country, or elsewhere if necessary, food, arms, fuel, and vital equipment of various kinds. Moreover, you and the United States government will make it your firm policy to assist us in establishing our government in southern Germany.

All this must be agreed to as soon as possible. We will have a representative at Wilhelm Platz in Stuttgart, May 1–7. If there is no representative from you or your government at that time and place, the body of William Barr will be delivered, with copies of this letter and the photographs and letter from William Barr, and other proofs, to the British government now located in Birmingham, at a time and place of our choosing. Your failure will become universally known.

Do not attempt armed attack or other typical American tricks in this matter. Send only one man who has full power to make the necessary commitments and arrangements.

Be assured we are utterly serious and determined in this matter.

> Most Sincerely,
> Hans Lauter,
> The New German People's
> Alliance.

Seeing that John Norris had finished reading, Richard Soble said, "The videotape is useless for determining location. The quality is poor, too." He took a remote control from his pocket and turned on the nearby VCR and TV monitor.

The poorly lighted scene that swam into existence showed William Barr, dressed in worn jeans and a thick, cable-knit alpine sweater, sitting in a bare corner of a log cabin. No window was visible. The camera did not pan left or right.

William Barr licked his upper lip as his eyes looked past the camera, to the left. He apparently got the go-ahead, for he coughed and said, "Hello, Julia. I hope you get this, as well as my letter. They want me to say something to further prove who I am. So. If Dick Soble

11

is watching, if he's still alive, this will have meaning to him alone.

"Dick, seven beats eleven any time." He grinned. "Remember?"

The lights failed and the picture went dark. Barr's voice said, "What? . . . So what do I do? . . . Okay. . . . Julia and Dick, they've blown the lights and don't want to tape outside in daylight because they think you could spot a landmark. So this is about all they'll be sending along. Hope to see you again soon. Good-bye for now."

The monitor screen went silent and black as Soble clicked off the VCR.

Soble said to Norris, " 'Seven beats eleven any time' is the punch line of a dirty joke Bill told me once, in the White House. It was the funniest joke I'd ever heard."

"You'll have to tell it to me sometime," Julia said dryly.

"It's very dirty."

"What did he mean by saying if you're still alive?" John asked.

Soble took a deep breath. He glanced at Julia and got a nod from her. "I've . . . I have congestive heart failure." He met John's gaze. "I've kept going lately on digitalis and diuretics. Bill knew I was reaching the end of the line."

Julia said emotionally, "You're a hero. You could have rested more. You could have had a year or more."

Soble shook his head. "I'd rather work."

There was an uncomfortable few seconds of silence.

"That's beside the point." Soble said. "John, I've recommended that you be the man to go to Stuttgart and deal with Lauter."

Julia nodded. "You are my senior special assistant."

John Norris wasn't surprised. He was the man who had risked death and managed to scramble the final programming of the Sword of Allah, the Moslem satellite armed to destroy cities and—as it turned out— destabilize the sun for one hour.

In that north African base, he had caused an unexpected, inexplicable twelve-hour delay of the intricately planned solar flare of radiation. He had thought the huge satellite was disarmed and rendered helpless by that final, irreversibly scrambled set of computer orders. But the actual result had been that Asia, Europe, and Africa had died, instead of North and South America and most of the Pacific Ocean. "The "wrong" half of the planet had been cooked.

Billions of people had died on the irradiated, daylight side of Earth. And, after the one-hour flare, millions more had died from the consequent devastating hurricanes, enormous tides, and searing, continent-consuming firestorms. The survivors of these disasters now faced starvation and erratic, murderous weather for decades to come.

The United States, largely because of new President Julia Waggoner's inspired leadership and organizational abilities, had managed to remain one nation and feed its people. Reconstruction progressed with amazing speed.

John Norris had frustrated the precise plans of a fanatic group of terrorist scientists two months ago, and he was now destined to deal with another power-seeking band of extremists.

He rose from his chair and stalked restlessly around the small, windowless conference room. They were on level nineteen in the president's executive suite, more than two hundred feet underground, below Wolf Ridge, in Josephine County, southern Oregon.

He stood well over six feet, weighed one hundred ninety pounds, and moved with pantherlike strength and grace. He was thirty-seven years old, until recently the best CIA field man Soble had, and he had seen more death, torture, and intrigue than a dozen agents. And still, he approached each assignment with a strange lust for what fate might bring.

John Norris asked, "What are my instructions?"

CHAPTER 2

Eᴙɪᴄᴀ Sᴛᴏɴᴇᴍᴀɴ sᴛᴀʀᴇᴅ ᴏᴜᴛ ᴏꜰ ʜᴇʀ Rᴏʟʟs ᴡɪɴᴅ-
shield and hated the cold, drizzling rain and the endless
puddles on the badly paved docks of Cardiff, England.

But a sense of urgency impelled her as she drove her
small party of managers and aides toward the ancient
World War II landing craft at the end of pier 30.

She stopped the Silver Cloud and stepped out. A gust
of cold wind whipped her long, wavy, blond hair. The
big black umbrella, quickly held over her head by a young
male aide, was almost torn from his grasp. Gusts of rain
pelted her hair and face.

Her blue eyes snapped with anger. She said viciously,
"Damn it, Greg, keep me dry!"

"Sorry, Mrs. Stoneman." He used both hands to hold
the umbrella against the sudden wind. His eyes showed
fear.

Erica wore her favorite long sable coat. She loved
sable. As the beautiful young widow of Bradford Collier

Stoneman, she had power and command over anything she wished. Instantly.

The more she delved into the Stoneman empire's holding companies—the interlocked lines of ownership, the conglomerates, the hidden chains of control, the agents, the bought politicians, the prostituted rulers, the leveraged media, the real estate—the more she realized just how impossibly powerful Brad Stoneman had been. And now, as his sole heir, his widow, the new chief executive officer of his empire, she realized how incredibly powerful she was!

Yes, immense wealth had been lost in the flare-ravaged lands, but some of it could be reclaimed. And a lot more wealth—which had belonged to others—could also be taken.

Eastern England was gone, having been licked, for a few horrible minutes, by the flare. London had suffered a million deaths, and millions more were dying of the effects of internal roasting. Their glands were all skewed and malfunctioning. The country had been mortally wounded.

Erica stopped at the gangplank before boarding the big, rusting hulk. The air rang with the sounds of reconditioning and repair. Work crews swarmed into the old L.C.T. With Erica's vast wealth and power, she could assume command over this work because of the men she owned in the new government. Prime Minister Edwin March's death in Geneva had been a special tragedy for England. He had been immensely popular.

Erica turned to her English manager. "Mr. Wright, it doesn't look big enough."

"It is deceptive, Mrs. Stoneman. It was designed to hold tanks, you see, and those areas are being altered to accommodate your armored Rover vans and three helicopters. There'll be plenty of room for everything, I assure you."

"And room for ninety-five men? And supplies?"

"Oh, yes. This expeditionary force will have fuel for three thousand miles of travel, all told. And it is anticipated that some food stocks and fuel will be found on the continent."

Erica nodded, studying the craft. "When will it be ready?"

"One week. Eight days at the most," Mr. Wright said. "The men are being organized in Axbridge. All top-rated mercenary soldiers and the experts in art and other specialties. You're getting the best, as well you should, for the money and shares you're promising."

"Are there other landing craft like this available? I want looting expeditions by the dozens, crisscrossing Europe, Asia, and northern Africa," Erica said.

Mr. Wright stiffened. "I would hardly describe—"

She laughed at him. "There's a new reality in place, didn't you know? I'm rerouting freighters from Panama and New York. They'll be floating bases for craft like this. I want a coordinated system of shuttle ships to carry the . . . loot . . . to our estates and warehouses in Trinidad and Tobago. If the true nature of this program is offensive to you, Mr. Wright, I can find someone to replace you."

Mr. Wright paled. "I shall carry out your orders to the best of my ability."

"And you'll be handsomely rewarded," Erica said. "Now, are there other craft like this, capable of ocean voyages?"

"We are scouting the entire United Kingdom. I'm afraid hundreds of Englishmen are already on the continent . . . looting."

Erica smiled and turned back to the Rolls. "Of course there are, but they can't get very far inland. They're disorganized, ill-prepared, and small-minded. When we go in, we go for the inner cities. We go for the treasures in museums, in bank vaults, in the sealed basement rooms of wealthy collectors. We go for precision tools,

17

spare parts, certain metal stocks, industrial diamonds. Your countrymen in their small boats are swarming the coast, scurrying around looking for diamond rings on rotting corpses. They can have those.''

She slipped back into the driver's seat. She said to the third man in her group, Sir Samuel TenEyk, who had not left the Rolls, ''I want you to sail in your yacht to South Africa. Three Argentinian freighters loaded with skilled workmen will meet you in Cape Town. You'll be in charge of preparing that area for colonists from Argentina who will follow in other ships. That country is better used than simply looted.''

Sir Samuel was stunned. ''That's a bold concept. I will of course . . . Will I have a title? I'll need a loyal force of armed men as well.''

Erica turned the Rolls to drive back to the luxury condominium building she owned in the center of Cardiff and had taken over as headquarters for her English and European operations. It was impossible to operate in London.

She answered Sir Samuel, ''Call yourself anything you like. King, if you like. Just remember the commander of your small army will be loyal to me, if royal push comes to Stoneman shove, and that the new South Africa will be owned, lock, stock, and barrel by Stoneman corporations and banks.''

Sir Samuel TenEyk said stiffly, ''Of course. And do you have similar plans for other prime areas of the empty lands?''

''Certainly. In due time, expeditions will leave Brazil, Mexico—perhaps even Los Angeles—for Taiwan, Japan, Hong Kong, North Korea, Arabia, and the Persian Gulf.''

Sir Samuel murmured, ''Breathtaking. Worthy of Bradford Stoneman at his prime.''

Erica smiled. ''Yes, I think Brad would approve.'' But then she frowned. She missed him. Old, cranky, demanding as he had been at seventy years of age, he had been loving, brilliant, shrewd, farseeing, and a force of character and personality she would never meet again. A part of her had died when those terrible strokes had claimed him in their underground Maine retreat, when it seemed likely the catastrophic solar flare would not end and the entire world would be destroyed.

Now she was alone, a virtual queen of the Earth, but alone in a way only the super-rich and powerful can be.

She glanced at Greg Albertson, her aide and occasional bed partner. His only value was his sweet mouth, agile hands, and fluttering tongue. He couldn't see past her unimaginable wealth, which petrified him, as it did most men. She reflected that it was a good thing she preferred to have oral sex performed on her. Greg wouldn't be able to keep an erection long enough to penetrate the cunt that ruled the world.

She laughed and ignored the puzzled glances from Greg, Sir Samuel, and Wright.

The car phone buzzed. She picked it up. "Yes?"

"Long distance from New York. Lane McDermott to Erica Stoneman."

"This is Erica Stoneman. Put him on." Lane was her number one man in the United States, as he had been for Brad. He knew all the secrets, all the plans. He was invaluable. She pulled over to the curb and parked. She heard a click and then the hiss of a long-distance connection.

Lane's voice came clear and strong. *"Erica? I have some incredible news. Are you in private?"*

"I will be in a second." She took a privacy mask from the car phone console and slipped it over the mouthpiece. When she brought the phone up to her mouth in a normal position, the mask adhered to her mouth and chin in a soundproof enclosure that allowed her to speak aloud but prevented anyone, even Greg, who sat next to her on the front seat, from hearing anything but a few low, muffled sounds.

She said, "All right."

"*Scramble. D-three-six.*"

She nodded and pressed special buttons on the elaborate console. "*Scrambled.*"

She heard a series of familiar wailing tones, and then the line cleared. Lane McDermott said, "*Do you hear me clearly, Erica?*"

"Yes, Lane. Do you still eat six apples a day?" The question was a confirming password. He had to answer, "I'm down to four this week." He did so.

She said, "What's so important?"

"*A special report from our man in the CIA. A terrorist group in southern Germany, maybe based in Stuttgart, says they are holding President Barr for ransom. They've sent photos, fingerprints, and a handwritten letter from him in which he gives facts only he could know.*"

"He's alive? Is he? Is the proof positive?" Erica's mind blitzed through possibilities, implications. . . .

"*The CIA specialists think so. Waggoner and Soble think so. She's sending John Norris over to negotiate. They want around twenty billion dollars for Barr.*"

"Bill Barr alive! If he gets back, Julia Waggoner is out, back to being a nothing vice-president. Bill, at least, cooperated with Brad on major foreign policies before the flare."

Lane said, "*We should be able to work with him a hell of a lot easier than with her.*"

Erica laughed, delighted with the news. "Oh, yes. Especially since she suspects I was behind that assassination attempt."

McDermott continued. "*The security lid is on this for now. No one but a very few in the administration, and the top congressional leaders, are supposed to know. Waggoner had to make a deal with the House and*

Senate leadership. They don't trust her to negotiate in good faith to get the president back. They fear she wants to continue as president, ruling by executive order in her declared national emergency."

"As a dictator!"

"Exactly. So they've forced her to send one of their own, Congressman James Lang of Missouri, on the trip with Norris. He's going to make sure Bill Barr stays alive and that the deal assures Barr's freedom."

"Isn't Lang one of ours?"

McDermott chuckled. *"Yes. He's been Stoneman-loyal since we made sure he was elected to his first term twelve years ago."*

Erica vaguely remembered the man. Short, energetic, a good speaker. Brad had seen him as a possible president—at least, a key committee chairman. Brad had made sure Jim Lang's friends and relatives prospered. Lang knew he was set for a fat job somewhere if he was ever defeated in a reelection, or if he ever decided to retire. Lang had voted the Stoneman way for his entire career.

Erica chuckled. "If something goes wrong in Germany, it could blow Julia Waggoner out of office, in spite of her precious national emergency powers."

Lane agreed. *"Yes, it's dynamite. We have to be very careful."*

"We win either way. If Barr is brought home safe and sound, Waggoner is out! If he's killed . . . then we get one of our people in congress to expose the truth. She'd have to accept impeachment or face a revolution."

Lane said, *"Yes, absolutely. And our man has further news about Richard Soble. Soble's heart trouble is worse, and he's close to dying. Waggoner has talked to our man secretly and will appoint him to head the CIA when Soble cannot continue."*

"Oh, how marvelous. Our fat little mole is getting up in the world."

"Things are going our way."

"Yes, and I'm going to make sure they continue that way. I'll call you back from headquarters. I'm in the Rolls now. We'll go over all this in detail."

"Fine. Scrambling out. Till later, Erica." Lane broke the connection.

Erica Stoneman put the car phone back in its cradle, made a pleased sound, exuberantly tossed her long, wavy blond hair, and turned to meet Greg's curious but wary brown eyes. She smiled and took a slow, deep, ecstatic breath. "Prepare yourself, Greg. I'm going to celebrate when we get to my suite. I'm going to require hours of your time and talent."

The two important Englishmen in the back seat exchanged amused glances. Greg flushed.

Erica didn't give a damn what any of them thought.

CHAPTER 3

HANS LAUTER ZIPPED UP HIS DOWN-PADDED JACKET EVEN further as he clumped along the narrow hallway of the chalet's attic level. He signaled to the guard in a small alcove. "Open. I must talk with him."

It was cold again today. Hans thought the weather would never change for the better. Southern Germany seemed cursed. For that matter, it was obvious God had turned His back on the common people of this world. How could organized religions survive this series of disasters? How could they explain the cruelty of their God of love?

The guard, Kurt Riste, rose from his chair and had to duck his head because of the low ceiling. Riste was six feet two. He asked Hans, "Have the Americans answered?"

"Yes. We'll have a meeting in an hour." Lauter could easily stand in the passageway. He was a small young man with shaggy brown hair and a precise, arrogant manner of speaking. He wore round, wire-rimmed glasses. He stroked his full beard as he waited.

Riste finally found the key in his pale, worn jeans and unlocked the padlock on the storage-room door. He drew his Luger and stepped back.

Lauter came forward and pushed the small door open. "Mr. President, are you awake?" He peered into the tiny room. A pale dawn light from a dormer window showed William Barr curled up in a cocoon of blankets on a mattress on the floor.

Barr stirred. "Yes." He emerged from the blankets, hairy chest bare to the waist. He wore only gray briefs. He shivered and reached for his ragged pants and shirt, the same clothes he had worn the day of the flare. He asked, "What do you want, Hans?"

Lauter went to the dormer window and checked the lock. He noted that recent dust had not been disturbed. He looked out at the small town of Waldshut a mile away, in the lower valley. A lucky town; it had been in the shadow of a nearby peak when the sun had spewed its hour of killing radiation two months ago. And this chalet had been equally lucky to have survived the terrible winds and to have been isolated from the track of the nearest firestorm.

The chalet's owners had not been so lucky, however; the flare had struck the houseful of people, roasting them in their own juices, bursting cans and bottles in the kitchen, exploding the burned-out Daimler's gas tank in a garage nearby. The fire had not reached the house.

This was a rare, quiet dawn. The usual tumbling, dark clouds were missing. There were now patches of blue sky. The wind seemed strong—the trees whipped spasmodically—but such winds had been common before the flare. Was it possible the weather could return to near-normal sooner than expected?

Hans turned to watch William Barr button his soiled white shirt. "Your government has responded. We just received a reply to our demands. They complied with our instructions in the letter. The correct time, the correct shortwave frequency; they even used the code we requested.''

Barr looked up, a spark of hope in his weary eyes. "What did they say?"

"Do you know a man named John Norris?"

Lauter observed the slight lifting of William Barr's stubbled chin, the momentary stiffening of his back, the quickly-drawn breath . . . and the attempt to mask those reactions with a sigh.

Barr said, "Yes." He pulled on his frayed pants. "Why?"

"He's the man they are sending to negotiate your ransom."

Barr nodded.

"Who is he? What is he?" Lauter asked.

William Barr decided to play it straight. He was at a disadvantage with Lauter in every way. "John Norris was a CIA field agent. I don't know what he is now."

"Ah. Would your government attempt a rescue?"

Barr smiled thinly. "I doubt it." He slipped on his tattered suit-coat.

Lauter said provocatively. "Or would the new president prefer you to die here as the result of a bungled rescue attempt?"

"Julia Waggoner wouldn't do that. And John Norris wouldn't go along with it," William Barr said firmly.

"No? John Norris is now represented to us as a senior special assistant to the president. Perhaps a taste of power has changed their minds," Lauter said.

"Hans, I know that's what you want—power," Barr said. "I know you'll do anything to get it. That's why I'm here. Your original plans were to grab me and blackmail the United States into abandoning attempts to destroy the Sword of Allah. You wanted to help Salamat, earn his gratitude, and be be given all of Germany to rule in true socialist splendor. Then—"

"We've had this exchange before, Mr. Barr."

"When we killed that damned satellite, you switched—"

"Shut your pig mouth, Mr. Barr, or Kurt will come in here and hurt you again," Lauter said.

Barr kept silent. Finally, he said, "I need to go to the bathroom."

"Yes, your privileges will continue as before. Kurt will take you downstairs to the outhouse in a moment. But first I want to know more about John Norris. Why would your Julia Waggoner make him a special assistant?"

Barr shrugged. He scratched his arm. "He was a good field agent. He got things done. I suppose he's been valuable to Julia during the situation they have in the States now."

"Describe him to me," Lauter ordered.

"Hans, I really do have to go to the toilet. Can't this wait a few minutes?"

"Pee in your bottle, Mr. President. Tell me about John Norris."

Fifteen minutes later, Hans Lauter went down the narrow, paneled stairs to the main floor of the chalet. He looked into the warm kitchen and saw Greta Verden sitting at the big table, drinking coffee with four others of the New German People's Alliance. A big iron wood-burning cookstove radiated heat in visible waves.

Greta's back was to him, and he appraised her for a few seconds. She wore a blue and yellow ski sweater, jeans, and boots. Her dark red hair was chopped short. He followed the line of her slender neck to her thin shoulders, to her narrow waist hidden by the bulky sweater, to her slim hips.

Greta was a beauty who tried to de-emphasize her body and face. She never referred to her years as West Germany's top fashion model. But she couldn't hide her startlingly lovely green eyes, the perfection of her nose, the full, sensual appeal of her lips.

And he knew the full, naked splendor of her body: her pale skin, long, slender legs, the firm, conical breasts with their swollen, knoblike areolae.

Greta was his lover. And now he had another use for her. Hans called, "Greta, I need to talk with you."

She looked around and smiled. She picked up her coffee mug and followed him into their bedroom.

"Close the door."

She obeyed. She asked, "Are you feeling passionate so early? Does success do that to you?" She crossed the room to sit on the bed. She walked around the large stain on the hardwood floor. An oval braided rug had been put down to cover as much of the discoloration as possible. A woman had died there. When the group had taken over the chalet, they'd found the burst, cooked body. Another corpse, that of a man, also ruptured from internal boiling, had been discovered in the bathroom. The tiles had been cleaned easily, however. Both corpses had been half-eaten by rats and dogs.

Hans stood by the window. "No." His mind sought correct approaches, proper phrasings for what he had to say. "I've just spoken with our prisoner. He told me he knows the man coming to negotiate details of the ransom. It is John Norris."

"So?" Greta arched her back and yawned, stretching. She hadn't really thought Hans wanted sex; he was too cool, too much in command of his emotions and his body. She respected that. It mirrored her own feelings. Sex was a tool for her to use when appropriate. The pleasure was incidental, pleasant, sometimes very intense, but not a factor which she could allow to matter.

She felt only contempt for men—and she had also known a few women so afflicted—who were dominated by their sex organs. Such people were weak, easily manipulated. When she had been famous a few years ago, she had deliberately humiliated many men by figuratively leading them around by their penises.

Sex with Hans was different. They both kept an inner distance, a final control, a perspective.

Hans said, "John Norris was the best field agent in the CIA. He is clever, strong, resourceful. He will be difficult."

"As we are. We will extract from the United States what we need. We will build a new, pure, socialist Germany," she said.

"Yes, but we must be careful with him. We must discover if he is really intent on negotiating the ransom, or if he has another aim."

"Yes, of course." She scowled. What was Hans getting at?

"I cannot go to Stuttgart to meet Norris," Hans said. "Where his plane lands will be his ground. He will have soldiers with him, maybe secret weapons."

Greta waited.

"I want you to meet him, insist he leave his plane and come here alone. I want you to guide him here, and during the time you are with him, test him, gain his confidence, in ways a beautiful woman deals with men. Make him yours, if you can. And if he has unexpected plans for us, or for our prisoner, I expect you to find them out."

"Ah, I am to seduce him." She regarded Hans mockingly. "You ask that of me?"

He smiled and pushed his glasses up his nose. "And, if necessary, you must be prepared to kill him."

Greta rose and went to Hans. "Naturally." She kissed him lingeringly on the lips. He didn't respond. His control was marvelous. She liked to test him on occasion.

She stepped back. "When do I leave?"

"Two days from now. Kurt and Helmut will accompany you. Take the BMW. John Norris is scheduled to land in Stuttgart on the morning of the sixteenth, eight days from now."

CHAPTER 4

SANDRA TIMMONS WONDERED WHY CEILINGS SIX AND A half feet high could seem so low and oppressive compared to the usual eight-foot ceilings in a normal room.

But nothing was very normal in this vast, twenty-four-level underground crisis center under Wolf Ridge, in southern Oregon.

She closed her book, *The Dynamics of the Debt Cycle*, and looked over at John Norris, as he did yet another series of fifty pushups.

He was startlingly naked. His sweat-glistening body seemed to dominate the small living room. His heavy breathing masked the ever-present buzz of the fresh-air vent in the wall by the brocade couch.

John's nakedness always disturbed her, even after more than a year of intimacy and an additional two months of living together in this cramped little apartment unit.

He was big—well over six feet—and beautifully, powerfully muscled. He wasn't tanned. Maybe that was part of the reason his nakedness was so disconcerting. His

skin was so white it somehow seemed to make his nakedness violent and unnatural. And there were the scars
on his body—from bullets, knives, torture. . . . The scars
really shook her up.

Yet Sandra shamelessly watched his large genitals
sway as he exercised. She smiled. It was amazing how
men had all their plumbing hanging out like that. So
vulnerable. She thought maybe that explained part of
the male psychology.

She said, "You've been doing a lot of that lately."
He'd been at it for the past two days, suddenly intent on
an even higher level of conditioning. As if . . .

A sudden chill ran down her spine. A faint nausea
claimed the pit of her stomach.

John grunted, "I need it." He reached his fiftieth
pushup and turned gracefully, easily, and began sit-ups.
He faced her now. His dark blond hair was damp with
perspiration. His gray-green eyes stayed on her as he
rose and settled back.

Sandra became self-conscious of her own body. She
wore only a semisheer blue nightgown in anticipation of
lovemaking after his shower. Her silky, silver-blond hair
tumbled free almost to her small breasts. She knew she
was too skinny, although John always said not, that he
preferred slender women.

She asked, dreading his answer, "Have you heard the
rumors that President Barr is alive in Europe?"

He nodded. He whispered, as he rose and fell,
". . . nineteen . . . twenty . . . twenty-one . . ."

"Are they true?"

"If he's alive, it has yet to be confirmed."

"What kind of an answer is that? Sounds like a government handout."

John stopped his sit-ups and said, "Sandy, the president has asked me to do something for her. I'll be away
for a few weeks."

The awful feeling in her stomach got worse. "What? Where?"

"I can't tell you." He stood up smoothly and padded into the bathroom.

Sandra clenched her small fists and followed him. Her nose stung with the beginning of tears. "I'm cleared for C-1 data. I'm one of her special aides, too!"

John stepped into the tub-shower enclosure, which was too small for him. He closed the shower curtain.

"Damn you!" Her throat tightened. "Let me guess! William T. Barr is alive, and you're going to risk your life to get him back! Is that it?" She felt tears rolling down her cheeks. She knew he wouldn't confirm or deny her speculation. The shower came on and she had to raise her voice over the spray. "How many times are you going to let yourself be used this way? How many times do you think you can come back in one piece?"

When he didn't answer, she whirled around and ran back into the living room, and then blindly into the tiny kitchen where she took down a bottle of vodka, yanked open the refrigerator, and took out the pitcher of orange juice. She made herself an impossibly strong screwdriver, tasted it, grimaced, and put it down. She heard the shower stop.

John called, "Sandy, I don't think this assignment is dangerous. It's just . . . negotiation."

She didn't believe that was all. And he couldn't tell her the rest. She picked up the drink and took a big swallow. She gasped at the explosion of heat in her stomach and at the strong taste. She emptied the glass in the sink. She went into the small bedroom.

There were no windows, only framed hologram views which gave a flawed illusion of depth and scenery. She hated them. She hated this underground warren of offices, apartments, storage rooms, machinery. . . . She wanted the government to move back to Washington, D.C.

When John entered the bedroom wearing a robe, she was in bed, arms crossed, still weeping.

He came to her and took her into his powerful arms. He brushed aside her silky hair and kissed her ear, because he knew she liked that, because it made her shiver and giggle.

Sandra shook her head. "Don't push my buttons. Damn you, I love you!"

John cupped her face in his big, gentle hands. "Sandy, love can't be a claim. It can't be a governor. I have to function. You want security—a man who will be with you all the time and live to be ninety and help you with all your needs. I want the edge, the gamble, the adventure . . . the risk of death. And after I've won, after I've pitted myself—my mind and my body and my skills— against those who oppose me, my president and my country, then I want intense pleasures of all kinds. I want the intensity!"

"You keep tempting fate."

He nodded. "It's my nature. I love you as much as I've loved anyone in my life, and love is a joy, a wonderful emotion, a wonderful state of being, but I accept that loving involves a terrible risk of loss. You cannot have the joys of love without the possibility of the pain of lost love."

"I know, I know, I know! Don't lecture!" She started to push his hands away from her face, then gripped them and kissed his palms. She pushed up the loose sleeve of his robe and kissed the ugly knife scar on his left arm that ran from elbow to wrist.

She lifted her head and asked, "When do you have to leave?" Her eyes showed anguish.

He took a deep breath. "Tomorrow," he said.

Sandra nodded. The dread still lurked in her belly. The fear. She smiled tremulously. "Then . . . let's make love intensely, now. So we'll have that at least." She melted into his arms and sought his mouth.

Briefly, in the following moments, Sandra was the

aggressor. She wanted to make this hour as memorable as possible, to brand herself in his memory so vividly that he could never forget.

She slid her hand inquisitively into his robe and found him growing hard. His size caused another ripple of awe and alarm as she couldn't quite believe she could take him in spite of the fact that she always had. She always would, as long as he was alive, and as long as he wanted her.

As long as he returned.

She played with him and laughed as he kissed her ear. She wriggled as he cupped her small breasts and tickled her nipples into small buttons. And she sighed as his mouth took them, and tongued them.

Sandra reached over to the bedside lamp and tapped the control for its lowest setting. The special lamp shifted to a rosy ten-watt glow. She liked to make love in a soft, dim light. The hard edges of reality disappeared and romance flourished.

She whispered, "Lie back." She kissed his deep, heavily muscled chest. His tiny, pebble nipples fascinated her. She licked them provocatively, and kissed the faint scars from the terrible, torture-inflicted burns he had suffered in Ubari only days before the flare.

Her soft hands caressed his hard, ridged belly, tracing muscles, sliding lower. She straddled his thighs and leaned over to kiss his "outie" belly button. Her breasts grazed his hips, his rigid organ.

Sandra glanced up self-consciously and saw a smile quirking around his lips as he watched. She giggled, "Voyeur!"

"Half the fun."

She experienced a shiver of delight and excitement and edged lower on the bed. She filled her hands with the thickness and power of him, and unhesitatingly took him into her mouth.

She liked the sense of control and mastery this act

gave her. She could feel his tightening, his intensifying pleasure. She could dictate to his body. She could make him hiss and grunt and thrash in the ultimate pleasure, if she wished. She could taste him and glory in that. She could deny him that, too.

Many times she had maliciously teased him to the brink, then made him lie still, frustrated, until she decided to begin again, and again bring him to the trembling, ragged edge of completion, only to take her mouth away and watch his huge organ stand in towering, pounding need.

They both knew she was punishing him, in her way, for not being the man she wanted, for being John Norris. John let her be bitchy that way, and his indulgence made her even angrier.

Now she considered doing that again, but knew this was a special time, a precious, loving, good-bye time.

She gave him pleasure with her mouth, but only for a minute. Then she crawled up his big, powerful body and let her belly press and warm him, and kissed him and whispered her desire.

John silently turned, holding her, and came over her. He knew how to arouse her, too, with his mouth on her breasts, and lower . . . lower . . until her breath caught and the simmering in her loins became urgent and she reached blindly for him, urging him up.

He loomed over her, supported easily on strong arms, massive shoulders, thick, powerful legs. Then she opened to him and gave a whimpering groan as he entered. She gasped and moaned and sighed and undulated under him as he moved in her.

Sandra's mind roiled with lust and anxiety and adoration. She quivered and panted spasmodically, helplessly, almost ashamed of her primitive submission, her swift climax. She clutched him and kissed him and cried out, letting her inhibitions peel away, as he continued to move, to thrust with such power and precision and skill.

She whispered, "John . . . John . . . John . . ." as a plea, somehow, to never leave. Hopeless. She clung to his neck and succumbed again, sweet moments later, to the frothy tide of pleasure.

But this time he was with her, now plunging with increasing ferocity and lack of control, letting go, letting go! He was breathing fast, sucking great lungfuls of air, groaning, gutteral in his lust, his thrusts becoming savage, total, jolting her, ravishing her.

She cried out, wanting this golden, glorious, overwhelming moment to never end!

But the rush of those fevered, agonized, intense instants ended, and too soon she felt the wave of passion, of sensation, of utter transport . . . fade. It was gone and she was lost, terrified she would never experience it again, terrified that this superior man, this enigma named John Norris, this man she loved, would never return.

CHAPTER 5

Erica Stoneman looked down on the devastated city of Rouen as her helicopter flew low through torrential rain. She could smell the stink from the city's 145,000 rotting corpses. The late winter cold had delayed decomposition, but now, with this warped spring coming on, the bodies were more than ripe.

They had been horrified when they disembarked from the L.C.T. in Le Havre. The harbor was a cesspool of disintegrating human and animal flesh, polluted beyond belief. The few survivors in the city had dumped thousands of corpses into the bay before giving up, more concerned with trying to resist the invasion of English looters who came soon after the end of the monstrous post-flare storms.

The English underclasses had swarmed into London and the eastern coastal lands before venturing across the channel.

The deadly radiation had lasted only five to fifteen minutes in central France during that terrible dawn, but it had taken only five minutes to kill ninety-nine percent of the people. The human body could not survive more than two or three minutes of internal broiling. Only a few, sheltered luckily by hills fairly deep underground, or protected by the heavy deck and hull plates of ships in Le Havre's harbor, had survived even that relatively short flare.

Western France had been spared the horrible death from the sun, but the terrible storms and massive killer tides that followed had devastated those areas. Government was virtually nonexistent.

The French survivors were looters, too, of course. Everyone on the continent had to be a looter to survive.

Erica consulted a map and indicated to the English pilot that he should fly north. That section of Rouen seemed to have escaped the hurricane-powered firestorm which had burned most of the small city, and there were some large machine-tool plants there, according to the lists made up by her Cardiff researchers. Diamond-tipped cutting tools were going to be more precious than diamonds themselves, and it would be years before production bottlenecks were alleviated and transportation restored to permit an adequate flow of such tools in the United States and Central and South America. In addition, the new colonies would need a supply of machine tools of every type.

Erica liked this kind of adventure. She knew it was dangerous for her, but she couldn't stand to be cooped up in Cardiff or back in the States while this vast opportunity presented itself—a gigantic once-in-a-lifetime chance to see and personally supervise the selective looting of a dead continent.

And, of course, the matter of President Barr would require her on-the-spot attention.

There would be time later—years and years—in which she would concentrate on macrostructuring a vast new power complex in the new world, the tremendously altered world as it now existed. But now . . . now her youth would be served.

Through the helicopter windows, streaming with rain, she saw what she wanted to see, then switched on the intercom. She had learned early not to try to shout too often over the roar of the helicopter engine, the added drumming of the vanes overhead, and the wild lashing of wind and rain. She said, "Cyril, circle this area for a few minutes."

The pilot nodded and began a slow turn.

Erica adjusted her earphones, switched from the intercom circuit, snapped on the radio, and brought the special privacy microphone mask to her mouth. "Rouen One to Zebra One. Over."

The voice of her task-force commander, Miles Webster, crackled in her ears. *"Zebra One. Come in, Rouen One."*

"Miles, the Gourmet Tool Works are intact. Send a van and truck there when you get here. How far away are you?"

"About forty klicks, I'd say. Two hours, unless we run into something unexpected. By the way, we found a village store with a cellar full of tinned goods. There are a lot of downed trees and poles on the road, you know. This damned weather—"

"Yes, I can see! I'll fly on to Paris for a preliminary look. I'll meet you here in two hours or find you on the road. Any armed resistance?"

"Not since Harfleur. Haven't seen anything alive."

"Fine. Out." Erica switched out of that frequency. She took a notebook from a pocket in her snug flight suit and flipped to a special page. She held it so the pilot could not possibly see it or read the new radio frequency she intended to use.

This was the shortwave setting for contact between the United States government and the terrorists who held President Barr. The frequency had been provided by Edward Marin, her invaluable mole in the CIA. She punched in the numbers and flipped the cover on the powerful radio console.

She tapped the pilot on the arm and pointed up, taking the mask from her mouth long enough to shout, "Ten thousand feet! Paris!"

He raised an eyebrow, but nodded. The armored helicopter began to climb. He wasn't worried about fuel, and there were no other craft in the skies. The buffeting winds and rain were not a factor. This was the finest all-weather copter in the world.

Soon after that height had been reached, Erica began broadcasting, with a directional beam, toward southern Germany. "Calling Hans Lauter. Calling Hans Lauter. Come in, please . . ."

It took fifteen minutes to make contact. They were flying over the suburbs of Paris when a response crackled weakly in her headphones. *"Lauter here. Who is calling?"*

"Someone who knows you have President Barr."

"Who are you?"

"I can't tell you now, over the air. I'm in France, coming in your direction. I'll contact you again, but on a new frequency . . ." She gave him a setting, repeated it, and asked, "Did you receive that?"

"Yes. How did you know—"

"I can't talk to you now, Mr. Lauter. The United States may be monitoring this frequency. I'm beaming toward you, but you're sending in all directions. Remember that. I'll call again in a day or two. Please don't make any hasty deals with the United States. I can offer you more than twenty billion in the long run."

Lauter said only, *"I doubt it, but you have time. Out."*

Erica smiled and switched off that frequency. She motioned to the pilot to go down. From this height,

Paris was a blackened smear glimpsed through rents in the fast-moving low cloud cover.

A few minutes later, they dropped carefully through the boiling dark clouds into a torrential world of wind and rain.

She knew the post-flare winds had reached beyond two hundred miles an hour, but their power and destructiveness were not clear to her until now.

The Eiffel Tower had been blown down; only a third of it stood, with the rest a twisted mass of girders fallen east onto the surrounding park and boulevard.

The city was a tragic crisscross of fire-blackened ruins. The twisting, looping Seine seemed dead, with bridges down and no boats moving. There was no sign of life anywhere.

Erica flinched from the sight below. She had visited Paris often in years past. She had loved the magnificent old city and its people. Now its corpse brought home to her as nothing else had—not even the sprawling, ravaged city of London, with its human maggots digging in its guts—the terrifying extent and finality of what had happened to half the planet during that awful hour, two months ago.

She stared down and felt sad and elated. This vast world tragedy was beyond recall, beyond mending; the world's fate had abruptly, irrevocably, changed—and she was the architect of the new future!

Erica Stoneman flipped an overlay over a map of Paris and studied the sites marked for inspection. She looked down. There was the Arc de Triomphe . . . and there! By God! The Louvre appeared undamaged! The priceless art in that building had to be taken and preserved.

She felt a spine-tingling frisson of delight and exaltation. By God, she was going to own the whole world before she was finished!

CHAPTER 6

THE BIG NAVY VTO, ITS WINGS ROTATED TO VERTICAL, its propjet engines clawing at the sky, sank slowly to a landing close to the center of Wilhelm Platz in Stuttgart.

The large square of ruined gardens and lawns had been difficult to find in the long-shadowed, burned city. Their flight from Sheffield had been delayed by bad weather, and freakish head winds had slowed the plane over France. But here, incredibly, the sun was shining, just beginning to set behind the nearby Black Forest mountains.

Congressman James Lang, wearing a navy jumpsuit and special bulletproof vest under his heavy flight coat, sat in his bucket seat, peering out at the devastated city. Here and there, a building or a neighborhood seemed undamaged, for no apparent reason; the firestorms, driven by winds of hurricane speed, had whipped in mad paths across the industrial city, before being quenched by monsoonlike rains. On the outskirts, in the heavy manufacturing areas, small mountains of coal still burned deep within themselves, sending up twisting columns of smoke.

Lang turned to John Norris, who sat on the other side of the utilitarian military cabin. He shouted over the rumble of engines. "You see anyone?"

John shook his head. He had been conferring with the marine sergeant, the leader of the five heavily armed soldiers who had accompanied them on the plane. He and the sergeant looked out at the square. Norris said, "One man by the statue . . ."

It was May fourth, well within the time frame for the meeting with Lauter.

The plane's wheels touched and crunched into a bed of struggling, unattended spring flowers. The wheels sank into the rain-softened ground. The pilot slowed the engines. He kept them vertical: the only possible take-off from this place was straight up.

Jim Lang stood up, grateful for the relative quiet, and walked toward the locked exit door.

"You don't go out yet," John said loudly. "We wait till we're contacted." He gestured to the marines. "Deploy—"

"I just wanted to stretch my legs! We've been five hours in this mixmaster. I'm a member of Congress, for Christ's sake, not some flunky! I am entitled to some courtesy and respect."

But John simply stared at Lang with calm, contemptuous gray-green eyes and said, "You could get picked off. We'll sleep inside tonight."

"Can't we use the radio to contact whoever is out there?"

"We'll try. But—"

A rifle slug hit the plane's armored side and splanged away. Lang cringed. The report echoed faintly nearby.

The pilot called back, "Want us up?"

John called, "No. Not unless we start taking heavy caliber rounds."

42

The plane was invulnerable to all but antiaircraft and antitank weapons. It would be a sitting duck for a small missile or cannon fire.

John's decision was a gamble. But whoever had fired that rifle was foolish to have wasted a bullet if he had anything bigger.

The marines were at the bulletproof windows, peering out at the surrounding buildings through binoculars. One marine called, "Sir, there's some fighting going on over there."

Norris crossed to a window and looked out. "Firefight." They could now hear small popping sounds and an occasional heavier-caliber gun.

John said, "They may be having a jurisdiction problem."

Representative Lang asked, "What do we do?"

John considered. "We have supper."

"But whoever is supposed to be meeting us may be in trouble," Lang said.

John took a deep breath. "Okay, you go out and find out. Do you speak German?"

James Lang flushed and kept silent. What had seemed, back in Oregon, a thrilling opportunity for prestige, a potential bonanza of publicity for himself, had turned sour and become an endless series of humiliations at the hands of Julia Waggoner's so-superior special assistant.

Lang settled back onto his bucket seat and stared out of the round window at the deepening darkness.

John called to the pilot, "Kill all lights. Open the door."

Two marines slipped out to take up nearby guard positions. They carried special night rifles and tiny, devastating body-heat missiles.

In the darkness of the cabin, John switched on a Secret Service com set. It hissed on its preset frequency. Lauter's terrorists possessed at least one com set, taken from the dead men of President Barr's Secret Service, and had decided on this method of initial contact.

The sergeant passed Congressman Lang a self-heating dinner pack and a can of self-heating coffee.

The battle out there in the ruins ended. Total darkness closed in. The engines continued to turn over in readiness for possible emergency takeoff.

After half an hour, John called to the pilot, "Kill the engines." An hour of idling would waste too much fuel; they had to have enough for a nonstop flight back to England, as well as a margin for a high lift to establish satellite communication with Oregon.

The muted rumbling stopped.

In the silence, the only sound was the sipping of coffee, a low-voiced conversation among the marines inside, and the continual hiss from the radio.

Lang didn't care to speak to John Norris, and he thought it beneath him to try to buddy it up with the young, grim-faced marines.

Abruptly, a woman's voice blared from the radio. *"The American plane. Hello. Hello."*

James Lang fumbled in his coat for his tape recorder.

John took the com set off the map table and brought it to his mouth. "Norris here."

"Yes. Hello. I am here as the representative of The New German People's Alliance."

"Fine. Do you want to come to the plane, or do we meet someplace else?"

"We will meet at six tomorrow morning. I will tell you where, tomorrow, before you leave your plane. Are you alone, John Norris?"

"No. I have with me Congressman James Lang. And I have five marines, a pilot and a copilot," John said.

"You were to come alone. We accept your marines and the pilots as necessary to you. What is the function of the congress man?"

"The president required me to take congressman Lang. He is an observer and a close friend of President Barr's. The marines will guard the plane."

44

There was silence. John waited for a moment, then put the com set back on the map table. It hissed quietly.

Lang started to say something but was cut off by the woman's voice. *"Your President Barr is not in Stuttgart. He is being kept in a place only I can take you to. I have a car. The congress man cannot go."*

Lang grabbed the com set and pressed the "transmit" button. He said loudly, angrily, "I have to go along! What kind of a trick is this?" He glared at John.

The woman responded. *"It is you who are trying to pull the tricks! The instructions were clear!"*

John took the small radio from Lang and broadcast, "President Waggoner decided to send Congressman Lang at the last moment. We have been sending a shortwave message to Hans Lauter for two days advising of this. James Lang, I repeat, is a close friend of President Barr's and will be able to make a confirming identification. He must accompany me."

"The instructions—"

"Lang comes along, or we leave now. Those are my instructions." John released the button and called to the pilot, "Start the engines."

Lang said, "Just a minute—"

John silenced him with a look.

The woman did not respond until after the plane's engines whined and sputtered to life.

"Very well. I have been on the road and waiting here, and have had no contact with Hans. But you two must be searched for weapons tomorrow morning. You will not be armed during the trip."

John replied. "Understood. Speaking of that, what was all that shooting about a few minutes ago?"

"That was very little. Some looters admired our car. We had to kill them."

"Is it likely to happen again?"

"It is always possible. Your landing has attracted

some attention. But we will protect you. When we meet tomorrow morning, you are not to be armed!"

"I agree. I will turn on this radio tomorrow morning at five-thirty. Anything more to say?"

"No. Have a good rest, capitalist pigs."

John laughed and switched off the com set.

CHAPTER 7

AT PRECISELY SIX THE NEXT MORNING, THE HISSING COM set quieted with a carrier wave, and the voice of the woman with a German accent blared, *"John Norris."*

John put down his can of hot coffee and picked up the small, short-range radio. "Norris. Where do we meet?"

"You will walk south across the square to Schaumburg Strasse. Walk south on that street for two blocks."

"Now?"

"Yes, now! And you are not to be followed by your marines!"

The marine sergeant put a blunt finger on the street map before him. The map was a blowup from a very recent satellite photo of the city and pictured the place where they had landed, Wilhelm Platz, and the blocks surrounding it, in great detail. "Sir, we won't be able to cover you once you're past the corner," John said. Schaumburg Strasse angled to the west from its southeast corner connection with the Platz.

James Lang stood by nervously. "We are going to carry guns, aren't we?"

John sighed. "No. We obey their instructions. We're going to be searched once we make contact. They're watching the plane. So we take only some rations and the case of equipment for exact, technical identification of President Barr. That's our deal."

Lang huddled deeper into his heavy flight coat. He peered out of a window. It was a cold morning. A gray sky wept a fine mist.

The sergeant spoke into his own com set to his two marine guards outside. "Norris and Lang coming out. No fire unless the g's start it. Keep your positions."

One of the outside marines answered, "I have one in my h.s. scope. He's in the left-corner window, second floor, building one, sector nine. He's got a rifle."

"Watch him. Lock on. Don't fire unless he fires," John said. He stuffed a dozen meal packs into his many-pocketed, zippered vest, picked up the large briefcase, and moved to the plane's locked and armored door. Lang hurried to load up and join him.

They jumped three feet to the soft ground and slogged through the muddy flower garden and a patchy, ankle-deep lawn. The grass was leprous and wild. Their breath fogged before their faces. The sweet smell of rotting flesh permeated the wet, frigid air.

John said, "Keep your hands out of your pockets."

Lang obeyed, but said, "It's cold!" He had forgotten his gloves.

There were no living people in sight. Abandoned and smashed cars littered the streets. There was no sound except a faint creaking in the distance. A dog howled.

They left the square and crossed the street.

Lang muttered, "Christ, this is eerie." He looked into a blue-white Porsche which had smashed into a bakery window. He recoiled from the putrescent corpse in the driver's seat. It had been a woman, and it had been partly eaten before it had spoiled too much for even the starving dogs and rats.

He backed away and almost stumbled against the jagged remnants of a grocery-shop window. "Damn!" He gaped at the shambles inside the store. The floor was ankle deep in ruptured, exploded containers of food, all of which were now spoiled and rotting. Glass jars, too, had exploded. The fierce radiation flare had caused all liquids and moisture within its penetrating reach to steam and boil. The internal pressures had burst every can and bottle and jar in the store.

Norris and Lang had traveled almost one block down Schaumburg Strasse when a tall young man armed with a Luger emerged from a doorway ahead of them. He wore a camouflage jacket and pale, worn jeans. He had on new brown boots. He said, in thickly accented English, "Here! Into this store you must go." He gestured to a shoe shop.

A second gunman appeared. He carried a hunting rifle. Norris, Lang, and the terrorists were hidden from the plane by the angle of the street from Wilhelm Platz.

The shop's plate-glass door had been shattered. The steel frame was bent. Norris and Lang entered the store and saw a tall, beautiful, red-haired young woman watching them from behind the counter. She wore a quilted ski jacket and ski pants. She held a Soviet MAK-18 automatic rifle.

She said, "Stop there." Her pale, freckled skin showed no makeup. Her eyes were startlingly green.

John noted that she handled the MAK-18 with casual confidence. She had fired it often and well, he concluded. He was intimately familiar with the weapon.

The two German gunmen had entered the shoe store behind Norris and Lang.

James Lang was relieved that there were no rotting corpses in the shop. He was feeling sick.

The redheaded young woman said, "Which of you is

John Norris?'' She looked at John. There was no question in her mind.

He said, ''I am.'' He nodded at Lang. ''And this is—''

''I know who he must therefore be!''

Greta Verden was impressed by John Norris, in spite of her bias. She sensed his strength under his bulky coat. He was big and tall and strong. There was something frightening about the smooth grace of his walk and movements, something disturbing in his calm, gray-green eyes. Something she wouldn't identify stirred in her lower belly.

She said abruptly, angrily, ''Put down that case! Step to the left. No, you, Lang, you go to the right. Three paces. Take off your coats—slowly!'' She moved the MAK-18 menacingly.

John and Representative Lang were searched thoroughly by the two young men. The leather briefcase was brought to Greta. She opened it and carefully inspected the tiny chemical refrigeration unit, the medical syringes for samples of blood, the special cameras, the papers and instructions. She looked up, smiling. ''This will convince you of your president's identity, all these testing things?''

John said, ''It'll be the scientific evidence they need in Oregon and in Washington, D.C.'' John nodded at James Lang. ''We both know William Barr, but we could lie.''

''Ah. Even you are not to be trusted. Governments are the same everywhere, aren't they?''

John nodded. ''Because people are the same.'' He asked, ''Who are you? What's your name?''

''I am Greta.'' She inclined her head toward her companions. ''The tall one is Kurt, the other is Helmut. Each of us is very good with guns.''

John said, ''Representative Lang and I are here on most important business. Can we get on with it?''

Greta smiled. She liked John Norris and did not want

to like him. She fastened her gaze on Representative James Lang. Of what use was this small, frightened man? How could he be used? This was a matter for Hans. She would concentrate on this John Norris.

She said, "You may put on your coats. We will keep your wonderful meal packs. We go to our car, now."

They walked, single file, south on Schaumburg Strasse, Kurt in the lead. Helmut and Greta brought up the rear. John had been allowed to carry the briefcase.

James Lang ventured, "This doesn't look so bad. The city, I mean." They were in an unburned strip of blocks. "Were all the people killed?" They passed an overturned city bus. It held only the green-uniformed driver. His head, exposed to the weather by smashed windows, was mostly skull.

Helmut muttered, "Ninety-nine percent."

"Well, in a city of seven hundred thousand, that means about seven thousand people are still alive. Where are they?"

"Looting. Killing each other over possession of a market, a shop, a . . . what you say . . . a supermarket."

Greta hissed. "Shut up! Keep silent! You are both fools!"

Helmut flushed and prodded Lang forward at a faster pace.

Their car was a black BMW sedan. Helmut drove it out of a locked garage.

Greta had posted Kurt, with the MAK-18, down the block from the garage. She took a pistol from her ski jacket and motioned Norris and Lang into the backseat. She sat uneasily to the right of John, her pistol pointing at him from her lap. She seemed tense.

Kurt joined them on the run and climbed into the front passenger seat.

Helmut drove fast through the dangerous streets. He swerved constantly around burned cars and trucks and bodies. He stayed on the wide boulevards as much as possible, as they allowed more room for maneuver. Several times he had to bump the heavy car over rotting corpses. He kept a southerly direction.

They passed through a devastated sector of the city. Here some buildings had exploded from rupturing gas lines or from the superheated air of a firestorm.

In order to make its way, the sturdy, beautifully engineered sedan rocked over rubble, timbers, and remnants of burned furniture. Even so, Helmut often had to detour down side streets, doubling back in a circuitous route, as if in a nightmarish maze.

The side streets were the worst: there, the sickening smell of rotting flesh was strongest, and the bodies more numerous. During those terrible moments of dying, everyone seemed to have struggled desperately to get outside, to get away from the place where the radiation had first begun to cook their flesh.

There were sickening sounds as the tires rolled over softened, liquescent corpses. Everything was wet from the continuing mist.

James Lang kept whispering, "My God . . . my God . . ." He held a handkerchief to his mouth and nose.

John asked Greta, "How long will it take to get to President Barr?"

She shrugged. "If we are not interfered with . . ." But she didn't give a time.

Helmut gained the suburbs of Stuttgart and, soon after, managed to gain access to the autobahn. The awful smell disappeared and James Lang rolled down his window a bit.

The six-lane autobahn rose above the surrounding land. There had been light traffic that dawn when the clouds had miraculously melted away, and the glaring sun radiated death to everyone in its light. Most of the trucks had gone out of control as the drivers realized, too late, they were being cooked to death, and they had plunged through the railings and careened down the embankment, to ditches below. Some had swerved, rolled over, jackknifed. All gas tanks had exploded and burned. Every vehicle was a blackened ruin.

Helmut was able to speed along nicely, with only occasional radical moves to avoid a two-lane wreck or small pileup.

"Gasoline must be hard to find," John said.

Greta nodded. "We have reserve cans in the trunk. But we are a target. Any moving car is now a great prize." She kept tapping her fingers on her thigh. Her green eyes darted from John to James Lang and back to John.

John kept his eyes on the road and the approaching intersections and overpasses.

The ambush came as they were speeding past the fire-ravaged town of Kirchheim.

Two burned-out trucks and a car completely blocked the southbound lanes. Helmut muttered, "Gott verdammen!" and slowed the BMW.

John leaned forward and peered intently at the blockage. He commanded, "Stop! That VW has been moved. It's been dragged to—"

A spray of automatic rifle slugs stitched the windshield. Kurt's blond head snapped back and the left rear of his head erupted with a spattering of bone and gray brain material which peppered John and Greta.

James Lang screamed—a high-pitched woman's sound. Helmut twisted the wheel and spun the car in a professional, skidding, 180-degree turn. Greta scrambled around, as the car was turning, to get a shot at the attackers.

Simultaneously, John lunged forward and reached over the front seat to grab the MAK-18 from Kurt's spasmodic hands.

The car lurched to a stop—a frozen moment—as its momentum was used up, and before Helmut could shift and accelerate.

More quick rifle shots smashed into the upper part of

the big sedan. The rear window spiderwebbed and showed ragged holes. John realized the shooters were deliberately aiming high to avoid hitting the gas tank and the engine. "Keep low!" he shouted.

Helmut gunned the powerful car. The engine roared and the sedan lunged back the way they had come.

But the ambushers had anticipated this maneuver. Two men had risen from the right ditch beside the highway when the BMW passed them and squealed into its turn. Now they opened up on the car from the side. Heavy-caliber slugs ripped into the doors and windows. The BMW jerked spasmodically from a stray bullet that cracked its distributor.

James Lang screamed again and sprawled loosely against John. Lang's left arm was shattered and there was a hole in his flight coat. Red froth suddenly appeared on his lips. His breathing was ragged and wet. "I'm . . . it hurts!"

The big car staggered forward with continuing, increasing speed. But Helmut was grunting with agony from the driver's seat. He was slumped forward against the wheel, dying. His foot was jammed down on the gas pedal.

Greta seemed unhurt. She singlemindedly smashed a loose, gaping hole in the limp rear window and emptied her pistol at the two men.

John realized the car was angling to the right and would, in a few seconds, plunge off the concrete into the deeply gullied center strip.

Bullets continued to whip past the roaring, jerking car. The engine fought itself.

John reached for Helmut and pulled the young man aside, away from the steering wheel. Helmut jerked sideways against the body of Kurt. Helmut was convulsing helplessly. He had taken a bullet in the neck. Part of his spinal cord was gone.

John grabbed the wheel and kept the car on the road.

Now Helmut's foot was off the gas pedal and the car began to slow.

Greta cried, "Oh, Gott!" when she saw that Helmut, too, was dying. She looked around, wild-eyed, and screamed at John, "This is your work! Your CIA!" She tried to shoot him, but her twenty-shot magazine was empty.

"Don't be a fool! I'm not interested in killing you or your men!" John shouted. "I want to get to Barr as much as you want me to!" He was hunched over the back of the driver's seat, awkwardly steering with one hand.

James Lang had slowly, weakly, slumped to the floor. He retched horribly, spewing blood and undigested food on the plush carpeting.

Greta returned to sanity. She twisted around to look out of the shattered rear window. "They're running after us."

"Christ!" John threw himself into the crowded front seat. The sedan veered drunkenly until he got into position.

Greta screamed, "Schweinhund! Give me my gun!" She grabbed for the MAK-18 that John had taken.

He handed it back to her, then concentrated on keeping the sputtering car going. The front seat was a blood-spattered mess. The still-twitching bodies of Helmut and Kurt crowded John and bled on him.

The heavy thunder of the MAK filled the car as Greta fired at the pursuing ambushers.

John saw them in the rearview mirror: there were eight of them and they looked like soldiers. They seemed strong and well fed. They were shooting as they ran. But Greta took three of them down with her first burst. The others dove for the center-strip gully.

Something cracked in the engine and the car lost all power. John shifted to neutral in order to coast as far as possible. In the silence he heard James Lang's labored, bubbly struggle for air. He heard Greta doing something with one of the guns. Probably reloading her pistol.

He asked, "Do you have any plans?"

"What plans? What do you mean?" She weaved her head left and right as she scanned from the shredded rear window.

"In case this happened." John cursed under his breath as he heard Lang's horrible breathing stop. He'd known from the instant the congressman had been hit in the chest that the man would die. There were no hospitals now, and no doctors. Any serious wound was a death sentence.

"No! No!" Greta cried. "Those men are soldiers. They are probably survivors from the French occupation forces, from the base in this state."

"How do we get to the president?" John said.

Greta didn't answer. She was examining James Lang. "He is dead. Your member of Congress is dead."

"I know." The BMW was creeping now, almost stopped. There was no point in staying in the car. "Which way do we run?"

Greta looked around at the countryside. "Those trees." She pointed. "We stay away from Kirchheim."

John braked the car to a stop and got out. He yanked open the rear left door and quickly surveyed James Lang's body. The bullet had splintered the man's left arm and smashed into his chest, leaving a neat hole in the so-called bulletproof vest. The attackers were using the new zeflon-coated ammunition developed for NATO and given to the French and Israelis.

This bullet, malformed by shattering Lang's arm, still had had enough force and slickness to slice through the laminated nylon and break a rib before shredding part of a lung and perhaps the stomach. Massive internal hemorrhaging had finished him.

John grabbed the briefcase on the seat and then reached for the MAK-18.

Greta pulled it away. She leveled her pistol at him.

John conquered his rage. He said in a controlled voice, "I'll need a weapon. That thing is heavy. If we're going to do a lot of running . . ." He glanced up the highway and saw a few of the soldiers climbing into view. Several others were probably coming forward under cover of the gully.

Greta's beautiful face twisted with indecision. "Take Helmut's rifle."

"It's under their bodies." He lunged back into the front seat and dragged the corpses away with savage strength. He found the Mauser on the floor, along with Kurt's Luger. He took both weapons.

Greta said, "Take the food! From their coats. The meal packs."

"Jesus!" John looked at the soldiers who were running, weaving, toward the car. They were still three hundred yards away. He rested the Mauser on the open rear door, aimed and fired.

One of the soldiers toppled. The others sprawled forward and began firing.

John levered another shell into the chamber and ignored the *splang* of slugs into the rear of the car as he transferred meal packs from Helmut's coat to his own jacket.

Greta had come to the other front door and was looting Kurt's pockets. She wordlessly handed John six spare clips for the Luger.

As the soldiers rose to dash closer, John put a rifle bullet into the gut of the soldier who seemed to be giving orders by hand signals and shouts. The man fell, writhing, to the gravel shoulder of the highway.

John and Greta sprinted across the concrete to the ditch, leaped over it and ran toward the small clump of blackened trees a hundred yards away, across a scraggly open field with dead vegetation. The unshielded ground had been irradiated to a depth of nearly two feet. All plant seeds were dead. During the flare the moisture in exposed trees had turned to steam and burst the tree trunks asunder, often sending shrapnellike splinters hissing through the heated surroundings.

The remaining soldiers on the highway did not bother to shoot at John and Greta. They closed in on the BMW. They wanted its gasoline.

As they ran, John admired Greta's lithe, strong body and her stamina. She carried almost as much extra weight as he, and seemed to carry it effortlessly.

They entered the thicket of shattered trees and dead bushes and stopped to look back. They were both breathing hard. They saw that they had not been followed. The soldiers were investigating the car.

John and Greta looked at each other. He asked, "How far?"

She brushed strands of red hair from her eyes. "We cannot walk. It is over two hundred kilometers."

"Then we find another car."

She laughed. "Maybe, if we are very lucky." She led the way through the ruined little forest and pointed to the hills. "It may be possible there. On the west slopes there may be houses which were in shadow during the Death Time, and there may be a car with gasoline still in it. But I think the people who survived will not want to give it to us, if they have not starved to death or been killed by looters."

John nodded. In the distance it was easy to see the shadow line: there were oblong patches of healthy green on the west slopes of hills and low, rounded mountains. Everything else was starkly brown and gray. But even the green areas were full of blowdown destruction, and some were disfigured by the ragged, blackened tracks from hurricane-driven firestorms.

It was twilight, eleven hours later, when John and Greta struggled up a twisting dirt road to a stone-and-wood house built into the side of a seared hill. The house was partly burned. Constructed of white stone, it had survived the blast of radiation from the sun, and its garage was sunk into the hillside.

This was the eighteenth house they'd found in the hills.

"If there's a car inside, it didn't burn," John said.

Greta slumped to the dead lawn. She pushed the carrying strap of the MAK-18 off her aching, blistered shoulder. She gazed at the house. It did not appear to have been looted. "Go and see," she said wearily.

John left the Mauser with her and approached the house, the Luger in his left hand.

The burned, surrounding forest was silent. There were no birds, no small animals, no insects. Only a faint, cold breeze stirred. He could hear himself breathe. He could hear Greta moan softly with discomfort as she shifted to a more comfortable position. Their all-day trek had exhausted her.

The padlock on the garage door was secure. He used a rock to batter the hasp loose. He didn't want the sound of a shot to echo for miles. When he pulled open the doors, a 1975 VW Beetle in superb condition seemed to smile at him.

They found the lower level of the house undamaged by fire or rain. There was a small, dry back bedroom. It held the possessions of a child.

There was a body on the kitchen floor, dressed in a moldy sleeping gown and robe. The upstairs front bedroom held the very badly decomposed body of a naked man. Rain had lashed in through a charred hole in the beamed ceiling.

Greta and John decided to spend the night in the house.

They washed in cold water from a protected water heater. They each ate a self-heating meal pack and drank hot coffee. They discovered a small bar in the living room and sat on the cold sofa and drank wine.

It was very dark now. An occasional furious little red glow from Greta's cigarette was the only spot of light. She held an ashtray in her lap.

Greta remembered the instructions Lauter had given her. The original plan had been for a one-night stop at a house near St. Blasien after a day of circuitous southerly driving. An ambush such as had occurred this morning had not been seriously considered.

The original plan called for her to use sex, if necessary, to gain John Norris's trust and any information that could be crucial.

Now that the opportunity for sex was present, Greta was not so sure John was a man who could be manipulated. And she was not sure she dared try to seduce him.

Her reluctance confused her. But if he gave a hint, a sign that he wanted her, then her duty would require her to go through with it. Her right foot tapped endlessly on the deep carpet. She was very nervous.

John sipped white wine and asked, "How do you people expect to make a country out of all this emptiness and chaos? How will you control the looters? How will you handle renegade soldiers like the ones who attacked us?"

She smiled in the darkness. "We will have money and supplies. We will attract men like that as a flame gathers moths. And we will have the keys to imported food and equipment from your country. We will build slowly, carefully, a new socialist state, here in southern Germany, and we will gain followers as we grow."

"It'll have to be a socialist dictatorship, of course."

"For a few years," Greta said.

"Forever," John rejoined.

"And do you think your country will ever return to full democracy?" Greta said lightly, tauntingly.

John laughed. He knew it was pointless to argue politics with a fanatic socialist. He said, "The United States isn't a democracy, it's a republic. But you may be right.

Like Rome, we will probably deteriorate into some form of Caesarism.''

"And would you resist your President Waggoner if she attempted to remain a dictator?"

John thought for a minute. "If it was blatant . . . yes.''

His answer surprised her. She believed him. She drew nervously on her cigarette. She changed the subject. "The death of Congressman Lang makes your mission more difficult.''

John grimaced. It sure as hell did. The leadership of the House and Senate would be very suspicious at the death of their man. They'd surely start to smell a plot, a trick, a secret deal. It could ruin the negotiations. It had suddenly become absolutely vital that President Barr be alive and that he return to the United States.

John knew Greta was probing for information, seeking an angle, an advantage for her side. Two could play that game. He said, "I may have to ask you to return with me if necessary to testify that Jim Lang was shot by one of the soldiers who ambushed us.''

"Oh?'' She was suddenly tempted—and, as quickly, very angry. She bit back a sarcastic comment about prison or execution for "terrorism" and kidnapping. She regained control. "Would I have amnesty? After I told what happened, what would happen to me?''

"What would you want to happen?''

Greta felt suffocated. She stubbed out her cigarette. She remembered her life as a top fashion model. The money, the luxuries, the privileges, the attention. She had rejected that soft, degenerate capitalistic life. And now she was doomed to live in this charnel house of a country, doomed to struggle, perhaps die . . .

She gritted her teeth. Damn John Norris! He was stirring up memories and attitudes and desires she wanted buried! But she had to deal with him for Hans's sake. For the sake of the new socialist reality.

She leaned back in the cold, clammy sofa and shivered in spite of her warm coat. "I'm cold," she said. "We should get to bed. How do you want to sleep tonight? With me?"

The choice was the sofa or sharing the bed in the child's room. The bed upstairs was ruined by rain and mold.

"With you, of course," John said.

She had expected that. She found his hand in the darkness and stood up. "Come, then."

They spread extra blankets on the bed and slipped between the two lower blankets. They needed insulation from the thoroughly chilled mattress.

Greta lay naked in the narrow bed, feeling the press of John's hip, the smooth, hard bulk of his arm and shoulder, the firm tree trunk of his thigh. His body seemed very warm.

She waited for him to touch her, to turn on his side and put his big hand on a breast . . . on her flat belly. She was exhausted from the day's action and the long trek, and yet she was excited and wide awake. Part of her mind was cool and calculating, but it floated on a turbulent pool of repressed emotion.

Finally, she asked, "Don't you want me?" Could he be playing a game? Could he really be like Hans?

John asked, "Do you want *me*?"

She had never wanted a man for sex. Was this one asking permission? Asking her to be as passionate as he? Was he one of the humble, considerate ones who would not dream of imposing his sexual needs on a woman unless she wanted it, too? Very well . . . for Hans, for the New German People's Alliance.

Greta turned toward John and pressed her firm breasts against his arms. She whispered, "Yes, I do want you," and the words which never failed, "You are so strong . . . so big . . ." She slid her hand onto his naked hip and to his ridged, muscled belly. She was disturbed to feel scars and vestiges of recent wounds. She found him hard, however, and surprisingly large.

She did not want to kiss him, but forced herself to do it. Kissing on the mouth seemed too intimate to her. It brought minds too close. It was a commitment, somehow, a form of sincerity from which she recoiled.

But this time, as John's arms closed about her and as he touched and pressed himself to her, and kissed her, Greta found herself experiencing an atavistic pleasure. For this was no ordinary man. She sensed great discipline and power in him, both physically and mentally.

There was a certain way he touched her, a certain assurance and skill in his caresses and kisses. . . . Greta sank slowly into a world of sensual gratification, of letting go, of reveling in the itchy spiking of her nipples, in the simmering, liquid heat of her loins.

When he moved over her and into her, she groaned from the pit of her stomach and dug her short nails into his scarred back. And when the endless deep movement and cumulative sensations tensed her body and compelled her to beg him to continue, as she hung in a sweet, convulsive oblivion, as she was wracked by pure, exquisitely intense rapture, Greta shuddered helplessly and yielded a part of herself she had never known to exist before.

When his powerful spasms came, she could not help moving with him, crying out with him, could not help wanting his pleasure to be better than hers, if that was possible.

Later, when she returned to the bed, she found John asleep. But she could not sleep. In a twitchy pool of weariness, she dozed, awakened, then dozed again. Her mind fought with itself as she struggled for balance and tried to reinforce her loyalties to Hans Lauter and revolutionary socialism. But however many times she reviled John Norris in her conscious mind as a capitalist tool, as a degenerate product of the exploitive American culture, a sickening pool of fear deepened in her guts.

Finally, she convinced herself she hated John. He had used her! She had allowed it in the mistaken belief that she could use him. But he had been too clever for her, this time. It would never happen again! It must never happen again!

CHAPTER 8

THE ROLLING HILLS OF LUXEMBOURG HAD ONCE BEEN beautiful. Now, on a sterile farm not far from the capital, Erica Stoneman had established a forward base. Most of her force was still in Paris, systematically looting that once-magnificent city.

The meadow on which her elaborate, multiroom tent was set up had been chosen for its drainage and view of the destroyed city of Luxembourg on the one hand, and for its view of the mountains to the south and east. Most important, the chance of disease from human and animal corpses was minimal.

Her aide, Greg Albertson, sat opposite her at the small dining table and tried to make conversation. "What is it you want from Luxembourg, besides the gold in the banks?" he asked.

Erica regarded him with amusement and exasperation. "The mansion of Simon de Bouvet contains some price-less Rembrandts and a very special Titian."

"God, I'd have thought you had enough old paintings by now," Greg said.

"This is a rescue operation as much as a looting expedition," she snapped. "If I don't get these art treasures into safe, air-conditioned rooms, they'll deteriorate even more and be ruined or stolen by careless, ignorant brutes who won't know how to treat them."

"A service to mankind," he said.

She caught his sarcasm and resolved to make him pay for it. Tonight. She had had just about enough of his insults. When they returned to England, he would be cast loose.

She put down her fork and rang for her servant, a young woman named Hulda. Cook, maid, and secret bodyguard, Hulda had been a detective on the New York City police force. Erica paid her more than she did Greg.

When the stocky, dark-haired, thirtyish woman entered the pale green room, Erica said, "We're finished now. We'll be in my bedroom."

Greg said, "It's only eight."

"So? You'll go down on me when I say, day or night, where I want, for as long as I want. That's what you're being paid for, isn't it?"

Hulda stood by, patient, observant, showing no expression.

Greg flushed and shot a shamed glance at Hulda. He hated Erica Stoneman. She constantly humiliated him in private and in front of her maid and her mercenary officers, whenever it suited her. If it weren't for the fantastic salary she was paying him . . .

A chime sounded. Someone wished entrance to the tent. Hulda went to see who it was.

A minute later, Lieutenant Granville entered the dining room. "Mrs. Stoneman, Radio has a call on the frequency you wished monitored."

Lauter! Erica nodded. "Good." She rose and said to Greg, "Wait for me in the bedroom."

When she climbed into the communications van, the radioman handed her his earphones and mike. He indicated the transmit button on the console. "Thank you, Michael. Leave, now," she said.

When the soldier-hand had climbed down and out and shut the door, she transmitted, "Is Hans Lauter there?"

His voice crackled in his ears. *"Here. I've complied with your instructions. I demand to know who you are."*

"This is Erica Stoneman, Mr. Lauter. I am in Luxembourg and I want to meet with you."

"Who is Erica Stoneman?"

"The widow of Bradford Collier Stoneman. I was his sole heir. I control all of his assets and I possess all of his power. I can help you more in the long run than the United States can, Mr. Lauter. If you really do have President Barr."

"I have him. What are you doing in Luxembourg?"

"My organization is carrying out a thorough, carefully planned, salvage operation. This is only our first large expedition. I'll be sending in many more in the next few months and years."

"Salvage? You are looting! Capitalist—"

"Mr. Lauter! I can move against you if I choose. I am here with a considerable force of very well equipped, armed men. But I would rather cooperate with you, if you will cooperate with me."

"I will kill your president before I'll submit to your plans."

"In many ways, William Barr dead would be better for me than William Barr alive. Kill him if you like, if you really have him. But I can use him, and you, in the future. I can send you arms and food and certain vital machinery to help you establish your new socialist state. I don't care if you want to be a king, a dictator, a premier, whatever. Your form of government and economy do not matter. All that matters is quid pro quo and strictly enforced trade and development agreements.''

"Spoken like a true bloodsucking exploiter of the people."

Erica was becoming impatient. "Are you making a speech, Lauter? Are you trying to impress your ragtag little band of opportunists? Are they listening?"

There was silence. The carrier wave buzzed lightly. Then Lauter said, *"Very well. I will meet with you. But you must be alone, with only one or two men as your personal guards. If you are as well informed as you seem, you will know I am about to meet with John Norris, a representative from the United States government."*

"Yes. I ask that you not tell him about me, and that you not make a deal with him until I can talk to you personally."

"Do you have a way of getting into southern Germany quickly?"

"Yes."

"Then come to the Bad Meissen Lodge three kilometers north of Waldshut, near the Swiss border. Can you do that?"

"Of course. When I am near there again, I'll radio you on frequency—" She gave him a setting. "We'll work out the details and safeguards at that time. Agreed?"

"Agreed. Till then." The carrier wave ended and empty static filled Erica's headphones. She took them off and leaned back in the cushioned swivel chair. She smiled. She licked her full lips as her blue eyes narrowed in thought.

So John Norris was now in Germany. Had he reached Lauter already? She had never met Norris, but had examined a dossier of him prepared by Lane McDermott, complete with nude photos obtained from the CIA files. The pictures had shown the ugly torture wounds inflicted on him by Calvin Bergendahl when he was captured in Ubari, just before the flare.

The in-depth photos also showed his magnificently muscled body . . . his heavy genitals. . . .

Erica closed her eyes and indulged herself in erotic reverie. She stirred in the chair and slowly brought her right hand to her left breast. She fondled herself through the tough, silken fabric of her semiformal jumpsuit.

Then she shook herself and stood up. She left the radio van. She had some intricate planning to do later in the night, and she thought more clearly if she was free of erotic pressures.

Three minutes later, when she entered her tent's bedroom, she smiled at the sight of Greg Albertson already in bed, naked, waiting to be used.

She stripped quickly and spread herself on the expensive orange nylon blanket. "Slow, at first, Greg, then faster and faster. I want you to do all your wonderful tongue tricks tonight." She pulled a pillow under her head and watched him. He was a slim, white-skinned young man with practically no body hair. His genitals were small, and even when erect, his penis was hardly worth noting. He was an androgynous male, with slim, soft hands and a natural talent for oralism.

She arched her back as she suctioned one of her large nipples into his mouth. Yes . . . yes . . . he was so good at this. . . .

Later, with his head buried between her trembling thighs, when his fluttering tongue drove her into a fifth—or was it her sixth?—orgasm, she noted with amusement from a small, observant part of her mind that he was grinding his loins against the slick, quilted surface of the nylon blanket. He was snorting with his own solitary pleasure.

Erica would never give him the satisfaction of her mouth. She had never done that for him, nor would she ever. Greg was not her lover; he was her employee.

As she panted into her latest, shattering climax, she thought of John Norris. Powerful, arrogant, totally masculine John Norris! How sweet it would be to have him do this to her! How fine to make him submit to her will! And how satisfying it might be to have him beg for completion by her mouth.

Erica knew herself to be an overwhelmingly oral woman. Her preference for that way of loving had attracted Brad Stoneman to her, and kept him loving her until he died. She had not made oral love to another man since Brad, and she missed it. She missed the pure pleasure of doing it, and above all, she missed the exciting power over a man it gave her.

But it could not be an ordinary man. It could not even be Lane McDermott, who served her so well in New York as he had served Brad for all those years. Lane was interested, but he was—bottom line—only another employee.

She wanted a man who was her equal.

CHAPTER 9

THE OLD VW BEETLE SOUNDED LIKE A HIGH-POWERED washing machine, but it did the job.

John and Greta left the hillside house at dawn and, with John at the wheel, made good time once they reached a southbound secondary highway. Greta consulted a map she had found in the glove compartment, and they rejoined the main north-south autobahn, far south of the previous morning's ambush.

The bug was much better able than the BMW to maneuver through sometimes awesome multicar pileups at what had been busy ramps that fed the autobahn from Metzingen and Reutlingen. Once they had woven their way through the congestion of dead cars and trucks at Pfullingen, the super highway had cleared enough for them to buzz along at over seventy kilometers an hour.

They saw occasional wisps of smoke from chimneys in isolated, distant houses, but no people were visible. Instead, John had to constantly shift lanes to avoid the sprawled, decomposed remnants of people who had escaped from their cars and died, cooking in their own juices, on the cold concrete that awful morning.

Greta was distant and cool toward John. She resented his smile, his clear-eyed, rested look, and his indifference toward her weariness. He did not care about her!

She had to admit he drove well. Oh, yes, he was skilled in many things.

When they reached Waldshut, where the Rhine emerged from Switzerland, she said brusquely, "We are here. Take the next exit."

He had to squeeze around a large, burned-out diesel truck that had jackknifed and turned over. Its load of bottled water had broken and been exploded by steam. Glass covered the ramp.

Waldshut was only slightly damaged by the hurricanes. It had not burned. A few starving people were about. They stared apathetically at the Beetle.

Soon after John and Greta drove into the mountain town, the right front tire blew, from a shard of glass picked up on the exit ramp, and John automatically slowed down. The car lurched and bumped on the flat tire.

"Don't stop!" Greta ordered. "Turn left here—Schneise Lein." She shifted the MAK-18 to subtly bear on him.

"How much farther?" John asked. The flat tire made steering difficult. It sounded as if it would come off its rim any second.

"I will tell you."

A moment later, she called over the loud *flub-flubbing* of the ruined tire, "There—the chalet. Left! Left!"

John studied the ornate white house as he wrestled with the wheel and drove the noisy, jolting little car up the long, steep, curving driveway. A young man holding a MAK-18 stood alert by the front door, and another stood, with a shotgun, close to the two-car garage. A third man watched from a small barn.

Greta waved from the car window. "I am back!" she shouted.

When John stopped the car in front of the house, Greta got out and said to the front-door guard, "Watch him." To John, she said, "Stay here. Don't leave the car."

"I wouldn't dream of it," John said, smiling faintly.

Five minutes later, two additional armed young men came from the house and escorted John inside. He was taken to the living room, where Hans Lauter was waiting for him. One of the men carried the briefcase. It had been opened on the porch and its contents examined closely. The briefcase was handed to Lauter.

Hans lounged in a big chair by the front window. He did not stand, nor did he offer his hand. He pointed to an identical chair by the fireplace. He drew his fingers through his long, clean brown hair and observed John closely.

John walked across the hardwood floor in his heavy boots and took the offered chair. He sat and waited for Hans to speak. The guards, with sidearms, stood inside the living-room archway.

After ten empty seconds, Hans sat up. "Greta told me you two had an adventurous journey here," he said.

"I think any trip in this country now is going to be exciting," John answered.

"Are you hungry? We have soup. Some coffee?" Hans offered.

"I'd like to see President Barr, if I may." John said.

"In due time. We must have some understandings, first." Hans touched his full, neatly trimmed beard. "I must know your powers of negotiation. I must see some identification."

From an inner pocket, John took out a waterproof packet of documents. He hesitated.

Hans smiled and said, "Toss it." He easily caught the packet, and studied its contents in silence. There were signed papers from President Waggoner identifying John Norris as her representative and official negotiator, and a letter from her to Hans. There were photographic and fingerprint proofs of John Norris and Congressman James Lang.

Hans looked up and asked, "How will the unfortunate death of Congressman Lang affect us?"

Greta entered the room at that point and sat in an armless chair next to the hallway door. Her left foot tapped nervously on the wooden floor.

"At the very least I'll need to take back with me a videotaped statement from Greta as to how he died," John said. "And a videotaped statement from you, testifying that she is your associate and that she is telling the truth. Both of you should mention that your side lost two men in the ambush. And all this should be done in President Barr's presence, with him in the picture, too."

"I will not be photographed," Lauter said coldly.

"President Waggoner will need everything possible to convince the leaders of congress that Lang's death was not part of a plot of some kind to keep President Barr a captive, or to have him killed," John said.

"Why will you need all that on videotape if you intend President Barr to return with you?" Hans glanced at Greta and saw the squinting hate-filled eyes she directed at John Norris.

Greta said, "If necessary, I could go back with them and be our contact, our ambassador to the United States. I could swear to the truth of the ambush, in person, and they could use a lie detector on me, or drugs."

Hans nodded. He watched her. "That could be done . . . if necessary." Then he asked John, "What proof of the lack of a conspiracy do you need, beyond the return of President Barr? If you give us what we want, you and your woman president will have no problems about the death of James Lang."

"First, I need to see the man you claim is William T.

Barr," John said. "If the claim is proved, then we can negotiate the ransom amount and terms. If all that is accomplished, I must then communicate with President Waggoner and perhaps with the House and Senate leadership by means of a secret, coded satellite relay from my plane. I will send back blood-sample analyses, photos, and videotapes. Experts in the United States must then examine what I send to determine if it is legitimate. I will make my report. I will also have to use my plane to pick up the body of James Lang."

"Delays!" said Lauter, shaking his head.

John continued, "I will then return, and you and I will talk again. We then may have a deal, subject to final approval by my superiors in the United States."

Hans adjusted his wire-rimmed glasses on his thin nose and said with deadly certainty, "The money amounts and the other demands in our original contact are not negotiable. We will be paid the full—ransom, as you say—or President Barr—and you—will be killed! And let your President Waggoner and those other superiors, those other leaders, consider how that event would, should it occur, affect their future in the United States, when your bodies were dumped on the doorstep of the British government, and the world was told."

John calmly met Hans Lauter's fanatic, willful gaze. "I understand your position, but the process cannot continue until I determine if Bill Barr is really alive," John said.

Lauter nodded. "But you will first be searched thoroughly. You will strip, and your clothes and your boots will be inspected. And your mouth and your ass will be investigated." Hans smiled with power and contempt. "You understand, that is necessary," he said.

"Here?" John shrugged. He took off his flight coat and began unbuttoning his shirt.

"Johann, Albert!" Hans snapped. "Take him into the kitchen and do it!"

When the "inspection" was over and John had dressed, he was given his briefcase and escorted, by Hans Lauter, up the narrow, paneled stairway to the attic.

As they walked down the hall to the low-ceilinged alcove, Lauter said, "You will find President Barr changed from his days in Washington."

"I saw the photos and videotape you sent," John said.

"Then you know what to expect. We do not live luxuriously here." Lauter was only five feet eight inches tall. He glanced at John, amused, superior in his own lack of height, as John had to duck into the small entrance. "Konrad, open the president's door," he said.

The young guard opened the low, padlocked door and stood aside, a P-38 cocked in his hand.

Lauter pushed into the tiny room followed by John, who had to duck even lower.

"Mr. President, you have a visitor," Lauter said. He stepped into a corner and watched.

The warm late-afternoon sunlight angled into the cubbyhole from the dormer window, and bathed William T. Barr in yellow. It cruelly detailed his gray-stubbled face, his dark-circled eyes, his bony thinness, the shabbiness of his soiled clothes. He was sitting on his blanket-covered mattress, his back against the wall, enjoying the sun.

But when he opened his eyes and, squinting, looked up and saw John, his face was transformed by a smile. He struggled to his feet. "By God! Norris! Am I glad to see you!" He embraced John and hugged him fiercely.

John returned the embrace and gestured for Barr to be seated again. "It's very good to see you alive, sir." He squatted on his heels and placed the briefcase on the mattress. He had known instantly this man was Bill Barr. He looked around at Hans Lauter. "I'd like to talk to the president alone," John said.

Lauter chuckled. "No."

Bill Barr grimaced. "Hans doesn't trust anyone. Sometimes not even himself. Ignore the bastard," the president said.

John smiled and turned his back to Lauter. "Sir, the situation in the United States is pretty bad. . . ."

He spent fifteen minutes outlining what had happened since the solar flare of deadly radiation had struck Europe, Asia, Africa . . . and spared North and South America. He sketched in the political situation, and ended by saying, "Erica Stoneman has been foremost in pressuring for a return to pre-flare markets and constitutional government, and she has many, many supporters in Congress."

" 'Supporters' is a kind word," Barr said grimly. " 'Prostitutes' is a more accurate description of her people. Jim Lang was one of them. Did you know that?"

"I suspected it," John said.

"Hell, I played poker with him every Wednesday for a year. No ethics, no morals, no shame, but a pretty fair poker player," Barr declared.

John opened the briefcase and took out various testing kits. "Sir, I have to take samples of your hair, blood, and some skin scrapings, for analysis and identification. I have a special camera here for pictures of your retinas and your teeth."

Barr grunted. "I understand. Do you have to fly back to the States with all this before you are allowed to do any serious negotiating?"

"There's a marine on the plane who is a trained lab technician, and there's a miniature lab aboard for him to use, with a computer. But if I'm ordered back, I'll have to go. They may want to question me in great detail, with drugs. James Lang's death will make the House and Senate leadership—"

"Yes, I understand," Barr interrupted. "What's that?"

John had taken out a special, high-speed miniature videotape camera. "It's something the CIA put together.

It will self-destruct if tampered with; it's self-powered and has a built-in recorder, with tape enough for three hours. I've been given a set of questions from the congressional leadership which only William T. Barr could answer. I'll record you as you read the questions and answer them." He handed Barr the question sheet. "When I get back to my plane, I'll use a special take-off to feed this tape's signals to the satellite and on to Oregon and Washington at the same time. The signals are coded for acceptance, and I don't know the code, so a false transmission is impossible."

Lauter muttered, "Such elaborate precautions!"

Barr laughed as he scanned the question sheet. "Trust Sam to ask about that!" He looked up. "Okay, turn it on."

John turned to Lauter. "I'd like Greta to come up and sit next to the president and tell how James Lang died."

Hans said, "She wants to go back with you."

"She can if I'm ordered back and if you agree she can return with me. But this tape will be transmitted as soon as I get back to Stuttgart, and it could speed up the pace of the negotiations. If I'm called back to the States to explain about Lang, the process could be delayed for weeks. And they'd probably send someone else in my place."

Lauter considered. He finally told Konrad to get Greta. He took Konrad's P-38 and stood just outside the open door of the cell-like room while waiting for her.

Eighty-five minutes later, the tests completed, the samples taken, the testimony by Greta and John photographed and recorded, with cross-examination by Barr and Lauter, John repacked the briefcase and snapped it shut.

He shook William Barr's hand. "I have to get back to Stuttgart now. I'll return as soon as I can, sir. We'll cut a deal and get you out of here."

Barr's handshake was firm and strong. "Seeing you has been a tonic, Norris. Take care."

Greta had sullenly, silently left to go back downstairs.

As Konrad locked the door, Lauter said to John, "I want the money quickly! I don't want to wait for months while you shuttle back and forth to receive 'further instructions.'"

"Let me fly here, then, to save travel time."

"No! How great a fool do you think I am?"

"I'll tell them you're impatient," John said. He and Lauter moved into the attic hallway and started down the narrow stairs.

"You will tell them President Barr will not be freed, under any conditions, until ten billion dollars are deposited in Zurich Credit Bank in my name," Lauter persisted.

John smiled. "In your name."

"Yes, to control the money, for legality. It is a formality," Lauter said.

"As you wish." John stopped in the second floor hallway. He was about to descend to the ground floor when Lauter pushed him abruptly to the right.

"No! You do not leave!"

John controlled the sudden, savage surge of rage the arrogant push had triggered in him. He allowed himself to be herded into a bedroom.

Lauter said, "Here you sleep tonight. It is too late to start back to Stuttgart now. We must find a new tire for that car."

John nodded. "I need to go to the bathroom."

"A guard will take you to our—what you call the outhouse. And he will bring you some food. There will be a guard at this door all night. We do not have electricity, but we see well in the dark. Do not try any midnight escapades."

John turned to survey the used, rumpled bed. "I'd like—"

Lauter pulled the bedroom door shut and locked it.

CHAPTER 10

LATER THAT NIGHT, AFTER A CANDLELIGHT CONFERENCE with most of the others in the New German People's Alliance—eleven young men and one other young woman—Hans and Greta lay side by side under heavy wool blankets in the first floor bedroom. It was directly below the bedroom which held John Norris.

Hans asked in a low voice, "Did you have sex with him?"

"No. We were both too tired after that ambush and after walking all day," she lied. "He was disturbed by Lang's death."

"I cannot imagine anything disturbing that man."

Greta did not reply.

"Why do you want to go to the United States?"

"I don't! If I have to accompany him, they will find an excuse to imprison me. Once they have Barr, I will be doomed."

Lauter was reminded of something Erica Stoneman had said during their latest shortwave talk. He had made sure none of the others heard him speak with her. She had said that once the United States had Barr back safely, it would renege on any deal made with Norris, and might even seek revenge by trying to wipe out the New German People's Alliance.

Of course he had known that. He was no fool. All governments were amoral entities.

Thus, perhaps he had to make two deals. The possibilities were fascinating.

Hans said, "You must go back with him to Stuttgart and you must do anything to assure the success of our strategy."

Greta sighed. "I know. I accept that."

He turned to her and casually, possessively, clamped his hand on one her of her firm breasts. He squeezed the flesh too hard. When she cried out and moved, he took it as a sign of passion. He whispered, "Soon we will have ten billion dollars! Ten billion!"

Maybe more, he thought, if the Stoneman woman could be milked.

He threw back the blankets and permitted himself to suckle cruelly on Greta's swelling nipples. He moved over her. She squirms nicely, he thought; the prospect of vast amounts of money makes women eager.

Greta stared up at the ceiling and could not help comparing Hans to John. She inhaled sharply as Hans forced himself into her, thrusting against dry tissues, bringing pain to them both.

Greta knew why he did this occasionally; it was a kind of payment made to offset his great inner joy—the money that he thought was coming to him, and the power. The pain was necessary.

She felt him push into soft, inner slickness and warmth. In a moment, the pain lessened and faded. He jerked into her with swift, increasingly frantic movements as his pleasure escalated.

She did not receive any pleasure from it. There was

only the drubbing, a constant, mild irritation. She waited
for it to end. She was surprised that Hans was losing so
much of his control. Was it the ten billion dollars? He
was panting now, gripping her shoulders fiercely, his
hoarse, fast breathing loud in her ear.

Greta felt compelled to fake pleasure. Her moans were
quiet, her movement mechanical. She felt a contempt
for Hans she had never known before. He was losing
her in his mad lust for money and power. The approaching reality of his dreams had warped him. She suspected
that even his dedication to revolutionary socialism might
be in danger.

As Hans spent himself, Greta wondered what John
Norris, overhead, was thinking. Could he hear them? A
strange ache suffused her emotions. She found herself
beginning to weep. She struggled to resist the tears.

When Hans sighed and rolled off her naked body,
Greta swiftly left the bed and went into the bathroom to
wash by candlelight from the bucket of well water on the
toilet lid.

As she shivered in the cold, she silently cursed herself, Hans, and John.

CHAPTER 11

THE LARGE, ARMORED TWIN-ENGINE HELICOPTER, CAR-
rying Erica Stoneman and six heavily-armed mercenaries,
fought for stability as the pilot struggled to land through
high winds and low, shredded clouds.

Below, perched on a mountainside, flanked by stark
outcroppings of black rock and deep, rotting snow, the
massive, one hundred fifty-seven-room Bad Meissen
Lodge provided only a marginal helicopter landing area
next to its parking lot.

The lodge had escaped most of the flare because of
the looming bulk of the mountain. But the lodge was
now abandoned. Its kitchens had burned along with the
exposed oil and propane tanks. One third of the huge,
timbered structure was a charred ruin.

Its parking lot had taken the full blast of radiation and
was host to row upon row of burned-out cars. With the
food stores destroyed by the explosions and fire, with no
heat, the guests and staff had trekked down the mountain, only to starve and die in the valley.

But there was now one undamaged car in the lot—a late-model Mercedes sedan—and there was one man standing in the lodge's ornate stone doorway, looking up at the wind-buffeted helicopter.

Erica shouted to the pilot over the roar of the engines and the gusting, shrieking wind, "Get us down, damn you!"

The big copter slewed and dropped, causing clenched jaws and instant nausea. The dark-haired young pilot fought the controls. He managed to hover at ten meters and lurch toward the landing area.

A freaky gust of wind tilted the copter on its side. The powerful blades almost chopped into concrete. He gritted, "Bloody fucking hell!" and again righted the craft. He took advantage of three seconds of wind lull and dropped to a hard, jolting landing. His hands flew as he feathered the vanes. "Get out and secure the lines" he yelled to the soldiers.

The men leaped out and began tying down the shuddering, skittish copter with nylon ropes and metal stakes driven, with small, explosive hammers, into the rock and concrete.

"Good job," Erica said, smiling at the pilot. She had been gripping her seat frame with desperate, white-knuckled strength, and she knew it had been a near crash. But now, as her heart thudded with adrenaline, she felt exhilaration. She lived a charmed life. Nothing could happen to her. She was destined to rule the whole goddamned world. The Stoneman empire was spreading, growing. . . . She was making history. She *was* history!

Erica unbuckled herself and jumped from the copter into a cold, whipping wind. She zipped up her fur-lined flight coat and looked up at the darkening sky. Storm clouds were boiling over and around the mountain peaks to the northwest. Damn this incredible weather!

She saw a short, bearded young man, in a heavy ski

parka, waiting at the doorway of the lodge. He wore a sidearm.

She called to her men. "Mathews! Salter! Come with me. You others cover us!" She headed for the lodge. The force of the wind made her stagger, and it ripped the quilted hood off her head. Her long blond hair whipped wildly.

When she was about thirty yards from the lodge, she called, "Lauter?"

The young man nodded and walked forward.

Erica told her armed escort to stay in place. She went forward alone to meet Lauter. This was the agreement they had reached a few hours ago by radio.

Lauter's eyes reminded her a little of Brad Stoneman's. They held the same fierce drive and were almost the same golden brown. But she thought there was a hint of wildness—or madness—in this man's eyes.

She said, "You're not alone, are you?"

His lips twisted. "My men are hidden. There can be no tricks," Lauter said.

"I'm not interested in double-crossing you," Erica said. "I want to make a deal. But I'm damned if I'll freeze out here in this wind! Let's go inside."

"Alone?" Lauter asked.

"Yes, damn it! I'll trust you." She had a small Baretta automatic in her coat pocket and a few other devices elsewhere in her clothing.

She went back to her men. She told them she would be in the lodge with Lauter and to come inside for her in exactly thirty minutes. Then she returned to Lauter and they entered the dark building.

The lobby was depressing and cold, but there were big, hand-built wooden chairs and tables. The thick-paned windows had survived the hurricane winds.

Erica sat in a chair and kept her hands in her pockets, one hand on the Baretta. Her eyes were attracted to a wide hallway on the far side of the lobby. The hallway led to a gaping, charred, snow-filled opening.

She shifted her gaze to Lauter, who sat opposite, slightly to the side. Her breath puffed into the frigid air as she said, "I want to claim credit for rescuing President Barr. In return for this, I will pay you one billion dollars in gold coins in advance and I will send in men and machines to get an economy and a government organized in this region. Your group will be in charge."

He laughed. "I am getting ten billion from the United States."

"Really? How will it be paid?"

"It will be deposited in my name in Zurich Credit Bank," Lauter said.

It was Erica's turn to laugh. "And you think you'll be able to walk in, withdraw ten billion in cash, and walk away?"

"I will take what I need. The rest—"

"You will be offered a fraction of that ten billion. If it is ever actually deposited in Zurich, you will probably be arrested there for your part in masterminding the kidnapping of President Barr during the flare. That's crime in Switzerland, you know. And by now, the CIA has agents there, waiting for you. If you are not taken in Zurich, they will follow you. And once President Barr is safely away from where you have him, they will move in and kill you. You, and as many of your pathetic little group as they can find."

"I am not stupid! I have anticipated those moves. There will be precautions," Lauter said.

"Why take a chance?" said Erica, aware of the cold seeping into her insulated pants and coat. She stood up and began to pace.

Lauter said, "You could cheat me, too. Why trust you?" He was impressed with Erica Stoneman. He sensed a savage mind behind those blue eyes and that lovely

86

face. She walked like a cat—a tiger. Where had he seen a walk like that? Yes—John Norris.

"Because I am setting up governments everywhere I can—France, Spain, Italy, South Africa. And I need ruthless, competent people to head them," Erica said.

"I will rule a socialist Germany, not a capitalist colony for you!" Lauter said.

"I don't care what kind of outer shell you present to the world, or to your people, Lauter. Any government is power over people. Any government has guns to enforce its laws. Any government lives off the people it controls. And any government makes trade agreements with international banks and corporations. I will deal with you on a strictly business basis. I will keep my word and I will expect you to do the same. There's wealth and power here for everyone."

Hans Lauter suddenly felt in over his head in these financial and political waters. He had not really thought beyond getting the ransom for Barr. He knew nothing of the technicalities, the structures, the dynamics of governing. He had thought vaguely of recruiting surviving professors and civil servants to form the infrastructure of a government.

But this woman had clear, precise plans, a master plan for the entire world! He began to be afraid of her.

"I will need gold coin to pay my army and my police," he said. "Can you provide that?"

"I told you I would give you one billion dollars in gold coin!" Erica said. "I have tons of it, from the treasuries of France and Luxembourg, from the banks, from private hoards. I can send you one billion dollars in gold and silver coin within weeks. You won't get that from the Swiss! They'll give you a computer entry on a piece of paper."

"I could not use one billion so soon," Lauter said.

"Of course not. But I can give you a letter of account which you can draw on as needed. I can give you a laser radio for special communications with my agents in France, and I will instruct them to honor your withdrawals. They will send what you need by special helicopter courier.''

Erica was bluffing to a degree; she did not yet have the organization set up in Paris to fulfill these promises. But for this one client, a special delivery by one of her helicopters could easily be made. Her main helicopter force, now traveling south toward Nancy, was carrying enormous cargoes of gold.

Lauter felt rushed, a bit overwhelmed. He had lived on the radical fringe of society for so long, had been poor for so long. . . .

Erica thought she had him. She continued, ''You could take over all of Baden-Wurtemburg, then Hesse and Westphalia. Eventually even Bavaria. A government needs people, and my experts think there may be as many as half a million survivors in southwest Germany. With a strong force, gathering recruits as you move, with food stores I have found and put under lock and key, you could take Munich and make that great old city your capital.''

Hans smiled. ''It is very tempting, the deal you offer. Especially the food. A man could now conquer the continent with food alone. But I will wait until Norris returns from Stuttgart. We will see.''

Erica studied him. She moved to a chair close to his. ''You let Norris see President Barr, didn't you?''

Lauter shrugged. ''He had to be sure.''

''I will have to be sure, too. This offer I have made, it's all contingent on my seeing the president. I have to talk to him,'' Erica said.

''To make a deal with him, too?''

Erica nodded, smiling. ''Something like that.''

Hans smiled, too. ''I will agree to that. But only you will see him. You may bring two men with you. And . . .'' He looked calculatedly at Erica's body. ''. . . you will

88

have to be searched in the nude. I would examine you myself."

Erica stared at him, color deepening high on her cheeks. He was demanding a malicious little victory, a young, pretentious male's humiliation of the world's richest, most beautiful woman. He was pathetic. When the right time came, she would have him killed.

She smiled wickedly, but her eyes were blue ice. "That might be fun."

CHAPTER 12

PRESIDENT JULIA WAGGONER SAT ALONE IN HER PRIVATE communications room in the underground crisis center in southern Oregon. She watched the color monitor for a scrambled satellite message from John Norris.

It was 4:00 A.M. and she was bleary-eyed. She sipped hot, black, sweet coffee and watched a woman technician through a soundproofed window. The girl switched in code circuits and verified sound levels. Then she gave a signal to the president and took off her headphones. She would monitor readings for picture stability and sound, but she would not hear or see any of the message itself.

Nevertheless, the transmission was being recorded on sealed tape machines, for later use by the president only.

The picture on Julia's monitor cleared and the white noise ended. John Norris's image solidified and his voice became clear and sharp. She could hear the faint drone of the VTO plane's engines. John sat in a small, quickly assembled broadcast booth in the plane, but it was not totally soundproof.

He saw her, too. The twin cameras atop the monitor before her stared, unwinking; she would never get used to those glowing eyes.

John said, "Mrs. President, are you receiving me? I have you clear."

"Yes, John. Everything is secure here. You can go ahead. Did you make contact with the New German People's Alliance? Where is Jim Lang?" He should have been sitting next to Norris; the booth wasn't that small.

"I'm sorry. Representative James Lang was killed in an ambush soon after—"

"What?" A terrible feeling of dread formed in the pit of Julia's stomach. "My God! What happened? *What happened?"* She dropped her mug of coffee to the carpet and hardly noticed.

John explained and detailed the events. Julia interrupted constantly. She learned in passing that William T. Barr was alive, well enough, and could probably be ransomed successfully.

Anxiety made her yell at John, "How could you let Lang be killed! The leadership will crucify me! Do you have his body?"

"Yes, the first thing I did when I got back to the plane was fly south to the ambush site. It was still there."

Julia pressed her hands to her face. "Can you prove any of this? Is this woman, this Greta, is she with you?"

"Yes," John answered. "She returned with me and will confirm what I've told you. Shall I have her do that now?"

"Yes, yes." The picture rippled and Julia became afraid the satellite link would deteriorate and break. "Quickly."

Seconds later, Julia stared at the beautiful red-haired young woman whose face filled the screen. Julia's apprehension increased. Even without makeup, with her hair cut crudely and in disarray, this girl was stunningly attractive. Who could take what she was saying seriously? The House and Senate leaders would laugh and make dirty jokes and then threaten an all-out investigation, an impeachment—except they could not do that until she reconvened Congress and returned the country to full constitutional government.

Julia felt trapped. She listened as Greta dismissed Lang's death as a minor inconvenience, a sad little event. What was more important was getting on with the ransoming of President Barr and the establishment of a pure socialist state in southern Germany.

That, at least, had the stink of reality, of greed and lust for power that marked a fanatic terrorist.

Julia interrupted the woman. "Miss Verden, you don't appreciate the problems caused by Jim Lang's death. Politically—"

"Two of my good friends died with him! Two good, loyal, dedicated socialists died in that same ambush! But you don't care about them, as I don't care about your precious Lang! What is one elitist capitalist pig, more or less? You have hundreds of congress men!"

Julia took a deep breath. "Yes, I see. Thank you for your . . . your testimony. I would like to speak to John again, privately."

"Scheiskopf!" Greta angrily left the booth.

When John confirmed that he was alone again, Julia asked, "Did she call me what I think she called me?"

"I'm afraid so," John confirmed.

"And I'm afraid that's mild compared to what I'll be called when I have to take this report to the select joint committee. But let's get on with it. I don't know how long this link-up is good for. Can you feed all the test data and video material through now?"

John checked out something in the booth, outside the camera's range. "Yes. It's set up for transmission. It'll be one hundred times normal speed."

Julia sat through several boring minutes as her screen went gray, and the mass of digital information piled up on high-speed tape machines in the next room.

Finally, John came back into the screen. "Data feed completed."

"How many people does this Hans Lauter have?" Julia said impatiently.

"I saw only eleven at the chalet. No one mentioned any other group elsewhere," John said.

"And there are three with you now, in Stuttgart?" Julia asked.

"Two down on the ground, and Greta up here with me," John said. "But if you're thinking of an armed rescue attempt . . . the weather is still freaky and Lauter is no fool. He will have moved to a different house by now, if not a different town. And in the event of any attack, we'd be unable to get to President Barr in time. He'd be killed. Lauter—and Greta—made that crystal clear before we returned to the plane."

"I see," Julia said. "Well, we must trust your judgment. So we must pay. How much, do you think?"

"It depends on what form of payment he wants, and when he wants it," John responded. "Lauter told me privately he wants the money in his name in Zurich Credit, and I don't think the others know that. He may be planning to run Venezuela."

"We can't send him ten billion!" Julia said. "I'm not even sure the Swiss would honor a telex of that size from us now."

"How much can I offer, then?"

"You're positive that man is Bill Barr?" Julia asked.

"Absolutely. Wait till you see the tape and the test results. Personally, I *know* that is Bill Barr."

Julia didn't doubt John. But she made a small face, a tiny grimace. She was of course vastly relieved that Bill was alive and that he'd be coming back to resume his presidency. But she had put so many important programs in place, had pointed the country in a different direction, one she felt was an improvement. She felt sure he'd change things, be influenced . . . but there was nothing she could do.

Julia said to John, "I'll have to take all this to the committee and to my advisors, and we'll have to contact the Swiss . . . John, what time is it there?"

"One-thirty in the afternoon," John said.

"Well, it's four-thirty in the morning here," Julia said. "You land in Stuttgart again and get a good day and night of rest. Get in the air again tomorrow at . . . can your pilot land at night?"

"It's risky," John replied.

"All right," Julia said. "Get into the air tomorrow at five in the afternoon and link with the satellite again. I'll have some decisions and instructions for you then."

"Yes, Mrs. President. Is that all for now?"

"Yes. Thank you, John, for the good job you've done. Till tomorrow." She signaled the woman technician to cut the link.

The monitor picture ripped and the image died.

Julia rubbed her burning eyes. This was going to be a long bastard of a day.

CHAPTER 13

Erica's skin still crawled from the touch of Hans Lauter's cold hands on her naked body when he had "searched" her. Now, ten minutes later, warmly dressed again, she climbed swiftly down metal stairs to the lowest level in the dead pumping station on the Rhine, a quarter-mile downstream from Waldshut.

She had giggled at his rude, intrusive, obscene touching in the station office, and she had acted cute; but in her mind, his last chance for a long life had disappeared. Once she had Barr . . .

Lauter was following her down, and one of his cohorts was leading the way. The air was dank and cold, and smelled of rotten fish.

She had left her two men outside in the armored van she had arrived in after an exhausting drive from Strasbourg.

Lauter had insisted she fly back to her main force and drive to Waldshut in one of her armored vehicles, and that she bring him a "downpayment" of 100 kilograms of gold coins.

But she had insisted the gold remain in the van until after she had talked privately with President Barr.

Now, as they reached the lower level, their bootsteps echoing in the big concrete and metal chamber which housed the turbine pumps, Erica asked, "Why do you keep him down here? You'll kill him with pneumonia."

"It is only temporary. We keep him warm." Lauter led the way to a solid metal door guarded by a young man with an automatic rifle. Lauter signaled and said, "Open the door."

"I want ten minutes with him alone," Erica said.

Lauter shrugged. "Yes, yes." He was thinking of imprisoning her, too, and holding her for a huge ransom. He had enjoyed humiliating this capitalist bitch up in the office. She was beautiful and had incredibly white skin, so soft. Her breasts were too small for his taste, but for a change . . . He wondered if her men would fight very hard for her. They were only English hired gunmen, after all. Yet she had a large force a few hours away. She had helicopters. Keeping her would complicate matters tremendously in the matter of Norris and Barr.

But the idea intrigued him.

He had personally searched her clothing, as well as her lovely body. She was not carrying to Barr a weapon of any kind. Let her make her deal with the man, if she could.

When the steel door swung open, Erica saw a man in a small machine-parts room sitting on a mattress. A kerosene lamp cast a dim glow of light. When he looked up, she saw a bearded, shabby William T. Barr, President of the United States. It was almost a physical blow to see him like this. He was gnawing on a piece of hard, pale cheese. A foul odor emerged from the room.

She walked slowly inside. "Mr. President, do you remember me?"

The steel door clanged shut, startling her. She felt a surge of panic. Would Lauter dare imprison her, too? She had to assume not. But the enormity of the risk she was taking struck her, then, and a chill of terror permeated her mind. Her mouth became dry.

Barr straightened. He peered at her in the dim light. There were no windows in this underground storeroom. He chuckled, and then laughed. "Erica Stoneman. Yes, I remember. We met at a reception in New York when your father was running for reelection in 1988. That was before you married Brad Stoneman."

She nodded and smiled. She came forward and knelt on the mattress, close to him. She could smell him—an acrid combination of sweat and urine. She noticed a shit bucket in a corner.

He asked sourly, "What the hell brings you here?"

She decided to be brutally frank. Bill Barr was reputed to be tough and realistic. "I think I can buy your release from this situation and get you back to the United States."

"That would be nice, but I don't think you can afford me." He gnawed another bite of cheese.

"I think I can. I can give all the gold coin in Europe. I doubt that Julia Waggoner would empty Fort Knox to ransom you."

Barr stared at her. "Assume for a moment that Lauter will sell me to you. There's a quid pro quo, of course. What do I do for you, once I'm back in office?"

"I want what everyone wants, a restoration of constitutional government, reopened stock markets, bond markets, credit markets. We all want full return to pre-flare equity in real estate and commodities."

Barr smiled and shook his head. "Everyone doesn't know how much of the country you own or control."

"The Stonemans have never abused their wealth and power."

Barr laughed.

Erica flushed. "You don't know what that woman is doing to the country. She's a damned socialist! She's become a dictator and she's using the national emergency to rule by executive order. She won't allow Congress to reconvene."

"I'm sure there are good reasons for that. John Norris told me the situation the country is in. The food emergency—"

"I'm not talking about simple food rationing! Of course that is absolutely necessary! I'm talking about a police state! I'm talking about thirty million men under arms, a total civilian work draft, and a total lack of democracy."

Barr said firmly, "I would have done the same thing! And I don't think I'd have been as forbearing as Julia has been concerning your underground black market activities. I'd have thrown Brad Stoneman in jail—and you, now—if I'd been in power during those first weeks."

He reached for a bottle of wine. Pure water was almost impossible to find.

Erica was barely able to control her temper. "Don't you know you'll be killed once John Norris gets you away from these people? Julia Waggoner has no intention of allowing you to take over from her."

"I don't believe that. I know Julia and I know John Norris. I don't know you . . . except by reputation."

Erica turned away. She controlled her breathing and calmed herself. She faced Barr again. A molten rage burned in her, but she was in control. "I can have you out of here in a week. All I ask is a return to constitutional government. Not immediately, but within six months."

Barr took a swig of wine and offered her the bottle. When she declined, he said, "I'll wait till Norris gets back. If it appears that Julia is deliberately delaying my release . . . then maybe I'll accept your kind offer."

"You know the negotiations will drag on for a year or

more! He'll shuttle back and forth. You're a fool!" Erica said.

Barr smiled wryly. "We're all fools, Erica, in different ways. But you know all this isn't really my decision. Hans Lauter has the final, greedy say in the matter."

"I can handle him."

"Be careful he doesn't handle you."

Barr's words triggered a flash of recall—the scene played out a few moments ago in the pumping station office: Lauter's hands squeezing and mauling her naked breasts, tweaking her large nipples . . . his lewd smile . . . his hand between her thighs. . . .

Erica spun away from Barr and went to the steel door. She pounded on it. "I'm finished in here. Let me out!" she shouted.

There was a terrible ten-second delay before the lock clicked and the guard drew the door open. She slipped through the opening quickly and strode toward the narrow metal stairs, ignoring Hans Lauter.

The door clanged shut on President Barr.

Lauter, who had been lounging against the damp concrete wall, called, "It did not go well for you?" He laughed. "Stop!"

Erica began to climb the stairway. She seethed inside and her mind raced with options, plans, schemes.

Lauter called again, angrily this time. "Stop!" And when she did not stop, he called to the guard at the top of the two-tier stairwell, "Walter! Do not let her leave the building!"

Walter called down, "Yah, I hear you!"

When Erica reached nearly the top of the stairs she saw the middle-aged guard filling the railing from side to side, pointing a deadly over-and-under 12-gauge shotgun at her. He said gruffly, "Halt!"

She stopped. She heard Lauter coming up behind her. She turned and shouted at him, "What are you trying to pull?"

Lauter took his time coming up the stairs. He did not answer. He had drawn his sidearm, a Luger. As he approached, he said, "Walter, stand by the door. Mrs. Stoneman, into the office!"

"I'm not going to let you rape me!"

He gaped at her for a second, then chuckled and waved the Luger, motioning her to the top of the stairs, at ground level, and into the office. "Rape is not my purpose. We have important matters to settle before you leave."

Erica warily walked into the office and stood beside one of the windows at the rear. She kept a desk between herself and Lauter. She nervously fingered one of the large plastic buttons on her heavy coat. "What do you want?"

Lauter closed the office door so Walter could not hear. "I want the gold."

"I'll unload it when I'm safely inside my van."

"No, you will order it from the van now. I haven't seen the gold. I do not know if it truly exists. You have gotten your visit with President Barr. Now I will get what I want."

Something in his tone—a subtle body-language movement—told Erica that the moment her two men emerged from the van with the heavy wooden box of gold coin, they would be shot.

She had not come unprepared. The large buttons on her coat contained batteries and a miniature radio-signaling device. The buttons were connected by wire "threads." Her coat contained a wire antenna.

She activated the radio. An alarm would flash in the van and the powerful van radio would automatically broadcast a prearranged distress call to her main force. Two heavily armed helicopters would be overhead, locked on her signal, within thirty minutes. Plenty of time before night settled in.

Erica looked at her watch. "If I'm not in the van in

five minutes, my men will kill you. A radio message has gone to my force in Strasbourg."

"If that is true, you will be dead, too," Lauter said.

She met his eyes and beat down his gaze. She said, "All of our great plans will be finished. Why let that happen? I gave you my word you'll get that gold. I'll keep my word. That little amount is nothing to me." She tried not to show fear. She kept the tremor out of her voice. Her mouth was very dry again. Her heart thudded, shaking her body.

Lauter said, "Your tons of gold. I want that, too. Your men will not attack if you tell them not to. You do not wish to die."

Erica could not keep from nervously licking her lips. "Hans, you're a fool, because you think me a fool." She ripped the radio button from her coat. "Break this open," she said, and tossed it to him.

Lauter let it drop and stepped away from it. "It will explode, eh? When I smash it?"

"It's a radio! Here—" She boldly stepped forward and picked up the button. She cracked it open on the nearest desk with a heavy metal bookend.

Lauter saw that she had told the truth. "So you have signaled." He realized she had made the game very expensive and risky. He smiled. He admired her nerve and anticipation. "We will bargain a bit more. I want the gold in the van . . . and I want the van. I have a great need for a vehicle such as that."

Erica studied him. "I'll have to use the van radio to countermand the attack and have one of my helicopters land for me and my men."

"Of course. But remember, I have four people hidden outside with heavy caliber weapons. If, after a few minutes, you and your men have not left the van, I will order it destroyed, and I will be gone from this area before any of your helicopters arrive."

Erica said, "I consider the van an extra gift, Hans. A

further token of my admiration for you. You've shown me you are really capable of ruling a country . . . a new Germany.''

He nodded, smiling. "And I've decided not to kill the golden goose.''

Erica relaxed. "I'd better make that call.'' She smiled at him. "You'd better tell Walter to let me out of this place.''

Lauter nodded and left the office ahead of her.

As Erica watched him walk cockily toward the older guard, she marveled at his stupidity. Didn't he realize she would have him killed at some time in the future, when he was of no use to her, when he had no leverage? He had forced her to strip naked before him! He had mauled her, violated her body! *Her!* He was so blind!

As she walked out into the greater cold and wind, she vowed that Hans Lauter would die before he could spend any of her gold or any of the dollars he extorted from the United States.

CHAPTER 14

WHEN PRESIDENT JULIA WAGGONER ENTERED HER PRIvate conference room, the babble of conversations stopped among those seated at the inlaid maple table. The three men and one woman rose to their feet.

Julia waved them down. She took her central chair and opened the embossed leather folder she had brought. Each of the others had a similar folder.

She took a deep breath that became a yawn. She felt dragged out. She knew she looked haggard. Each morning the mirror showed more lines in her face. Her fortyfifth birthday was coming up next month . . . and she looked sixty!

She found herself facing Edward Marin, acting CIA Director. "How is Richard doing?" she asked. Richard Soble, the Director, had collapsed earlier in the day. He and Edward Marin had flown from Washington, D.C., to the huge underground Oregon Crisis Center, at her insistence. Soon after an initial meeting with her at 9 A.M., he had slumped to the floor in the executive restaurant on level 19.

Marin licked a neglected fleck of pastry frosting from his upper lip and said, "Not well. His heart is leaking. It can't get enough oxygen . . . An operation is impossible."

Julie bowed her head. She rubbed her weary eyes. "I've got to get down to see him." Before he dies, she thought.

Richard Soble had been invaluable during those terrible hours and days during and after the fire. Without his knowledge and integrity to lean upon, she would have been unable to assume the presidency and cope with the enormous disaster which had assaulted the nation.

Marin continued, "His heart can't pump well enough to maintain adequate pressure. Water is accumulating—"

"Yes, thank you!" She turned to Harvey Crenshaw, her political advisor. "How am I going to tell the Select Committee of Jim Lang's death? What's the best way? They'll go for my throat."

Crenshaw nodded. "Especially Senator Diller. He's paranoid as it is." Harvey glanced around at the others, then met Julia's haunted gaze. "We have everything Norris sent—the girl's statement—and we have complete and total confirmation that President Barr is alive. That fact overrides Lang's death, since he was sent only to further verify Barr's identity. The fear of your enemies in Congress was that the president, if alive, would be killed or that he would be discredited as a fake and ignored."

Selma Kaplan, a tall, skinny black woman, an anthropologist and now Julia's secretary of social services—a vast, growing, multifaceted bureaucracy—interrupted to say, "We could defuse the Lang matter by making him a hero. State funeral, all-com link, features on TV—"

"We don't have his body yet, and we'd have to surface the news that Bill is alive and being held for ransom. That would play into Lauter's hands. He'd ask for the moon!'' Julia said.

"And we'd have to pay. The people would demand it. You'd have no options," Edward Marin said.

"What options are there?" Julia stood up and walked a few feet to a serving table. She poured herself black coffee.

"With John Norris's cooperation—a swift commando attack to free the president," Marin said.

The third man present, General Conrad Steiger, commander of the recently created elite army Lightning Force, spoke for the first time. "We don't have enough specific, hard intelligence. We can't drop in based on what little we know. Too risky," he said.

"And Norris warned against something like that," Crenshaw said. He turned to Edward Marin. "Don't we have any spy satellites that fly over Germany?"

"Not southern Germany. Half of our spies were destroyed during the flare."

Julia stood behind her chair, sipping the strong coffee. She said to Marin, "What about those reports from England about a Stoneman expedition into Europe? Are they anywhere near?"

Edward Marin closed his eyes in thought. "Ahh . . . yes. That little . . . ah . . . expedition . . . The last reports I've seen had it in the Netherlands, heading north toward Amsterdam."

"Damned looters!" Julia said.

Marin looked unhappy. He changed the subject. "The immediate problem is the Select Committee. I worry about how long they can keep all this a secret."

Julia made a face. "If one of them talks to the private media, my hands will be tied. I'd be forced to go on an all-net hookup and tell the people everything."

"Don't tell the committee about Lang. Stall them," Crenshaw said.

Julia shook her head. "It's been six days since Norris

and Lang left England. The committee was promised a report after a week. There's no point in delay. In a few more hours, I have to get back to John with instructions.''

Selma Kaplan had been studying the photos transmitted by John via satellite. She flipped her folder shut. ''Mrs. President, above all, President Barr must be brought home alive. There is no way you could survive his death in Europe now, no matter how he died or who or what killed him. There is so much suspicion of the emergency measures you've had to impose, so much resentment, so many rumors and lies floating around, that you would be judged in almost every citizen's mind to have had him killed in order to stay in power.''

''I know,'' Julia said, shivering.

Selma Kaplan went on. ''The people are literally starving. We've had to cut food rations below sustenance level. Slow starvation creates an incredible anger. At a certain point, lethargy and weakness set in. But now . . . the least incident could trigger a terrible rebellion. It's quite simply a race, now, between mass famine and our first harvests.''

''What about the fisheries?'' Julia asked. ''I thought the expanded fishing fleets were bringing in millions of tons of migrating fish.''

''They are, and the coastal cities are eating more fish than they like. The problems are still processing and transport. We're losing enormous catches due to spoilage.''

''And in the meantime food riots in the middle west are straining the army to the limit,'' General Steiger said. ''People hear about people on the coasts eating roast salmon and white fish every day and they go crazy!''

''Millions of people are leaving their jobs, work crews, and just heading for the east coast. Whole families. Sometimes whole towns pick up and go,'' Selma Kaplan said.

Julia felt an almost overpowering urge to throw her coffee mug at the paneled wall. "I know all that! I read all your damned daily reports! I know that freak hurricane wiped out two hundred greenhouses in Tennessee and Georgia and Alabama. I know sixty-five people were shot for looting in Kansas City, and forty-one in Seattle. In one day!"

She glared at Selma. "And I know children are selling themselves for a meal. For a piece of bread!"

Julia watched Edward Marin rise from his chair and walk around the conference table to the serving cart. He had taken two oatmeal cookies and was pouring himself a mug of tea when she screamed, "Damn you! You gluttonous pig! Sit down! Stop eating for two minutes and pay attention! Or, by God, you'll be outside working in a road gang, clearing a highway!"

Marin scuttled back to his chair, white-faced.

Julia shook with rage and guilt. She stood, breathing hard, fingers clenched around her mug, and became aware of hot coffee slopping over onto her trembling hand. The silence in the room was ugly.

Julia deliberately threw her mug against the wall behind Edward Marin, who ducked. Steaming coffee splashed on the shiny tabletop. The mug didn't have the decency to break.

She took three deep, slow, quivering breaths and willed herself to relax. She moved to an empty chair near the end of the table, next to Harvey Crenshaw. She said to him, as if nothing had happened, "Agreed, Jim Lang's death is secondary to Bill Barr being alive. But I'm going to need . . ." She paused to think. Her mind refused to work.

Crenshaw said, "Throw the problems at the committee. Ask them to decide what to do about Lang's death. Let them wrangle about the negotiations with Lauter and his New German People's Alliance. Let them take some responsibility."

Julia scowled. "That's weakness. I'm supposed to make the decisions."

Harvey said, "You're sharing. You're bringing them into the decision-making process. Stroke them. If you don't like their suggestions, send Norris the instructions you prefer. But let the committee think they're important. Let them think you value their thinking."

"I was never good at that kind of devious manipulation of people."

He smiled. "Mrs. President, it's all a matter of semantics. Think of it as the grease that turns the wheels of government."

"I thought that was bribery," Julia said. But she nodded. She wished she had John Norris here. More, she wished she could call in Richard Soble for some frank talk. She sighed. "All right. Set up the teleconference with the committee for as soon as possible."

CHAPTER 15

Greta stood in darkness on a second floor balcony of the Greit Pfad Hotel, overlooking Wilhelm Platz, and watched the big American plane squatting obscenely in the once-beautiful square. Its windows showed bits of inner light through blackout covers. Its engines remained vertical, but silent.

She fingered the small radio clipped to her belt. She constantly shifted the heavy MAK-18; its carrying strap bit into her already sore shoulder.

She wondered what John was doing now, in the plane. Eating one of those delicious meals in self-heating packs the American military possessed? Writing endless reports? Playing cards with the marines inside?

She lifted night binoculars to her eyes and studied the area around the plane. There . . . and there . . . the two marine guards. One of them was watching her with his special infrared viewer. She smiled and waved. He waved back.

The night sky was black, with swiftly scudding clouds.

The deserted streets of Stuttgart were silent. The air stank from the continued rotting of the seven hundred thousand corpses that inhabited the dead city.

Greta moved restlessly along the small balcony. She didn't want to go inside; the air in the room was even more oppressive and foul.

She had a fine room. No one had died in it. The bedding was clean, though stale.

Albert and Walter, her companions on this trip, were in the next room. They had discovered a bottle of schnapps in an upper-floor room and were now, she was sure, drunk. Walter was a great one to drink.

She knew why Albert had been sent along with her and John. Albert was a spy, a watcher, for Hans. She resented that. If Hans could not trust her, who could he trust? She smiled cynically to herself. No one.

She kept watching the plane. Her fingers stroked the cool plastic housing of the small packset. She wanted to call John, but had no reason.

She muttered a curse at herself and was about to go into her room when she saw a flicker of movement on Reisestrasse, an angled street the marines could not see.

She brought her glasses up to her eyes. The special lenses made the blackness grey. Yes—there! A large animal—a tiger—was moving among the cars, sniffing the decaying corpses on the street and sidewalk.

It must have somehow escaped the Fellbach Zoo, months ago, and been feeding on human and animal flesh ever since. But now the flesh was bad. The tiger was a rack of bones. Starving. It was desperately seeking fresh meat. As she watched, it sniffed the foul air. It seemed to come alive with hope. It loped toward the corner, toward Wilhelm Platz. It smelled the marines.

Greta unclipped the radio and brought it to her mouth. She pressed the transmit button and said softly, "Norris!"

Four seconds later, the packset crackled and John replied, *"Yes?"*

"An escaped tiger is coming toward the plane from my street, now. He's starving, and he wants one of your marines."

"Thanks."

Greta watched the drama with her glasses. The big cat crept into the platz, using shrubs and high grass and wild spring flowers to mask its advance. She saw the two marines receive an alert from the plane.

The poor animal did not have a chance. The marines spotted it by its body heat, and a roaring, withering crossfire tore it apart. Its leaping, snarling, convulsive death spasm lasted only a few seconds.

For some reason, Greta felt a sting of tears in her nose and a tightening of her throat. But the beast was better off dead.

Seconds later, Walter and Albert burst out onto the balcony next to hers, their guns ready. She called to them, "They killed an animal. It's nothing."

Walter peered down at the platz. It was too dark for him to see anything with the naked eye. "A big animal? Would they shoot like that at a dog?" His voice slurred. He could barely stand. The quick surge of adrenaline which had sobered him for a moment was now fading.

Albert looked down, too, trying to see. He was less drunk. He said, "A bear, maybe? Escaped from the zoo?"

Greta gave him grudging respect. Albert was smart. She said, "Yes, a tiger."

He commented, "The creatures will come for it." He referred to the skeletal men and women who had somehow survived for this long in the city. All the food stores had been looted, and all the homes. A few survivors had all the clothes and shoes they needed, but they were eating each other, now. They would risk death for the carcass of the tiger.

Walter staggered back into the room. "Let them have

it.'' He had eaten well the last few days on food packs from the plane.

Albert looked silently at Greta for a few seconds, then said, ''I may sleep a bit. Wake me at one in the morning, and I will stand guard till dawn.''

Greta nodded.

He turned and reentered the room he shared with Walter.

She knew there were survivors in the area. They had been watching all the time. The plane had been watched. But the starving ones knew better than to try to attack the marines. She suspected there were few guns among the city survivors, and little ammunition. Disease among the survivors was undoubtedly taking its toll.

She was suddenly completely revulsed by her world. She felt absurd and helpless. What was the point of all this money and power-game playing? To become so powerful that this could not happen again?

Greta's thoughts spiraled to John Norris. She made a face, turned quickly, and paced the balcony. She told herself she hated him.

But she brought the radio to her lips. ''Norris.''

''Yes?''

''I must speak with you, alone.''

She waited long seconds for an answer. Then, he said, *''All right. Where?''*

She said softly, ''Downstairs, in the lobby.''

''Five minutes.''

She clipped the radio to her belt and entered her room. She let herself out into the totally black hall. She speared the darkness with the small, powerful flashlight given her by John when she had been up in the plane for the satellite link to President Waggoner.

There were no creatures in the hallway, nor in the stairwell, nor in the lobby.

She was sitting in darkness, in a large, overstuffed, horsehair-upholstered couch beside the side entrance to the restaurant, when John slipped into the lobby from a side entrance.

Her eyes had adjusted as much as possible to the darkness, yet the large areas in the lobby were still masses of blackness within blackness. She sensed his presence more than she saw or heard him. She whispered, "Here."

Seconds later, he settled down beside her. He wore nightsight goggles, but she could not see that. He asked, "What's the problem?"

"If . . . if I returned to America with you . . . how would I be treated?"

"That would depend. If you help me, if you are really turning, the president—Waggoner or Barr—would be grateful. I doubt that you'd go to prison. We don't have the luxury of prisons anymore. Every convict is out and working. They would probably love to be back in their cells with their TVs and free meals."

She leaned against him and rested her head on his big, powerful shoulder. She trembled, and was not sure why. She was no longer sure of anything. "I was a model, a professional fashion model before. . . . I was internationally known. I made enormous amounts of money."

"Then that's an area you could work in, eventually. You're at ease before a camera."

"Could you promise me a position? You are the president's special assistant."

"I have no real power."

Greta turned to him and insinuated her hand into his shirt. She felt again the ridging of hard muscles, the warmth of him, and the scars. She playfully fingered one of his tiny nipples. She giggled, a girlish sound that surprised her and then embarrassed her. She was glad for the darkness.

"What is it like in America now?" she asked. "Are people starving there, too?"

"A few," John said. "Most are simply losing weight.

The whole country is on a diet. The hurricanes and deluges destroyed whole crops. The transport system stopped dead for a week, more than that in the west. But we're harvesting huge amounts of fish, and processing plants are being put on line.''

Greta began opening his clothes. She whispered, ''The last time we were alone together was very good.'' She urged his head lower, to kiss. It was she who was asking for sex, who was the slave of her body. She didn't care.

When she found his mouth she moaned and kissed urgently, passionately. Suddenly she ached for him, yearned for him.

A moment later when he pulled her shirt free of her jeans and filled his big hands with her hot, firm breasts, Greta shivered with delight and excitement. Her passion was not faked, not a duty. She was astonished at her own lust. She surrendered to it again.

The horsehair couch was their bed. In the almost total darkness, she stripped naked and opened her long, slender thighs to receive him. Her hands trembled when she touched him, and her flat belly sucked and bloated when he thrust deep.

Greta panted and keened during the golden time that followed, as he covered her with his massive body and yet did not crush her, as he filled her and jolted her and wrung great, shuddering gasps from her sweetly tormented body and soul.

In those final moments, even John's attention was riveted, concentrated on his pleasure.

They did not see and could not hear the opening of the stairwell door near the dead elevators. Albert Ranker, his MAK-18 ready, slipped into the lobby and swept the area with his night glasses.

He saw Greta and John, and smiled without humor or indulgence. He watched silently as their lovemaking reached its peak and Greta screamed in her final climax.

Then he backed into the stairwell and let the door close soundlessly.

Greta lay limp, overwhelmed, her mind disengaged, her naked body chilled by a sheen of drying perspiration. Her inner thighs still trembled, and her belly jumped and flexed from the sweet aftershocks of their lovemaking.

John stood beside the couch, dressing. He sighed, and she sighed in echo. He had been so incredibly savage in those last few moments. He was without control, without limit! She couldn't believe she'd survived. The power! The terrifying thrusts! And his deep-throated grunts of pleasure! She felt proud of having given him her body, and of satisfying him.

She instinctively regretted having that year-long contraceptive injection in Berlin five months ago. Something deep within her wanted to have his child.

She loved him.

And his tenderness, his gentleness and concern for her enjoyment, until he became unrestrained, as he let himself go, that proved he loved her, too. Didn't it?

CHAPTER 16

THE NEARLY DEAD RAISED CLAWLIKE HANDS AND GAB-
bled weakly in French for food and water. The stench was
sickening.

Erica Stoneman walked quickly past them down the
aisle of the huge, old, stone Catholic church. She was
inured to it now, the ugly reality of starvation and disease in this terrible, hellish landscape.

Strasbourg had taken almost a full hour of murderous
solar radiation on that horrible morning two months ago,
and great winds and greater fires had swept over the city
later that day, and in the days following.

But this church had survived. And these pathetic remnants of the city's population had sought refuge here, in
their faith. Apparently, the priests and nuns had cared
for them and fed them as long as humanly possible.

Individually, these people had been only partially
cooked; somehow they had escaped most of the radiation. But their organs and glands had been severely
damaged and they had come here for nursing and food.

Erica had, early on, issued strict orders that no food or water be given by any of the survivors, no matter how pathetic they were.

Of course that edict was violated almost daily, as attractive young women survivors approached her men and exchanged sex for food. Erica accepted that.

This church boasted a solid gold crucifix and gold candleholders. There were said to be jeweled and gold ceremonial staffs and crosses. Her soldiers were breaking down doors in the sacristy and other private areas.

Erica climbed onto the altar and ordered two of her soldiers to unfasten the huge crucifix from the wall. It certainly looked like solid gold. In the past week, she had become somewhat of an instant expert on precious metals and jewels.

Her thoughts kept returning to the encounter with Hans Lauter in Waldshut. A cold rage burned in her.

One of the soldiers inspecting the wall mountings of the gleaming crucifix called for a metal-cutting power saw.

An aide ran down the aisle and called, "Mrs. Stoneman, we have a coded message for you, from Paris."

She gave further instructions to her soldiers and walked out of the old church, past the piteous, mewling near-corpses lying on foul, stained mattresses in the spaces where several rows of pews had been removed.

The starving priests and nuns who had been caring for these dying things were, by Erica's order, locked in a chapel. There was no food left in Strasbourg. All that remained was death. Maybe that is what those awful creatures were really begging for: a bullet in the brain. She decided she could give them that, in a few hours. She would make the same offer to the priests and nuns.

When she emerged from the communications van ten minutes later, Erica ordered a helicopter fueled for a flight to Paris. After refueling at her base there, she would fly on to Cardiff.

She read again the decoded message she had printed out herself: VITAL NEW INFO FROM M. NEED CALL ASAP. LANE.

"M" was that fat, cowardly little toady, Edward Marin, the Stoneman mole in the CIA for a decade, now acting CIA director. Brad's investment in the man was now paying off.

She had to be in Cardiff, at her headquarters there, to make the scrambled private phone call to New York.

She refused to speculate on what the vital new information might be. It was important enough to require a conversation and critical, top-level decisions. Something Lane McDermott couldn't handle.

It was a four hundred-kilometer flight to Paris through a slashing cold front that made the mountains of Lorraine extremely dangerous.

Erica held on grimly as the copter was buffeted by winds of ninety kilometers per hour and bulletlike sleet. It was not comforting to her to see sweat beading the pilot's face as he fought the controls.

Part of her was exhilarated by the danger and positive she would make it through. She led a charmed life; she had a destiny to fulfill. But another, acidic little voice ate away at her confidence by recognizing the frailty of the helicopter, human error, and the storm's total indifference to her existence. If there is no God, the voice whispered, there is no appeal, no fate, no predestined greatness, and all her illusions, all her great plans, were only phantoms, only collections of electrons in her brain, in her megalomaniacal, solipsistic mind.

She was confirmed in her beliefs, however, when the helicopter broke through the front over Bar-le-Duc and flew on through clearing weather. The sour little voice faded from her mind.

Her Paris base was a soccer stadium near St. Ouen. As her pilot landed in an area marked off at one end of the field, she viewed with satisfaction the huge accumulations of precious metals, crated artworks, key machine-tool parts, rare books and letters from the National Library, the treasures from museums—all securely boxed and crated, all under acres of heavy-gauge plastic sheeting.

Her Cardiff organization had quickly sent follow-up crews and experts to do this work. Already there were convoys of trucks with guard vans escorting them to the coast, where her ships were loading.

Erica didn't feel comfortable shipping all this wealth to the United States or England. The ships were destined for "The Stoneman Islands," shown on the maps as Trinidad and Tobago. That small island republic and its rulers had been owned by the Stonemans for a hundred years.

She ordered the pilot to inspect and refuel the helicopter while she made a swift inspection of the base. A reserved, upper-class Englishman, Sir Henry Benford, the newly impoverished Earl of Norfolk, escorted her to the stadium and a private suite reserved for her visit.

"We just now have it ready, you see. Raided some unburned homes nearby for the furnishings. This used to be the suite reserved for the soccer team's owner, but it was atrociously decorated. Really awful. I had to throw it all out."

Erica hardly glanced at the place. She shut the door on him and headed for the bathroom, which was clean and elegant. In addition, the plumbing worked. That was the major miracle wrought by Sir Henry.

A few minutes later, drinking a can of low-cal Coca-Cola which had been brought in from Cardiff, she was admitted, with the Earl, into the team dressing room which now served as a vault.

Here were the gold and coin and jewelry accumulations. Here, in special steel cases taken from the French Treasury, were tons of pure gold bars, tons of gold coins, and the jewelry of dead wealthy French women taken from bank lockboxes.

Special teams of looters, working with portable generators to power their drills and saws and using explosives for primary entry, were systematically going from bank to bank, from security company to jewelry company, blowing safes, forcing lockboxes.

Erica stood surrounded by billions of dollars worth of treasure, and laughed. She was flushed with a kind of mad rapture, of triumph and possession.

The flight of Cardiff was largely uneventful. As they flew over Kent and East Sussex, Erica switched the radio to the government's AM station and picked up a revealing news broadcast:

". . . were shot. The army has mobilized one hundred thousand men and is sweeping slowly through greater London, meting out severe punishment to the organized gangs of looters and resisters who insist on pitting themselves against the rule of law. The unfortunate acquisition by these forces of large stores of military supplies shortly after the flare, and the deplorable revolt by several groups of soldiers in Kent, has vastly complicated matters, as these men are trained in the use of advanced military technology. However, there is no basis in fact for the rumors that these rebels against the Queen are in possession of operable U.S. cruise missiles armed with nuclear warheads. Were that the case, Her Majesty's government would not be pressing forward its campaign to subdue the resisters and bring peace and order to the eastern counties.

"Good news will soon be forthcoming from the fisheries, as the Channel is yielding extraordinary catches of bottom fish that are leaping at any bait put in the ocean, since their usual food, the smaller, surface fish, were largely killed by radiation from the solar flare. The home secretary has put every boat in the water that can float, and conscripted everyone who ever put hook in water to man them.

120

"The dairy herds of Devon and Dorset are yielding normal amounts of milk, in spite of the ten percent loss of cattle during the post-flare extremes of weather. "The—"

Erica turned it off. Cardiff was only a few minutes away.

Finally in her suite in the Avon Building, Erica banished her servants from the dozen rooms and put through an unscrambled contact call to Lane McDermott in New York. "Lane, I'm in my suite in Cardiff now. Call back in fifteen minutes." That would give him time to have the circuits run for taps. Every precaution had to be taken.

"Fine, Erica."

She started a hot tub and began to undress. Her mind percolated with ideas for further exploitation of Europe. Word had come that the Mafia had survived the flare nicely in mountainous Sicily and was moving formally to take over the island. Further, they were organizing to invade Italy, not as an army, but in a loose alliance with local underground and criminal groups. Rome was a mass of putrescent corpses. The Pope was dead, the Vatican empty of life—except for those few looters greedy enough to try to rape the Eternal City's accumulation of treasures.

She couldn't go in there, however. Tough, fanatic Catholic gunmen, local Mafia, and other ruthless survivors, were coming down out of the central spine of the mountains and killing as many of the sacrilegious looters as they could catch. She didn't doubt a new pope would be "elected" soon by surviving low-level Italian priests.

Erica settled into her large, ornate tub and soaked luxuriously in the steamy water. She had bound up her long blond hair. It needed washing and setting, but Maria would do that later.

Now, Erica just wanted to relax.

Her mind would not cooperate. She knew the Po River valley in northern Italy was a vast triangle of death. No one could have survived in Venice, Padua, Verona, Milan . . . Millions of bodies were rotting in the intermittently hot spring. If a six to eight-ship convoy of surplus semi-skilled Brazilians could be sent there to occupy and exploit that region—that Fiat complex, for instance, and the art treasures of Venice—the proceeds could repay the costs of establishing a colony in the fertile area. They could fight off the mountain survivors and the Mafia, and stay for a thousand years. Of course they would forever be at war with southern Italy, but—

The phone beside the tub rang. She had plugged in the privacy attachment and scrambler box before slipping into the tub.

She languidly brought the receiver close and said, "Erica Stoneman."

"Erica, this is Lane McDermott. Are you in private?"

She slipped the privacy mask over her mouth and chin. "Yes, now."

"Scramble. F-three-nine."

She carefully pressed the buttons on the box. The line wailed and popped, then cleared except for the usual long-distance hiss.

Lane asked, *"Do you hear me clearly, Erica?"* He always used the same words.

"Yes, Lane. Do you still run four and a half miles a day?"

He answered correctly, *"I'm down to three."*

She said, "What's so important?" She leaned back against the warm, slanting rim of the big, round tub and let herself float in the hot, soapy water. Her breasts made small white islands with angry red "mountain" cones. Her flat belly was a shoals. Her thighs were unstable long sandbars.

"Erica, Julia Waggoner has decided against a rescue

attempt to get Barr out. She's going to offer a smaller amount than ten billion dollars to the New German People's Alliance, and she's going to stick with John Norris as negotiator."

"That was predictable." Erica yawned and felt tiredness seep into her bones. She idly used a free hand to touch her water-excited nipples. She liked the tiny shivers this caused. "Why the emergency call?"

"Representative James Lang was killed in an ambush just south of Stuttgart, carried out by renegade French soldiers. John Norris survived and went on to see President Barr."

Erica sat up fast. Water sloshed across the six-foot-wide tub. "Beautiful! What luck!" Her blue eyes glowed. Her mind worked like a suddenly activated computer. "Where is Norris now?"

"According to Marin, he's probably now on his way south from Stuttgart, to meet with Lauter again."

"What is the deal he's to offer?"

"One billion dollars now, payable in any form Lauter wishes, and four billion dollars as soon as Barr is safe in the United States."

"That's it?"

"That's it. No post-ransom help. Politically impossible. The Congressional leadership agreed to all this, by the way, though they were mad as hell and suspicious about Lang's death. This is a dynamite story, Erica. It's not likely to stay secret much longer."

"Yes, I agree," Erica said. "Tell me, can Marin plant counterfeit data in the CIA files, in memory banks, and so on?"

"To a limited extent, I imagine. Here and there."

"Is Richard Soble dead yet?" Erica said.

"Yes, he died last night."

"And John Norris's plane is in Stuttgart, right? How is it guarded?"

"Five marines and a two-man crew."

123

"That's his only link to the outside world? No other planes coming? No Lightning Forces flying in to help him?" Erica asked.

"A special helicopter was sent to pick up James Lang's body. It's on its way back the the States now. Beyond that, no, nothing. Norris is there now with just the one VTO plane and a few men."

Erica took deep, fast breaths. Her heart thudded. She saw her small breasts tremble from the heavy heartbeat.

Lane asked, *"What are you thinking, Erica?"*

She skated the pink tip of her tongue along her lush, red lips. She swallowed to relieve a dry mouth. "We'll go for her! Tell Marin to insert little indications, little pieces of evidence, into the CIA files to indicate indirectly that Julia Waggoner conspired with John Norris to assassinate President Barr in a way that would make Barr's death seem an accident or the result of forces beyond Norris's control. If it can be hinted by fragments of information that Jim Lang's death was arranged by Waggoner and Norris, fine."

"I see. That puts Marin at risk, you know. After all these years of—"

Erica overrode him. "Now—next, I will send a combat force to Stuttgart with one of my attack helicopters. That should be enough. They'll catch that plane on the ground and destroy it, wipe out all the marines. No survivors."

Lane made a wary sound. *"I see where you're going with this, but it's dangerous as hell. You must use overkill here. You must make sure, absolutely sure, that plane is wiped out, and that no survivors be around to describe who attacked. You'd better send your turret vans, too, and enough of your best, most ruthless soldiers to make sure everyone in and around that plane is killed."*

"Yes, yes! I know that! I'll pay them a huge bonus, a multimillion-dollar bonus."

"And," Lane ventured, *"am I to break the news to the public that President Barr is alive and being held for ransom by terrorists in Germany?"*

"Exactly!" Erica had become tremendously excited. "And hint strongly that John Norris, Waggoner's ex-CIA killer agent, her "Special Senior Advisor," is alone now in Germany, ostensibly to negotiate Barr's release, but actually, it is rumored, to make sure Barr never gets back to the United States alive. Julia Waggoner will stop at nothing to keep the presidency and to continue as de facto dictator."

Lane McDermott filled in with, *"And the suspicious death of Jim Lang, the only neutral observer, a respected member of congress, tends to prove the conspiracy. They had to get him out of the way."*

Erica nodded, delighted. "Yes! We bring her down! We now have Roland Lewis in place as her vice-president, and we own that old fart from toes up."

Lane said, *"Fine so far. But that leaves Norris and Barr."*

She pressed the phone more tightly to her ear and mouth. Her voice sounded odd because of the muffling of the privacy mask. She was very tense. She said, "Once my men have eliminated the plane and the marines, they turn south and close in on Waldshut. At any cost, they wipe out the terrorists! They kill Barr and Norris and Lauter!"

"Erica, it sounds perfect, but it is infinitely dangerous. If Barr, or even Norris, survives—"

"I'll join my forces! I'll personally direct them! Once they get close to Waldshut—"

McDermott interrupted her. *"Norris is notoriously hard to kill. He—"*

"LANE! I will not be interrupted like that!" Erica screamed.

"I'm sorry, Erica. But why do this at all? We can wait for events to unfold naturally. If Norris fails, Waggoner

is in the soup without such drastic interference and risk of exposure on your part. If Barr is freed, we can probably work with him. He—''

"No, we can't! I talked with him in Waldshut. I tried to make a deal, but he's as socialist-minded as she is! And she'd be back of him, vice-president again, and Roland Lewis would be bumped back to Speaker of the House.''

"You talked with Barr? How?''

"I cut a small bargain with Lauter. A little gold. He's a—I want him dead!''

Lane tried again. *"But you're risking too much. You'll still have all the expeditions, the colonies, the puppet governments. You might still—''*

"I don't trust Lauter. I won't try to deal with him again.'' Erica picked up a soft bar of castile soap. She tightened her grip and sank her fingers deep into the perfumed, pink ovoid. "This is my time, Lane. This is the way the entire planet can be locked up for us. This is the way I get even!''

"Erica, Brad wouldn't have—''

"My husband is dead, Mr. McDermott! Would you like to join him?'' Erica shouted.

There was silence on the line.

Erica smiled and rubbed soap on her shoulders. She had to let McDermott wrestle with his loyalties and insecurities. He was to her an old man, and old men were too cautious. They tended to make small, devious moves.

In her rush of power and planning and revenge, Erica forgot her recent terrifying experiences, her vow of security and low-risk-taking. This was different! She would be in command all the way, with overwhelming firepower.

Lane finally said, *"I'm with you all the way, Erica. I'll rock the country tomorrow with the Barr-is-alive-and-being-held-for-ransom story.''*

"With the sidebar of conspiracy and assassination!''

"Yes, of course. Editorial speculation. Rumors. Suspicious circumstances."

"Good. I'll be on my way back to Strasbourg in a few hours." Erica laughed. "If worse comes to worse, Lane, we can retire to Port of Spain, or Cape Town." She hung up and continued to luxuriate in the bath. She even enjoyed the delicious feeling of fear that claimed the pit of her stomach. This was really playing for high stakes! God, she felt sexy now! She regretted not bringing Greg Albertson back with her.

She picked up the phone and punched a number. When it was answered, she said, "Maria, would you like to substitute for Greg for an hour, right now?" Maria knew what went on between Erica and Greg. Maria had been hired with the possibility in mind that she would sometimes serve this purpose. Erica had specified that. Every employee was specially screened and investigated, even here.

When Maria answered, Erica smiled. "Good. Come back into the suite. Only you. I'm in the tub, now."

Erica put down the phone. This would be interesting. She'd never been serviced by a woman before. Who knows, maybe Greg would be out of a job.

CHAPTER 17

THE DRIVE SOUTH FROM STUTTGART HAD GONE WELL. John drove because he was now familiar with the wrecks and pileups on the autoban. The old Beetle, although loaded with four people and their supplies and guns, zipped along nicely.

He and Greta had decided it unlikely that the ambush group would have stayed in the Kirchheim area. The few surviving renegade soldiers had taken severe losses in the attack, and had lost their leader.

John approached the Waldshut exit and slowed down to maneuver around the jackknifed diesel truck which sprawled amid its shattered load of bottled water. The last time through, they'd picked up a shard of glass and blown a tire.

He steered onto the grassy shoulder and gunned the racketing little engine.

Albert, in the back seat with Walter, said, "Verdamnt! Take the next exit and come back! This is—"

The small car rocked into a grass-hidden gulley and

nearly tipped over. John braked abruptly and started to back up. The engine died.

In the silence, they all heard the distant hammering of an automatic rifle, then firecracker snaps from smaller caliber guns.

"An attack!" Greta shouted, and looked at John. "Schwein! Liar!" She pulled an automatic pistol from her belt.

In the back, Albert and Walter rustled and cocked their weapons with deadly swiftness.

John held up his hands, away from the wheel. He said calmly. "Not from my side. Not by the United States!"

"We must get up to the chalet! Drive!" Greta said urgently.

John started the overburdened engine and skillfully guided the small car past the overturned truck. Getting back onto the ramp required negotiating a steep, slippery mud slope. The grass here had been killed by the flare as the radiation cooked out all its moisture and baked the ground six inches deep. "A couple of you might have to get out," he said.

But the rear tires were almost new, and the tread gripped enough to pull them up and onto the ramp. John drove recklessly through the small mountain town. At the entrance to Schneise Lein he stopped. "Listen!" he demanded.

The firing had become intermittent. The sounds came from the right of where the white chalet stood, partly hidden by withered trees.

"We get out. On foot, now!" Greta ordered. They left the bug and moved carefully toward the sounds of rifle fire. As they crept around a curve in the road, they saw the situation.

A house that had been sheltered from the flare and had escaped the winds was now burning. The owners had realized they would be desperately short of food and had built a large, secure greenhouse adjoining the sunny-side of their two-story house.

And now, some of their starving neighbors, seeing the growing cabbage, peas, and beans, wanted that food. The greenhouse glass was riddled, shattered. Several of the attackers lay close by, one a middle-aged woman, another an older man.

The house burned loudly, crackling and snapping. Red and yellow flames leaped high as they consumed the dry frame, the shingled roof.

There did not seem to be any survivors of the attack.

Walter spat on the dusty road. "Fools! Not even peas would be ready this soon!"

But they saw other, timid survivors creeping into the area, willing, and eager to take and eat what could be found. In minutes, the home of the attackers would be invaded and ransacked.

Greta sighed. "Let's go up to the chalet."

When they drove up the long, curving drive to the chalet, Greta knew instantly that something was wrong. The cars were gone. There was no smoke from the chimney. Every window was shut. There were no guards.

John realized it, too. His gray-green eyes darted from the small barn to the stable to the corners of the house. When he cut the engine, the silence was oppressive and ominous.

"Where have they gone?" Walter said, nervously.

"Let me out!" Albert said.

Greta sprang from the car, pistol ready, and Albert climbed out after her, his deadly MAK-18 cocked. John got out more slowly. Walter shifted his bulk to the right and climbed out that side.

Albert sprinted for the closed door of the chalet, and burst inside when he found it unlocked.

Great whispered worriedly, "Where are they?"

Empty seconds ticked by. Albert emerged from the house. "No one! The food is gone. All the guns. Everything is wrecked. Somebody—" He sprinted toward John. *"What happened, Amerikaner?"* He seemed on the verge of shooting.

One of the terrorist women, Frieda, emerged from the barn, carrying a sports rifle. There was straw in her short brown hair and she appeared sleepy. She called, "Don't worry. Everything is moving according to plan."

Greta stiffened. "What plan? Hans didn't tell me—"

"He decided to make a move—to be safe—just in case of a double cross by that one, there." She pointed her rifle at John. "I was left here to take you to the new place."

Albert put his MAK-18 on safety. "Hans trusts no one among us, it seems." He asked Frieda. "Why is the house such a mess inside?"

"When the others left, the starving ones came and searched. I had to hide, with my pack. Then I came back." She said accusingly, "You were gone longer than we expected."

Greta waved a hand. "He had to wait for the woman president to make up her mind."

John slipped back into the driver's seat of the VW. He had been searched for weapons earlier, soon after he had left the plane, and he felt incomplete without a gun. He could kill swiftly with his hands and feet, with a stick, a knife—anything!—but a sweet little nine-shot double-action Benelli automatic was quicker. He was here strictly as a negotiator, but he had a strong premonition of acute risk and danger, and that his killing skills would be required.

It was crowded in the bug, as Frieda directed him to a mountain road that twisted insanely along the side of a peak ten thousand feet high. This area was the northern fringe of the Alps.

The new headquarters of the New German People's Alliance was a large, two-level cabin built of stone and massive timbers. It had survived in the lee of the towering mountain when the flare struck, and had been solidly constructed, in lieu of the high winds to which this area was accustomed.

Several guards with guns watched as the bug labored up the final grade to the cabin. Twilight had merged with darkness, and it was difficult to see the rutted road.

John knew better than to use the headlights; they would be seen for miles and would probably attract the strongest and boldest of the local survivors. The noise of the engine was bad enough, but the sound would be impossible to pinpoint from the valley as it echoed and reechoed.

Hans Lauter came out of the big cabin to greet them. He seemed pleased with himself. He kissed Greta and shook hands with Walter and Albert. "Any trouble? No? Good." He smiled at John. "Come inside. In private I will talk to you now, over food. We had to dispose of two—how is it said?—squatters, in taking possession here three days ago. They had hidden some tinned fruit in the cellar. We will share one of the peaches tonight."

Greta clearly resented being excluded from the meeting, but only glared at Hans, who ignored her. The others muttered among themselves. They did not like the secretiveness and eliteness of their leader.

Nevertheless, a few moments later, behind a solid, locked door, Hans settled down at a table and poured John some brandy. A great deal of wine and liquor had survived the flare, since it was most often stored in basements and cellars.

"We have some cured ham with potatoes and some young onions that have appeared lately. That will be served in a moment. Drink. You've had a long trip. You must tell me of your long-distance talks with your president."

John shrugged off his heavy coat. The room was too hot from a roaring fire in a huge cast-iron stove.

Hans wore only slacks, a pale green shirt, bulky socks,

and leather slippers. His long brown hair and full beard were neatly trimmed. He took off his wire-rimmed glasses and polished them with a piece of paper napkin. His brown eyes stared nearsightedly at John. "I have been talking with *my* president." He laughed at his small joke. "President Barr is anxious to be back in America. He might be inclined to punish anyone who obstructs his return."

John settled into the offered wooden captain's chair and took up the snifter of brandy. He sipped. "I'd like to see President Barr, to see if he is still alive," he said.

Hans snorted. "I would not let him die. He is too valuable. You may see him after we have completed speaking. I must know what was decided."

John contemplated this bold, power-hungry twenty-six-year-old fanatic. It was difficult not to admire his daring.

John said, "President Waggoner is making this offer after having conferred with the House and Senate leadership. They all agreed this is the best offer the country can manage at this time. There were conferences by satellite with Swiss authorities. There is a limit to the amount of credit the Swiss will give, even to the United States."

Hans slipped his glasses back on. "I do not like the implications of what you are saying, Mr. Norris. What is this "offer" you are talking about?"

"One billion dollars in cash now, to be paid in any form you wish—gold, Swiss francs, dollars—and four billion dollars after President Barr reaches the United States safely. His arrival is to be verified by the Swiss ambassador who will meet him in New York or another port of entry," John said.

"No! No! It is not enough!" Lauter screamed.

"The full amount, five billion dollars, is on deposit now in your name in Zurich Credit Bank. You can withdraw or transfer one billion of it anytime you like.

It's yours now, with no conditions, as a payment in good faith. But if you don't free President Barr, the four remaining billion will not be released.''

Lauter threw his own nearly empty glass at the stove. The snifter shattered, and brandy flared on the hot metal in a brief dance of purple flame. "How great a fool do you think me? We kidnapped Barr in Geneva! Are we not wanted for that crime in Switzerland? I would be arrested!''

John said, "You specifically asked that the ransom be deposited in your name in Zurich Credit Bank. Didn't you realize the Swiss would seize you if—''

"No! It did not occur to me then! No doubt, you have CIA agents in Zurich, now, waiting for me, as well.'' Lauter was beginning to think Erica Stoneman's predictions correct and her offer far better.

John reached over to his coat and withdrew a thick packet of documents from the inside pocket. "We anticipated that. We had a lot of trouble with the Swiss. They don't like giving amnesty and protection to a person or persons wanted in their country for high crimes. You embarrassed them, even with the flare an extenuating circumstance. They are not happy. But they will cooperate to help free President Barr.''

Hans settled back into his chair. "Go on.''

John opened the packet and took out several copies of a multipage agreement printed on official United States treaty paper. He handed the copies to Lauter. "Read all the clauses,'' he advised. "The Swiss army and police are instructed to allow you freedom of movement in their country for a full year and will provide you with official protection.''

Lauter eagerly scanned the relevant Swiss clauses in the agreement.

"In addition,'' John continued, "there is a pledge by the United States government not to interfere with you, not to harm you, not to follow you to, in, or from

Switzerland. And we pledge not to attempt to harm you or any of the New German People's Alliance members before or after President Barr is released."

Hans Lauter slowly relaxed as he studied the document. But he said warily, "These promises are easy to put into print."

John sipped brandy and waited.

Finally, Lauter put down the pages and said, "It is satisfactory as far as it goes. But there is not enough money. We must have ten billion now and ten billion in follow-up aid, and diplomatic recognition of our government."

"I'm sorry, you're not going to get it."

"Then you are not going to get President Barr."

The two men stared at each other.

John said, "Why don't you let your alliance members vote on this offer?"

"That is an insulting offer! I would not dignify it by asking them to even look at it."

John then understood Hans Lauter completely. He leaned forward and put his elbows on the table. He said confidentially, "I am empowered to make you one more guarantee on a private basis. If you wish, you can be given a permanent visa to the United States. You could transfer the five billion to one of the big New York banks and live in America, or South America, if you like. Rio, for instance."

Lauter stiffened, but he listened.

"On a personal basis, you now have the problem of being a billionaire and not being able to spend that money anywhere but in the western hemisphere. Soon there will be a return to pre-flare freedom in the United States, and with some cooperation from a grateful Barr administration, you could easily change your name and even your appearance, if you like. It would be no problem."

Lauter asked softly, "The other four billion . . . it also is in my name?"

John restated the clauses. "There are five billion dollars—*five billion dollars*—in your name now, in Zurich Credit Bank. One billion is yours now, no matter what happens. The other four billion dollars will be released to you personally when President Barr reaches the United States safely. You don't have to go to Zurich to claim your money. You could go to New York and transfer it from there, for instance."

All you have to do, John thought, is desert your friends and keep all the money for yourself. That's what you've been maneuvering toward from the beginning.

Hans said, "How can I trust you?"

"Get a promise in writing from President Barr. For obvious reasons, I couldn't bring along a written promise from President Waggoner. But she did in fact make those promises and told me to offer them in her name. The fact that President Barr is alive is known to too many highly placed people in the United States now. We can't keep the lid on much longer. It's in Julia Waggoner's best interests to have Bill Barr returned safe and sound as soon as possible. She'll be crucified if he dies over here or if these negotiations are delayed."

"That would seem to be an open invitation to delay, to wait until the news gets out, and then demand anything we want, since then your public would demand him back at any price."

John nodded. "Except that if it goes public and you delay and extort outrageously, both Waggoner and Barr will be mad as hell at you, and the public could easily turn on you after he is returned. That's a double-edged sword, Hans, and dangerous."

"What we are doing now is not dangerous?" Lauter interjected.

John added, "There are powerful private interests in the United States and elsewhere who would gain from President Barr's death here after the news of his being alive has surfaced. They might try to influence events here. The longer you delay, the more time and opportunity you give them to act."

Lauter said, "I see. Yes." He wondered if Norris was talking about the Stoneman forces. Much diplomacy and negotiation, he realized, involved talking around things instead of about them.

Lauter felt leery about Erica Stoneman. She was close. Somewhere in France, near the border. A few hours away at most. She was a ruthless woman, recently come to great power, savoring it, using it. She was playing for the highest stakes in this affair. The world was at risk. He sensed he had mishandled his contacts with her. She could not be trusted. His instinct told him to avoid her. He had some gold from her, and an armored turret van. Leave it at that.

Norris and Barr were alone, stripped of real force, far from the plane in Stuttgart. And he had these papers with all these promises in writing. Maybe one billion in hand was worth—how did it go?—more than two in the Stoneman bush. He laughed.

John reached into another of his coat pockets. He handed Lauter a telexed guarantee of safe passage from the Swiss government. It was his final card to play.

"Ah." This further bit of proof was impressive. Lauter's fingers trembled just a bit. The billion dollars had become very real. He licked his lips. "I will speak to President Barr about these matters." He slipped the telex into a pocket. "If he agrees to these things, then I will have to travel to Zurich to verify the money—the deposit."

"How long will that take?"

"One day at most. Perhaps only hours. It is only forty-five kilometers to Zurich. The Waldshut bridge is still up. If the highway is clear . . . not long."

John leaned back. He nodded. "Do what you have to do." He turned his attention to the brandy.

CHAPTER 18

SERGEANT MACKAY JERKED AWAKE AT 5:34 A.M. WHEN private Jordan buzzed from his guard position near the statue and reported, *"I'm getting a lot of heat from Freudenstrasse. Can't see anything."*

Mackay had slept in his uniform again, as they all had in the big VTO, since their arrival eight days ago. The duty had been mostly a bore, once the disgust at the rotting bodies passed.

The incident with the starving tiger had been the only diversion, aside from Norris's return with that beautiful redhead. Since Norris had left with the terrorists to go south again, Wilhelm Platz had been a tomb of silence and boredom.

Predawn light pearled the sky when Mackay settled into the big cannon turret that was topside and put heat-seeing glasses on.

Freudenstrasse was a wide street directly east of the plane. A large department store faced the platz and took up the whole block. Its windows had been shattered, its interior razed and looted.

Mackay scanned the long storefront. Yeah . . . there . . . and there . . . and more there . . . fringes of body heat. A couple of them were moving deeper inside the store, but carefully, keeping low. Lots of people in there.

He switched on the plane's com system. "Gunther! Get up in the saddle. We might have to go up in a hurry."

The pilot stumbled, cursing, toward the cockpit, pulling on clothes as he went.

Peter Nance, the other marine guard, in the low hedge near the tail of the plane, reported urgently, *"Heat from Schaumburg, at the west corner of Reise. The tobacco shop. Three or four in there."*

Mackay swung his glasses north to check out Gestrickstrasse. More heat from the demolished restaurant. All he could see were hints, faint glows, as the people kept below the windows. They had to be lying flat and crawling.

The plane was surrounded. The movements spoke of military deployment patterns.

Mackay said, "Gunther, wind them up! Nance, Jordan, get inside on the double! Ivansie, man the door!" He switched on the turret and set the big twenty-millimeter cannon to autoload. The gun went "live." Servomotors whined as he swung the gun toward the department store.

The engines coughed as Gunther hit the instant-start buttons.

All hell hit the plane.

The glowing fringes of body heat rose to become hot yellow forms, moving, firing at the VTO. The quick thudding of a heavy machine gun counterpointed the impact of the slugs against the plane's armor.

Mackay triggered the cannon and raked the store with a

139

pounding string of shells. Wood, glass, plaster, and brick erupted in spraying showers.

There was a sudden racketing roar overhead as a military helicopter appeared above Reisestrasse and loosed two missiles at the plane.

Mackay didn't see the chopper or the missiles; they were behind his right shoulder.

Nance and Jordan saw death coming as they were about to climb into the plane. They hit the ground and clawed the dirt. They screamed as the missiles struck.

One missile hit the left vertical wing between the engine and the fuselage, precisely in the center of the left primary fuel tank. The thin armor yielded like tinfoil. The wing blew apart in a tremendous orange explosion.

Nance and Jordan were partially incinerated in a split second.

The VTO lurched drunkenly to the right.

The second missile simultaneously struck the ground directly ahead of the plane and blew dirt and dead shrubbery in a high geyser.

Gunther, the pilot, was killed as the force of the explosion hit the wing, which collapsed, shredded the cockpit, and coated the interior with burning fuel.

Mackay had not had time to get into the turret harness or don a helmet. The missile hit caused his head to bounce off the cannon. His skull cracked.

Of the two remaining marines inside the plane, the radio man was switching on his broadcast power when a hail of heavy-caliber, armor-piercing, teflon slugs from the restaurant on Gestrickstrasse riddled the plane, shattered his left arm, and tore through his chest.

Ivansie had been holding open the door for Nance and Jordan, when the wing exploded. The jolting lurch of the plane to the right threw him outward into the fireball.

The copilot took a spray of teflon slugs into his belly, hips, and thighs, as he tried to enter the nose turret.

Five seconds later, the helicopter put four more missiles into the plane.

The other fuel tanks went up and the VTO leaped as the dying tiger had leaped. It settled into a shattered hulk, a roaring red and black inferno.

CHAPTER 19

JOHN NORRIS SAT IN THE WIND ON A ROCK OUTCROPPING, a hundred yards above the cabin. The late morning sun warmed him periodically as it blazed down between fast-moving clouds.

Above him and fifty yards to the left, Frieda lounged on a hidden rock shelf, on guard. She knew where he was.

Greta appeared below on the path but ignored him as she climbed up to talk to Frieda.

John admired her sleek body and dark red hair. Her insulated jacket hung open to show her pointed breasts under her shirt as she climbed. She carried a heavy hunting rifle with a scope.

After a few minutes, Frieda clambered down the slope to the cabin.

John watched the road. Hans Lauter had taken one of the group's Mercedes sedans early that morning to make a quick trip to Zurich, to test the truth of the deposit and the safe-passage guarantee.

John hadn't heard what he told his followers, but Lauter had publicly ordered Greta and Albert to shoot John if he, Lauter, was not back by six o'clock the following night.

It should only take an hour to reach Zurich, if the road was clear. Swiss radio broadcasts said the highway was open. Waldshut was on the German side of the bridge over the Rhine. Koblenz was on the Swiss side and held the Swiss border guard.

Greta called down softly, "John. Come up to me."

John sighed and knew he had to go. He might need her in a critical moment if Lauter did not return, or if Lauter decided to pull something, later.

But she was as unpredictable as a bottle of nitro. Her emotions were throwing her in all directions. Dealing with her was like walking a mine field.

He moved silently, further to the left, so as to disappear from view of the cabin below. He climbed a difficult line in loose shale and finally joined Greta on the hidden rock shelf.

She was lounging against the granite backwall, luxuriating in the sun, her jacket off, her plaid shirt loose from her jeans and wide open. Her naked, conical breasts were startlingly white.

Greta smiled and patted the smooth rock beside her. "I am relieving Frieda for her lunch."

From this extra height and different angle it was possible to see a longer stretch of the mountain road. The wind blustered constantly, whipping her short hair, riffling their clothes.

She said, "I could never have a tan, before. It was always too many freckles. A model cannot have freckles. So I always avoided sun." She rested a hand on his thigh. "Now it does not matter."

"When do you think Hans will get back?" John asked.

She shrugged. Her exposed breasts moved enticingly.

"I won't let anyone shoot you. Don't worry. Hans is too greedy."

"How so?"

"We all think so. We talk. We have the right to participate in the decisions. We are socialists, not a communist dictatorship or a manipulated capitalist democracy." She raised her right knee. She began nervously tapping her boot toe.

"Except Hans is the one who decided to go to Zurich alone." John said.

Greta appeared uncomfortable. "There was only a safe-passage paper for him. He is accountable to us!"

John decided not to press the matter.

She began to caress his thigh. "Besides, I will be going back with you and President Barr to America. I am not concerned if Hans tries to cheat the others." Her hand moved boldly to cover the bulge at his crotch. She regarded him from the corner of her eyes. She licked her lips. She smiled.

John didn't react. He supposed she wanted to have sex again. He asked, "Could we hear Frieda when she returns?"

"Oh, yes, from far blow. The path rattles." Her hand began a gentle, seductive squeezing. "You enjoyed our lovemaking very much in Stuttgart, did you not?" Greta asked.

"Yes. But I'm tired today. I didn't sleep last night," he said.

"Ah. Yes. The talking, the talking, the seeing of Barr and more talking." Greta breathed faster. Her nipples had spiked. She seemed to be more aroused from fondling him than he was. Her toe kept tapping, tapping, tapping.

She closed her green eyes. Her left hand continued squeezing. She said, "I have had many, many men love me before you. But I never loved them. Hans loves me, in his cold way. I felt, from my childhood, sex was a thing to use. Most men are such fools over sex. For me it was too much trouble with them. Such a sweaty, grunting business.''

"Many women feel that way.'' John wondered, did Greta really think he loved her?

"But you have such control. You are the master of your body.'' She squeezed him in a different, more rhythmic, sensual manner. "Even there. Especially there, where most are slaves.'' She turned on her hip and looked up at his face, her green eyes wondering. "You can be in total command of your body and you can as you wish become totally animal!'' She shivered. "And you can conquer me in a way I never knew. I never thought possible. Me! I have become . . .'' She searched his face. "Will you use me as I have used so many? Will you keep me, in America? Will your job—will the president require that we be married?''

John said, "I never use women that way. I can't promise that you'll even—''

Greta put her hand to his mouth. "Listen!''

They froze. But there was only the sound of the wind. Nothing from below, from the cabin, from the road.

She whispered, "I thought . . .'' She smiled and shrugged. "John, do you want to make love?''

"I don't think it would be a good idea.''

"We have time!'' She fondled him and discovered him softening. "Are you embarrassed? In the day, like this?'' She knew that could not be true. But she was impelled to make him lose his control. She had to try to bring him down to the level of other men. She was humiliated to want him so much, and sense his not wanting her. His damned self-control!

Greta began to tear open his pants. When he tried to stop her she cried, "Let me! I love you!''

John regretted having sex with her before, in that half-burned house, in the hotel lobby. She was tormented now, self-deluded, trapped in powerful emotional crosscurrents that sprang from deep in her subconscious. Her sexual behavior and tactics, her becoming a model, renouncing that career for a fanatic embrace of radical, terrorist socialism—all these violent life-moves betrayed a fundamentally disturbed personality.

Now he was enmeshed in her turmoil.

She exposed him, lowered her head and filled her mouth with him. She sucked frantically, feverishly.

John said, "Greta, don't. Not now. Not for the wrong reasons."

She willed herself not to hear his words. He could not resist this! She used skills learned during her masked childhood, from the times she never remembered. She only knew she had always been able to do this—and this—and this! She had always been able to reduce men to helpless, jerking, spasmodic beasts this way!

But the organ in her cunning mouth would not harden! She reared up, eyes blazing with shock and hate. "You don't want me! You don't love me!"

"Greta, I never said—"

She flushed beet-red and her lovely face writhed with self-hate and revulsion. She scrabbled away from him and grabbed the big hunting rifle. She pointed it at John. She was wide-eyed, panting with rage, now directed outward, at him. The rifle barrel shook in small, erratic arcs. Her naked right breast pressed against the cool blue steel.

She choked out, "I see! I know! You were trying to get me to love you, so I would betray my comrades! So I would betray Hans! You scheismund!" She pressed off the safety. "We do not need you alive!"

"Kill me and you kill the deal! I'm the only link—" Using the pretext of quickly closing and zipping his pants, John shifted position. Only four feet separated them on the granite shelf.

"Pig! I am going to kill you because you attacked me! For this gun!"

146

John gestured toward the road. "Look! What will Hans say if you—"

Greta's eyes darted to the road. A cloud had shifted low against the mountain and obscured a far turn. She strained to see through the gray fog. The rifle wavered for a fraction of a second.

John moved with lightning speed. His gesturing arm whipped forward and knocked the rifle aside. The power of the blow tore it from Greta's grasp and caused the rifle stock to bruise her naked breast.

John simultaneously lunged forward and pinned her violently to the rock. Her head bounced on the granite and her green eyes lost focus. She lay dazed for a few seconds.

John took up the rifle and switched it back on safety. Then he sat back and held the gun on her as she blinked and became fully aware of the changed situation.

Greta sat up and stared at him with awe and loathing. She tenderly rubbed the back of her head. She winced. John said, "Listen to me, Greta. I will take you back to the States with us if you wish. But I have someone in Oregon I do not want to lose. I could not have a personal relationship with you back home. But I will help you find a place—"

"Stop this stupid talk." She spat at him. "I only had sex with you on Hans's orders. I do not love you. It was a good acting job, ja?" She buttoned her shirt. She spoke impassively, her expression frozen. "My instructions were to seduce you, to bind you to me if possible. It did not work. So. I was also told to kill you, if necessary." Her eyes showed the glow of hate. "That may yet be necessary."

"I understand." John took the cartridges from the rifle's magazine, and the cartridge from the chamber. He put the gun down and moved it to the left of the shelf. "I'm going back down to the cabin for some lunch. I'll leave these on the rocks where I was sitting a few minutes ago.

Greta said nothing.

Six minutes later, as John was about to enter the side door of the cabin, he heard the distant, purring sound of the Mercedes's engine.

CHAPTER 20

BEFORE HANS LAUTER POCKETED THE GILT-EDGED ACcount book, his eyes lingered on the enormous figure on the first page: over three billion Swiss francs!

He was also flushed from the praise by his companions. He met their admiring gazes in the flickering light of the kerosene lantern.

Albert asked, "The other thirteen billion francs, is it there?"

"Yes. It is in a separate account and will be released to us when Barr reaches the United States. The Swiss ambassador himself will make the satellite call to Zurich Credit Bank. I talked with him personally on the phone, to confirm what the Americans had promised. They roused him early from his bed to take the call."

Sitting opposite Lauter at the big wooden table, Greta said, "It is too easy. They agreed too quickly. We could have gotten more."

Frieda nodded. "And I do not like . . . I do not like that it is in your name."

Lauter felt anger rise. A flush of rage colored his neck. He turned quickly to her and raked her with his hard, cold, brown eyes. His glasses glittered in the flickering yellow light. "I explained there was no way the bank could create an account for the New German People's Alliance. We are not yet a recognized government. We are not a business. We are only a name. For the time being, the account has to be in my name. I am your leader. It was my idea to take President Barr and to exchange him for what we need. Where would all of you be without me? A few still alive, scrabbling for food, maybe. But most of you probably dead, rotting in Munich!"

"But how do we get some of the money? We have a right."

"We are socialists!" Hans stood up. "See what is happening? A little money and all your eyes gleam with greed. You want to get your fingers on it, to spend it. Never mind the impossibility of spending money here! But you will not destroy our dream! I will guard the money. I will decide if our plans are correct and if the spending is for the right things. We must be careful now. We cannot fall into pieces over this. I want you all to think of ways to use our new power. We are an alliance. All of us are allies!"

Lauter moved toward his bedroom door. He was tired. The stress of the trip into Switzerland, the dangerous driving alone, and now this hours-long discussion and argument with his "allies." They were small minds, all of them, incapable of thinking in terms of government. Almost all of them had spent the last five years, at least, evading government, sabotaging government, scheming to overthrow government! They could not now think of *being* government.

He signaled Greta to join him. He was not happy with her for posing difficult questions for him to answer. She was suddenly wanting to destroy the agreement with the

Americans. She did not understand that original demands were always exaggerated for bargaining purposes. She was a compulsive idealist, one who could not compromise. And there was something dark in her character. He had sensed that from the beginning, when they had met at a party, when she had been so rich and famous.

He did not believe she had given up her career and her fame and money out of dedication to pure socialism and a new order. There was a deep, disturbing element. . . . Secretly, he did not think Greta was sane.

But he did not wish to bother with such thoughts now. He wanted to relax with a bottle of schnapps and with her body. That would be nice.

He flopped on the bed and sighed. Greta came into the bedroom with a candle. She closed the heavy door and locked it. When she turned again to him, the candle light cast evil shadows from below, giving her beautiful face and dark red hair a menacing appearance. Her green eyes looked black.

She put the candleholder on the bedside table and opened the lower drawer in the dresser. She said, "I'm feeling strange. Billions of Swiss francs. That is amazing." She took a bottle from the drawer and pulled the cork. She swigged a mouthful of vodka and shuddered as it went down. She came to the bed and handed him the bottle. She rested her head on his thigh. Her breath warmed his crotch. She whispered, "I'm feeling erotic."

Hans chuckled. "I, too." He drank a full mouthful of the liquor. He made a face, but the exploding warmth in his belly made him happy. He felt himself harden.

Greta said, as she sat up to undress, "I'll let you do anything to me you like. I will do anything you like."

"That offer is something I cannot resist." Hans felt a chill and wished the cabin had more than one fireplace, more than one big iron stove. Once the door was closed, the oppressive heat from the big main room was shut out and the bedroom cooled too quickly. "Let's get under the blankets."

They stripped and snuggled under the heavy woolen blankets and comforter. Hans drew the covers over them both and in the warm darkness reveled in touching and stroking her soft, warm flesh. This evening he feasted on her hardened nipples and then quickly, selfishly, held her head and pressed himself deeply into her willing mouth. This was good for a change. This was the easy way to pleasure.

In the darkness under the covers, with their breathing loud in the enclosing pockets of air, Hans once again maintained marvelous control of his reactions. Ah, Greta was gluttonous, superb! She had willingly done this for him at that long-past meeting, at her twenty-second birthday party, to which she had invited some of the roughest socialist scum in Berlin. She had seemed to be asking to be raped, in one instance by a dirty gang, and to be seeking degradation. Punishment, he had thought, then, for her new wealth, for her easy success built on nothing but her beauty and small modeling skills.

That had explained her renunciation of her status, and her spending all of her money on stupid socialist campaigns.

But now, in the hot darkness, as his pleasure ripened and bloomed in his guts and exploded in her mouth as he fiercely would not cry out, but contained the enormous sensations within his body and mind . . . now he thought she was possessed by a terrible need to be used, and a corresponding terrible need to seek revenge for having been used in this way far earlier in her life.

Hans put it together, then, as she sucked him with feverish intensity and wrung from him every drop of semen, and continued, still, with compulsive need, to try to make him whimper or plead or command her to stop.

Yes, he understood then. She had learned all this from

her father, the tall, lithe, professional skier whose picture she kept hidden, who had died at age forty-seven, shortly before her twenty-second birthday.

He gritted his teeth and hissed as the pleasure came again, and the afterpleasure was too keen, too intense to be endured, even by him! He roughly pushed her head from his sweaty, naked loins and pulled the covers away from his head. He panted in the cool air and pulled her up for air, too. Her hair was damp with perspiration.

Sex with Greta was a contest of wills, a game of pretenses and domination. He had played for years, but would not be playing much longer! With thirteen billion Swiss francs he could . . .

Greta pressed against him. She clung to him passionately. "Did you like that? I know you did! All that money—for nothing!—makes life more interesting, more exciting. Hmm?" She pressed warmly against him. Her thighs enclosed his left thigh and she undulated against him in naked masturbation.

Hans said, "We earned the money. We risked our lives for it!"

She murmured, "Yes, we did. We are wringing some treasure from the capitalist octopus. But it should be more. You know it should be more."

"More is not possible."

She clung and moved. . . . She said dreamily, "We should show our displeasure to Barr and the president Waggoner for the small amount offered. It is insulting." She bit at his shoulder. She breathed fast.

Lauter wondered what she was getting at. He grunted noncommittally.

Greta stopped pressing her loins against his thigh. His skin there was now wet. She melted against him. She kissed him briefly. After a moment she whispered, "We should punish them."

"How?"

"It is necessary that Barr reach America, yes. But

could we not kill Norris, to show our anger? To show our power and our dedication to the revolution? To show that we are not to be so poorly treated without some reprisal?''

"I don't think—"

"He is arrogant and comtemptuous! We should kill their most trusted and valuable agent to prove we are not to be humiliated!''

Lauter heard the hatred in her voice, the virulent intensity. He felt her trembling. This was not a rational thing she was proposing.

Lauter frankly liked John, even admired him. He saw in John something of what he felt he possessed, too. He knew Greta had had sex with John, at least once, probably more than once. He was not jealous; he had instructed her to offer her body to the man.

But, in Greta's voice and desire to have John killed, Lauter heard a woman scorned. So John had won that sexual contest with her. He, too, had great self-control.

Lauter said firmly, "What you say is true, but we know that both President Barr and President Waggoner think very highly of him, and that his death, even if it were contrived as "accidental," would likely be blamed on us, and they would probably find a way to retaliate. We would not see the other payment. It is likely that Swiss or American agents would seek us out for retribution.''

Greta started to make a hot reply, then bit her tongue to keep silent. She had lost and she knew it. Hans would not put at risk the other billions. She whispered grudgingly, "You are right.''

After a moment, Lauter slipped from the bed and began to dress. "Stay here. I have some things to do,'' he said.

"What?'' Greta asked.

He didn't answer.

Five minutes later, Lauter went into the kitchen of the

cabin and said to Conrad, a slight, wiry young man with a scraggly beard, "I have to speak to Norris."

Conrad put aside his MAK-18 and unlocked the utility room door. He offered Lauter a pistol.

Hans shook his head. "That is not needed, now." He took a lighted candle and entered the small room.

John was sitting up in the cot. The water heater and washing machine had already been disconnected and thrown out. The window was boarded up.

Lauter placed the candle on the boards covering stainless steel wash-trays. He drew up a stool and sat facing John. "I have decided to let you and President Barr leave as soon as possible. I will let you use our radio to call your plane."

"The sooner we get to New York, the sooner you get the remaining four billion." John reached for his boots.

"Yes, and I will give you a friendly warning: be wary of Greta. She hates you."

John smiled faintly. "I know."

Lauter echoed the smile. "Do you want her?"

"No. But I offered to take her with us if she wants to go."

"Ah." Lauter stood. "She is free to go. I would not be sorry. She is geisteskrank—insane, I think. Dangerous."

John nodded. He finished lacing his boots and stood, too.

Lauter led him to a corner of the main room where the portable shortwave radio rested on a desk. He switched on the power and asked, "You have a special wavelength?"

"Yes, and a code word. May I?"

Lauter permitted John to sit at the radio. He and two other armed members of the New German People's Alliance watched as John set the dials and spoke into the mike.

There was no response from the plane.

Thunder rolled in the valley near the cabin. Lightning sizzled the black sky, shockingly close. Rain drummed abruptly against the windows.

John kept trying.

"The storm?" Lauter suggested.

John shook his head. "They've got the best equipment in that plane. Computers are supposed to be scanning the bands for my voice twenty-four hours a day. I told them to listen south."

John and Lauter checked the power, the settings. John called repeatedly.

After ten long minutes, Lauter asked, "Could they be asleep?"

"They'd better not be!" John kept trying.

After a longer period, Lauter said , "Try again tomorrow morning. Get back to bed."

When John had been escorted back to the utility room and locked in, Lauter said to the radioman, 'Listen on the frequency he used, and on the others I have given you."

Lauter wanted to intercept any messages he could. Knowledge was more than power, now; it was a matter of life or death.

CHAPTER 21

Erica RODE IN THE BUCKET SEAT, NEXT TO HER DRIVER, in the largest armored van in her convoy. She was in the lead van. There was a certain amount of danger in that, but she knew Waldshut better than any of her other men.

She had left most of her force in Strasbourg. With her now were her most trusted mercenaries. They had destroyed the American plane in Stuttgart, and they knew they would be killed by the United States or England, if caught, if exposed. They were each richer by millions of dollars in gold, and they expected more millions.

She had nine vans, three helicopters, and thirty top-notch men, all told. That should be more than enough.

She leaned forward against the restraining safety belts and pointed. "That's the road to the pump station."

Michael nodded and made the turn. The powerful van took the river road out of Waldshut.

The radio crackled and Miles Webster's tinny voice said, over the whining roar of his helicopter engine,

"We're over the pumphouse now. No sign of life. No smoke or lights." It was twilight. The long black shadows of the mountain had long since crept over the river and were now dissolving into the deepening darkness.

Erica had ordered a quick move to Waldshut that afternoon, the moment she had joined her attack force south of Stuttgart. She had flown over the still-smoking plane and was satisfied the job had been expertly done. She had interviewed Webster and learned the details of the attack.

Now, Norris and Barr had no easy way out. She was closing in on them and Lauter and his ragtag bunch of stupid terrorists. They didn't know the meaning of the word terror!

She ordered Webster, "Stay up there. We'll arrive in a few minutes." She called, "S-1, are you still over the bridge?"

"Still here. No traffic. I saw a car coming off on the German side this noon when I arrived, but I couldn't find it when I got closer. Running very low on fuel."

"Stay up till a van gets there. Then come to the pumping station." She ordered a van with six soldiers aboard to interdict the German side of the Rhine bridge by towing derelicts to block the entrance and staying there on guard.

She switched channels to the two remaining combat vans. "Salter. Mathews. Pass me and get your men into that pump station immediately. If you draw fire, take no prisoners!"

The two armored vans roared past her.

By the time she arrived at the pumping station, she learned the place had been abandoned.

Furious, Erica looked back at the town of Waldshut. It was a cold night, and she spied several wisps of smoke rising from scattered chimneys into the almost-black sky.

She gestured Miles Webster over from his helicopter.

She pointed. "Check out those houses." She spoke sarcastically. "If you discover the New German People's Alliance, call me. If you don't, find out from the native survivors where they went to. Survivors survive by knowing where others are."

She decided to camp in the wide, dead-grass area around the pumping station. She ordered her multiroom tent set up. The kitchen van carried it from place to place.

Webster reported three hours later. It was pitch-black. The moon and stars had disappeared behind thickening layers of rain-heavy clouds. The only lights were from the tents of Erica's soldiers and the grounded helicopters which were being serviced.

Erica heard his van growl into the encampment and stop beside her tent. Almost simultaneously, the sky muttered with oncoming thunder. Far down the Rhine gorge, a stab of lightning flickered in the darkness.

Erica was sitting at her folding dinner table, eating a heated Prestige Dinner, served with wine by her woman aide, Hulda, when the first spatterings of rain hit the nylon roof of her tent.

Webster clumped into the small dining room. The nylon walls began to billow slightly from a sudden wind.

After her shower, Erica wore only a thin dacron jumpsuit and slippers. Her long blond hair was damp from washing. She looked up, her fork poised before lush red lips. "Well?"

Miles said wearily, "We had to torture a few of them, and even then we didn't learn much. The group we're after left a few days ago. They went east, into the mountains. There are hundreds of cabins in that area, most of them formerly owned by rich Germans, a few by Swiss."

"Did you find out where they had been staying in Waldshut?"

"Yes. That is no secret. It's a chalet at the end of the

159

road. I forced one of the suvivors to take us there. It was empty, looted. Nothing there worth looking at. Not a clue.''

The rain came down hard, machine-gunning on the tent. The wind blew harder. Crashing thunder boomed and echoed in the narrow valley. Lightning ripped the sullen black night.

Erica nibbled at a piece of Swiss steak. She smiled at the coincidence. "Maybe there is a simpler way of finding them. Maybe they'll tell us, themselves." She left the table. "Hulda! Bring my rain gear!" she yelled.

A few minutes later, Erica climbed into the radio van and told the technician to get out. She adjusted the shortwave setting and switched to "broadcast." She called Hans Lauter.

It took only a few minutes to make contact. She smiled as she realized he must have had his radioman routinely monitoring the wavelength.

When the speaker crackled, *"Lauter here."* she said, "Mr. Lauter, this is Erica Stoneman. I want to meet with you again. I have a larger offer to make."

"Where are you?" Lauter asked.

She quickly looked at a map on the van wall. "I'm in Neustadt."

"You must be closer. Your signal is very strong in this storm."

"I have a powerful radio. What difference does that make? When can I meet you?"

"I am no longer interested in your offer," Lauter intoned.

"You haven't heard it yet. I have the entire French government gold hoard available," Erica said.

There was no reponse.

"Lauter?"

The link was gone. All she got was static. She threw down the microphone. "Arrogant bastard!" She changed the wavelength setting and turned to leave the van. She flipped up her plastic hood and raged out of the van.

Miles Webster was there in the heavy rain and wind, waiting for her. She snapped, "All right. They're somewhere close, and they're not going anywhere tonight. Tomorrow at dawn, send up all three helicopters. I want those people found!"

"If the weather—"

"They go up! I'll see you at five tomorrow morning."

"Yes, Mrs. Stoneman." He didn't salute, but he spun in a military manner and strode away.

At five-ten the next morning, in cold, still, predawn gray light, Erica watched the swift conversion of the helicopters to silent-running mode. With the added secret mufflers and engine baffling under a quickly-attached cowling, the choppers would be whisper-quiet, at the cost of increased fuel consumption and shorter range.

They rose silently as soon as the light was good enough. The copters had special heat sensors and radar.

Erica paced in the dead, powdery grass near the pumping station and commanded in her mind, the results she wanted. Norris, Barr, and Lauter would not get away! An entire world and trillions of dollars were riding on this plan. They had to be found and killed!

An endless, frustrating, enraging hour passed. The sun came up and shone brilliantly for a few minutes, before a thick vise of clouds slid shut. It began to rain again, but only a drizzle.

Erica paced beside the radio van's open door, listening to amplified reports from the helicopters. Nothing. Nothing. Nothing! In addition, the van at the bridge reported no contact, no suspicious sighting. And the weather was getting worse. The helicopters would have to return soon. Visibility was deteriorating in the gorge.

Then: *"S-3 to base. S-3 to base. I have one of our*

vans leading a two-car, one-truck convoy on the west river road, heading for Sackingen. Do you copy?"

Erica leaped into the van and snatched the mike away from the technician. She said excitedly, "Copy! How far are they from Sackingen?"

"Ahhh . . . I'd say thirty klicks. Repeat, thirty klicks."

Erica looked at the wall map. She radioed S-1 and two. "Join S-3 and attack! Repeat, attack that convoy. It must not reach the Sackingen bridge. No survivors! No survivors!"

"Right. Acknowledged. This is S-2. I only have ten minutes flying time left."

The other helicopters echoed they were all low on fuel.

"Do your best! Stop them!" Erica returned the mike and jumped from the van. "Webster! They're on the road to Basel! They're going to cross into Switzerland on the Sackingen bridge!"

Miles Webster barked orders, and within a minute, a force of vans and trucks was racing up the road to Waldshut. The van guarding access to the Waldshut bridge was ordered to join them.

Erica road eagerly in the radio van.

CHAPTER 22

PRESIDENT JULIA WAGGONER RUBBED HER TIRED EYES and reached for her third cup of coffee of the morning. She grimaced as she sipped the hot, strong, artificially sweetened brew. She wondered what all this black acid was doing to her stomach and guts. But she didn't like taking drugs. Uppers. Yellow dynamite, as some of her staff called the capsules they washed down.

Carter Holgate, a FEMA official from the next level down, sat opposite her, near her big executive desk. The room was a close copy of the naval office in the White House in Washington, D.C.

But this was the nineteenth underground level in the Oregon Crisis Center.

She said wearily, "The more of this stuff I drink to get through the day, the more it keeps me awake at night, and so I have to drink that much more the next day. It's a damned rat race."

Holgate nodded sympathetically. "I've been in that vicious circle myself. I simply take sleeping pills."

"Uppers and downers." Julia took up the situation report they'd been about to go over. "All right. These estimates. Is two weeks enough time for an orderly transition back to Washington? You have me flying back this coming Friday. Shouldn't I be the last to move?" She adjusted her wig slightly. Her scalp was sweaty again. Perspiration was irritating the nearly healed wounds she had suffered from the assassination attempt five weeks ago. The doctors had shaved her head and now she had a gray-blond stubble which made the wig business worse. She still thought there were some wooden splinters in her scalp the doctors hadn't found. She still woke up occasionally at night with that enormous explosion echoing in her mind from when that booby-trapped school doorway had erupted into millions of deadly splinters traveling at bullet speed. The next instant, Secret Service men and soldiers were sprawled around her, on her, dying, screaming, and her head had been afire with pain.

If the explosion had been triggered a second earlier, she would have been killed, her head and face pierced by dozens of the largest of the jagged wooden shards.

Holgate said, "We don't have to transport records and files; it's all been duplicated there by computer and printer and staff. All we move is people."

"You hope," Julia said.

"Well, there's no physical danger to the government now that the last Soviet nuclear-armed submarines have been accounted for. There's no rational reason for not moving the government back to the capitol. And it would be a good sign to the people, a sign of the return to normalcy."

Julie felt rushed. There were so many balls she had to juggle, so many irons in the fire. What was happening in Germany? She wished to God that John Norris would make a report. And she knew that the moment she moved back into the White House, every member of the

164

House and Senate would howl for her to give up her emergency powers and return to constitutional government. How could she oppose them?

In her opinion, the country wasn't ready for that. Not for months.

It seemed too soon to allow that political game to resume. Demagoguery would flourish like weeds in a garden fertilized with a ton of manure.

She looked over the schedule Holgate had prepared. "How about the weather? Can we be sure we won't have another string of monsoons sweeping east, as they did last month?"

"The latest forecasts are amazingly promising." He rubbed an itch on his chin. "The farmers are getting in a huge amount of corn and soybean planting. And with the clearing of the highways from Eugene, south to San Francisco, and up to Portland and Seattle, we'll be able to run trucks again and move produce and lumber in huge amounts."

Julia watched him scratch his chin again. Why did it itch so? Was he nervous? She was amused. She said, "Food is most important. One thousand calories a day, on the average, for our people isn't enough."

Debra Wiley, Julia's appointments secretary, burst into the office, "Mrs. President—"

Julia's phone buzzed.

Julia knew with complete certainty something dreadful had happened. She put her hand on the phone and said to Debra, "What is it?"

"On the radio—the news channel—they say President Barr is alive in Germany, being held for ransom!"

The phone continued buzzing under Julia's hand.

So the news had surfaced already. Julia knew this development would tie her up for hours. She said, "Thank you, Debra. Please cancel my appointments for the rest of the day."

She turned to Carter Holgate, who seemed stunned.

"Proceed with the scheduled move. I won't be able to talk with you any more today."

He nodded and almost stumbled from the office. The phone continued to buzz, demanding that she answer it.

Julia tilted her head back and stared at the white brocade ceiling for a second. Then she took a deep breath, lifted the receiver and said, "Yes?"

Brenda Ingram, Julia's congressional liaison assistant, said hysterically, *"Mrs. President, tune to channel thirty! It's awful! May I come in?"*

"Yes, of course." Julia needed Richard Soble now, and John Norris. But Richard had died yesterday and John was out of reach. God! Let him bring Bill Barr back quickly!

She pulled out a desk drawer which held a communications console. Radio—she punched for channel 30.

A newsman's voice emerged from a hidden desk speaker. ". . . repeat this bulletin! Reliable sources revealed a few moments ago to WPI that President Barr is alive. He is being held in Germany by radical leftist terrorists for a huge, multibillion-dollar ransom. These sources also reveal that John Norris, a special assistant to now-President Waggoner is alone in Germany to negotiate President Barr's release. Other informants told WPI that John Norris was, until recently, a top CIA "dirty tricks" agent. They wonder why he was sent, instead of a high-ranking delegation of State Department and Treasury officials. Rumors are now surfacing, in Washington and in England, that President Barr is actually being held in Germany by order of President Waggoner, and that the terrorists were controlled by her, but are now double-crossing her and demanding a ransom for President Barr. Other rumors, all unsubstantiated— let me make that clear—are that ex-CIA man Norris is in Germany not to negotiate President Barr's release but to see that he is killed. Please stay tuned to WGGT-New York for further details as they come across the wires."

Julia punched off the sound. She sat stunned. A chill rippled up her spine.

Brenda Ingram came into the office. With her was Dell Prentiss, Julia's national security advisor. Brenda blurted out, "It's outrageous! Those lies—"

"Dell, who is behind this?" Julia cut her off. "Who leaked the ransom story?"

Dell started to rub his bald head, as he did when speculating, caught himself, and self-consciously dropped his arm. "World Press International is owned by Houseman Limited in England. They've been a reliable news service. The misstatements come from the "other informants" who were quoted. I would say—"

"It's the Stoneman empire at work!" Brenda said loudly. "It's Erica Stoneman. She was in England the last we heard. She tried to have you killed last month and now she's trying to destroy you this way."

Julia asked, "Do you agree, Dell?"

"Mrs. President, it's highly unusual for a responsible news agency like WPI to go with such virulent, blatant slanting, unless very intense ownership pressure is applied. I'll bet some executive editors quit or were fired before that stuff went out."

Julia persisted. "But who owns Houseman Limited?"

Prentiss frowned as he searched his memory. "Ahhh . . . API Associates has the controlling interest. In turn controlled by the Farnham Group . . . which is majority owned by The Stoneman Foundation." He smiled, proud of his encyclopedic memory. "High finance and corporate linkages are a maze."

Brenda said, "More like a spider's web—with Erica Stoneman, the black widow, in the center."

Julia nodded. She knew how powerful the Stoneman interests were. Erica was moving extremely fast to exploit the burnt lands, and this move was a bold and clever tactic. Julia's phone rang. She answered it and listened to Herbert Werty, her Press Secretary, ask for something to release to the media. "Mrs. President, the story—all the wild accusations—is being spread across the country like wildfire! Everybody is picking it up and it's being made worse! We must release a statement!"

She snapped, "Quote. I categorically deny that I caused President Barr to be kidnapped and held incommunicado, and I categorically deny that my special assistant, John Norris, whom I trust and value, is in Germany now to kill President Barr. And, more, I will make a special all-net report to the people of the United States and to the world about this extremely sensitive matter. Selfish, ruthless multinational interests have deliberately created this crisis and spread these lies in order to destroy me and to gain even more power and control than they now possess. End quote. Get that out immediately, Herb."

"Yes, Mrs. President!"

Julia put down the phone. She turned to Dell Prentiss and said, "I want a full investigation into the origins of this story. Bring in the Justice Department, the FBI, MIA, NSA, and the CIA. And I want a report in my hands by . . ." She checked her desk clock. "two-thirty. I'll be going on the nets at three-thirty."

Julia said to Brenda, "Set up the broadcast and coordinate with Dell. I will go without a script, except for notes. Start the announcements immediately. I want *everybody* to see or hear me. Declare a stop-work period of half an hour—three-thirty to four, PST. Send out portable radios to work crews."

Julia was operating on rage, now. If Erica Stoneman was so eager for a knock-down, drag-out power fight, she was going to get one!

Prentiss had turned away to leave the office. Julia called, "Dell, contact John's plane. See if you can get some word from him in the next hour. I have to know if a deal has been made."

He nodded and left.

Julia's intercom buzzed. "Yes, Debra?"

"Mrs. President, General Steiger wishes to see you on an urgent matter. And Mr. Crenshaw wishes to come in, too."

"Send them in." Julia braced herself. Steiger wouldn't bother her unless—

The general entered swiftly, trailed by Harvey Crenshaw, her political advisor. Steiger didn't stand on formality. "The Mexican government has just stopped pumping oil into our tankers at Alvarado. They're cutting us off until we allow two million wetbacks into our country."

Julia felt sick. "We can't feed that many more people! We're all slowly-starving, now!"

Harvey said, "The American people won't stand for it."

Julia's mind darted for a solution. The country had to have that Mexican oil! The Persian Gulf area was totally empty of life. The oil fields, the oil ports, the storage tanks—all were burned out—dead. America's underground national emergency reserves were almost gone. If the transport system was allowed to grind to a halt. . . .

"Can we get oil from Venezuela? From Alaska?" Julia asked.

"Yes, given time," Harvey replied. "But the Venezuelan port facilities and transport system were more heavily damaged than ours. The Alaska Pipeline is still out, broken in dozens of places."

"There are thousands of Mexicans coming across the border or sailing around it every day, as it is," General Steiger said angrily. "We need at least ten thousand more guards and a thousand more vehicles to really seal the border. And more Coast Guard, too."

Julia felt a familiar despair at the enormity and complexity of the problems of the nation. She said wearily, "If we submit to the Mexican blackmail, we'll be flooded with people. If we take in even two million more, our own people will revolt. The southwest will crumble into anarchy. We've just lately been able to put down that Albuquerque revolt. And all those little, independent "kingdoms" are still waiting to be forced into line."

Crenshaw said, "We're still a month away from getting the Galveston oil terminals into even partial function . . ."

"How could anyone think I want to keep this job?" Julia said. "Dear God! Bill Barr can have it! Just let me be an ignored vice-president again."

No one said anything. Finally, Brenda Ingram, who had been silent, spoke up. "We could send some agriculture advisors into Mexico, couldn't we? Some equipment—tractors and such? Help them grow more food."

General Steiger snorted. "They'd eat the seed grain. They've already slaughtered and eaten every farm animal they had." He looked around at Brenda and Harvey, finally at Julia. He said quietly, "We could send a Lightning Force to Alvarado and take over that port. We could hold it indefinitely. The Mexican army is a shambles and spread so thin it hardly exists. We could take selected oil fields and fill tankers for a year or more at minimal cost in men and materiel."

Harvey Crenshaw looked thoughtful. "And we could send some food into the area, as a bribe to locals. After a few weeks, they'd fight to keep their own army away."

Julia sat back in her big chair and stared with tired, pale blue eyes at the two men. The idea sickened her. But it made sense. She said softly, "The increased oil supplies would allow us to recover faster and allow us to pay very high compensation to Mexico, later. They would benefit far more that way."

Steiger said loudly, "Hell, yes! We're their best hope. If they flood us with starving wetbacks we'll all go under, or you'd have to do what I recommended after the flare."

Julia said, "Under no circumstances will I make the

border between the United States and Mexico radio-active."

General Steiger shrugged. But he clearly saw his solution as the only cost-effective method of closing the border.

Julia said, "All right. Harvey, work with Prentiss and the general on a contingency plan for an intrusion into Alvarado and the best oil fields in that area. I want pros and cons, worst-case and best-case scenarios. I want the plan tomorrow." She rubbed her neck. "Thank you, gentlemen. Brenda, get moving on my broadcast."

As her office cleared, Julia's phone buzzed again. She sighed and answered it.

It was Herbert Werty, her press secretary, again. "May I come up, Mrs. President? There have been new developments in the media. The Washington News-Telegram has a special edition on the streets—don't ask me where they got the newsprint—which has a front-page editorial calling for your resignation. WPI is running a quote from Vice-President Lewis saying he is shocked at the cover-up of the Barr ransom story and of the death of Representative James Lang."

Julia snapped, "Damn him! He promised not to break the Lang thing! That two-faced old bastard!"

"Yes, ma'am. But you'll have to issue a response. It's a well-orchestrated attack. We don't know what bombshell will come next."

"Yes, I know. Come on up, Herb." Julia cradled the phone and stood up. Her back and neck still throbbed with pain from the minor spinal injuries suffered during the assassination attempt. She'd been pushed down so hard, so fast, and crushed under her guards so brutally, that several back muscles had been torn, and a vertebra or two sprung.

Nevertheless, she paced around the large room. It was now clear she'd blundered in naming Speaker of the House Roland Lewis as her vice-president. There had been good reasons: direct line of succession, assuring the country a semblance of constitutional government, his appearance of aged wisdom and stability, tradition, . . . and she'd thought the old man would put his country ahead of the Stoneman interests he'd been serving in Congress for forty years.

But this latest statement of his, apparently right on cue, proved he was part of an organized power play against her.

Julia's thin lips pressed together. She still ruled this country by executive order, and martial law was still in effect. By God, a lot of the Stoneman hierarchy in New York and Washington would be in jail by this time tomorrow!

Dell Prentiss thrust open the door. He was white-faced. He held a telephoto in his hand. "Forgive me, Mrs. President, but John Norris's plane has been destroyed! We just got this from the VXT satellite as it passed over Stuttgart." He ran across the room and placed the photo before her on the desk.

CHAPTER 23

Hᴀɴꜱ Lᴀᴜᴛᴇʀ ᴅʀᴏᴠᴇ ᴛʜᴇ ᴀʀᴍᴏʀᴇᴅ ᴠᴀɴ ʟɪᴋᴇ ᴀ ᴍᴀɴɪᴀᴄ. The road to Sackingen was a narrow, two-lane blacktop, slippery as hell with early morning dew. The clouds were low, occasionally covering the road. Every other curve seemed to bring a dead car or truck, some in the ditch, some simply dead in the middle of the road, with a moldering corpse at the wheel.

John Norris, President Barr, and Greta were crowded into the rear of the lurching, bumping van. Albert rode in the passenger seat next to Lauter. Walter sat in the elevated bucket seat manning the small turret machine gun.

Behind the van, two sedans and a truck tried their utmost to follow it. The whole of the New German People's Alliance and all of their possessions were fleeing the Waldshut area.

John monitored the van's radio. It was preset to the frequency used by Erica's forces—including the helicopters. He had been listening to their searching.

Last night, Lauter had placed a man in the van to listen, and had learned of the arrival of Erica and her force, and had known the bridge was blocked.

Lauter had decided to sneak through Waldshut before dawn and try for the Sackingen bridge into Switzerland.

John called to Lauter, "One of the helicopters has spotted us."

Lauter shouted, "Verdammung!" He veered around an overturned produce truck that had spilled its load of cabbages when the flare struck. The cabbages had cooked and rotted.

President Barr sat with his back against the driver's seat. He was bearded, unkempt, but grinning.

Greta sat on a pad at the rear of the heavy van, peering out the firing slit. She held her MAK-18 ready.

"Christ!" John said, as he reacted to a transmission. He reached up to the wall-mounted radio and flicked a switch.

The voice of Erica Stoneman blared into the van. *". . . join S-3 and attack! Repeat, attack that convoy. No survivors. No survivors!"*

President Barr swore incredulously. "That's Erica Stoneman! What in hell is she trying to do?"

"Right, acknowledged. This is S-2. I only have ten minutes of flying time left."

"She wants you and me dead," John said. "It simplifies things for her."

"S-1 down to nine minutes."

"S-3 down to seven minutes."

"I don't believe it," William Barr said. "Why? Just because Hans decided to sell me to the United States instead of to her?"

John shook his head. "With all of us dead, she can bring your body back and accuse Julia Waggoner of having you held and then killed. She could plant evidence. She can manipulate the news and she owns at least a quarter of Congress. She wants Julia Waggoner

174

out of the way because she owns the next man in line for the presidency, Roland Lewis.''

President Barr had paled. He became grim. ''I see. I think you're right.'' He held out his hand. ''Give me a microphone. I want to talk to her.''

John said, ''Sir, if you broadcast, she'll know you're in this van and not in—''

''Damn it, Norris. Let me talk to her!''

John hesitated, then obeyed. He unclipped a headset with attached mike from the radio and handed it to Barr. He flipped another switch on the radio and said. ''Two way, now.''

The radio speaker blared: *''Do your best. Stop them!''*

John called up to Walter, in the turret chair, ''A helicopter will be attacking from our rear. Maybe two others in a minute or two.''

''Ja.''

Lauter yelled back to them, as he drove, ''That bitch! I should have killed her!''

President Barr had donned the headset and adjusted the mike. He said, ''Erica? This is William Barr. What in hell are you doing? Call off your attack! These people are taking me into Switzerland.'' He paused. ''Erica?'' He looked at John. ''Is this thing working?''

John switched the switches and telltale lights. The headset was plugged in. He nodded.

Then Erica's voice came loud from the speaker. *''I'm willing to talk, Bill. Stop your convoy.''*

John shook his head. Barr understood. ''I don't think so. They're helping to get me back to the United States. Order your helicopters to back off. You're making a mistake.''

''No. I'm trying to kill John Norris and Hans Lauter. They're the ones who will kill you, Bill. Norris has orders from Julia Waggoner to keep you from returning to America at any cost.''

Walter called down from the turret, ''The helicopter is

175

attacking." He fired a shatteringly loud burst from the swivel-mounted Bingham 7.62.

Greta poked her MAK-18 out of the firing slit and tried to spot the chopper.

Lauter began evasive driving.

President Barr yelled into the mike, "Bullshit, Erica! We heard you order no survivors!"

"That was before I knew—"

Everyone heard the terrifying *pum-pum-pum-pum-pum-pum* of a small cannon. No shells hit the van. Walter shouted, "The truck!"

"Stop the attack!" Barr shouted. "Stop the attack, Erica. By God, I'll have you shot for treason! This is—"

Walter fired a long burst. A cascade of spent shells fell down into the van. Overlaying the Bingham machine gun was the sharp, explosive roar of Greta's MAK-18. And over it all, the deadly, no longer distant, sound of the cannon. PUM-PUM-PUM-PUM.

The turret bubble shattered at the same instant Walter was smashed down from the seat. His body fell heavily to the van's metal floor. His chest was a bloody ruin. His back was a fountain of red flesh and bone. There was a ragged hole at the base of the front passenger's seat. The shell exploded under the van, lifting it momentarily. At virtually the same instant, another armor-piercing shell tore a hole in the top of the van and punched through Albert's neck, sending his head flying. It holed the storage compartment and passed on to explode upon impact with the blacktop.

The van shuddered and leaped from the twin explosions, but the engine miraculously kept running, and Lauter kept it on the road. Simultaneously, other shells pocked the road behind, beside, and ahead of the van. They tracked ahead, then stopped.

John's ears were ringing. President Barr still screamed into the mike. Greta had stopped firing; she could no longer see the helicopter.

Lauter was wild-eyed as he drove, now. He kept having to push Albert's fountaining body away.

John leaped up into the turret seat. Wind hit him. The stressed plastic bubble had disintegrated. Only a shattered sawtooth rim remained. But the machine gun was still operative.

He couldn't see or hear the chopper. He saw the two sedans following behind the van, weaving.

Lauter took a curve, and the new angle showed more of the road behind. The truck had overturned and was a mass of flames.

A second attack helicopter was coming up, low, near the surface of the Rhine.

John swiveled around and saw the first chopper wheeling into sight. He knew the British machine. He knew its vulnerable spots. But if it kept out of range and simply shredded the van with its cannon, there was no chance.

John deliberately tilted the machine gun down and to the left, as if it were out of commission. He slumped in the turret and let his head loll back on the turret cover. His head bounced painfully, but he had to make the helicopter pilot think the van was helpless.

He yelled down, "Greta! Don't shoot until I do!"

She sensed his trick and yelled, "Yes! I understand!"

President Barr shouted, "You win, Erica! You win! Stop the damn attack! I'll do anything you say!"

There was no answer.

John watched the closest helicopter from a corner of his eye. It was flying silent. He noticed the special cowling and mufflers. It whirred closer, like a monstrous, curious insect. The nose cannon always pointed at the weaving, squealing van.

The second copter was approaching. John saw six missiles mounted under its belly. And far back was a third helicopter.

The narrow, twisting road climbed the side of a rock

mountain, now. The river side became a sheer drop to the swift-running water.

The two sedans, heavy old Mercedes X-6s, had closed up on the van. Several of the terrorists were shooting rifles and MAK-18s at the cannon-armed chopper.

The chopper drifted closer—into John's range—and began blasting at the cars. It moved alongside the van, only fifty meters from the road, slightly higher. The sedans braked and dropped back hurriedly.

John came up, swiveled the machine gun, and aimed. There were a series of hydraulic pumps in the belly, just behind the landing skids. He sent a hail of 7.62mm high-velocity slugs into the helicopter's underside.

Greta poked her MAK-18 out of a side port and loosed a long, roaring blast into the cabin.

For long seconds, the pilot didn't seem to realize he was under heavy fire. Then the big chopper jerked and shuddered. The tail rotor lost power. The machine spun, out of control, and reared upward, toward the rock face of the mountain. The pilot desperately tilted away and applied full power, but the fatal momentum could not be overcome in time. Still spinning like a top, the chopper drifted gracelessly a meter too far. The vanes chewed at solid rock and destroyed themselves. The helicopter fell and smashed on the road behind the second Mercedes.

Greta screamed, "We got him!"

The radio blared, *"Base, S-3 is gone. The bloody fuckers shot him down!"*

Norris aimed at the approaching missile-bearing helicopter. Too far.

President Barr yelled into the radio mike, "Call it off, Erica! For God's sake!"

Erica's passionate voice blared over his, *"S-2, use your missiles! Use your heat-seekers!"*

"Will do." The second chopper turned back and put two miles between itself and the convoy. It loosed a missile.

John yelled down to Lauter, "Brake and spin on command!" He watched the flare as the rocket approached, a brilliant yellow framing a deadly black center. "NOW!"

Lauter hit the brakes and savagely twisted the wheel. The van skidded into a slewing, off-balance turn on the slick road.

The missile sensors, losing the van's hotter exhaust, switched in a microsecond to that of the rear Mercedes. A split second later, the car blew into an orange ball of fire from which spewed jagged fragments of metal.

The first Mercedes, a few meters ahead of the other, took the full force of the blast. It was thrown forward and careered off the edge of the narrow shoulder. It fell, twisting, to the rocks on the river edge, seventy meters below.

Greta screamed at the sight and Lauter cursed. Their friends had just died.

John called down to President Barr, "Bill, shut up! Pretend you're dead!" Greta quickly reached up and flicked off the two-way switch on the radio. They could now hear Erica and the two helicopters, but would not be broadcasting.

The van had stopped in the middle of the road, almost facing the helicopters. Lauter hesitated to turn and make a further run for Sackingen. The van's engine was still alive, roaring, but in neutral.

"Base, the two motor cars are destroyed. The van is not moving."

Erica broadcast, *"Barr? If you're still alive, I'll make a deal with you. Barr?"*

The President looked up to John. "Is she serious?"

John shook his head. "Trick."

"Lauter? Are you in that van?"

Lauter said, "That hündin!"

John climbed down from the shattered turret. "Any flares in here?"

They searched the van. They had to move and move again the grisly bodies of Walter and Albert. After a moment, President Barr opened a metal wall box and called, "Here." He took out a packet of emergency road flares.

"Lauter? If Barr is dead, I can still use you."

John said, "When I call for a flare, ignite one and drop it out the back. She's going to send more missiles. But missiles are stupid." He climbed back up into the turret and watched the two remaining helicopters, which hovered over the river two miles from Waldshut.

A silent moment passed. One helicopter pilot reported, *"Base, the van is still not moving. It's twisted around, broadside on the road."*

"Barr? Lauter? Last chance to deal."

John said, "I think she'd like to save this van if she could."

One pilot radioed, *"Base, S-1 has five minutes of fuel left. Must return."*

"Base, S-2 has only six minutes left. Visibility worsening."

Erica said viciously, *"All right! Destroy that van! After that, land on the road if you have to. We'll bring fuel to you."*

President Barr cursed. John called down, "Okay, Hans, go! Don't bother with evasive action. Flat out to Sackingen! Greta, ready with those flares."

"Ready."

Lauter shifted into a gear, twisted the wheel, and gunned the van around. He quickly built up speed.

"Base, the van is moving!"

"Kill it!"

Ten seconds later, John saw a missile launched. The rocket approached with terrifying speed. He shouted, "Flare!"

Greta pulled the igniter and dropped the red cylinder out of the van's rear firing port.

A second later, the missile was drawn to the flare's intense heat and blew a four-foot-wide crater in the blacktopped road, only thirty feet from the rear of the van.

Metal shrapnel peppered the rear of the van. The shock wave gave the van an added push, lifting its rear wheels off the pavement.

Lauter fought for control. The van slewed and wobbled, but straightened. They went around a sharp curve and were hidden from the choppers by a wall of rock. But the next curve would expose them again.

John called, "Get ready with a flare."

They came into view of the helicopters.

John saw another missile launched. "Flare!" he called.

Greta sent another flare blazing from the van. But the helicopter pilot was very good and very smart. He launched another missile five seconds after the first.

The explosion of the first missile obstructed John's view of the chopper for a few seconds. Through the temporary afterimage from the explosion behind the van, he suddenly saw the second missile, almost upon them, heading true. The pilot had keyed a homing delay into this one.

"Hard left!" John shouted. There was no time for a flare.

Hans had nowhere to go at 70 kph. To the left was a small ditch to catch rain and small fallen rock from the granite wall. To the right was a narrow shoulder and emptiness—an eighty-meter drop to the Rhine.

He did the best he could. He reacted instinctively by again slamming on the brakes and again spinning the van to the left. The tires shrieked as the van skidded off-balance sideways, into a high-speed drift into the ditch.

The missile struck the blacktop, eight feet short of the van. The shock wave blew the van over onto its right side. It crunched and rolled, wheels up for an instant, and then heavily over onto its left side, and for an instant on its front wheels—the tires blew—and it careered into the rocky ditch, bucking its rear high, still rolling, till it crashed on its buckled right side and rear.

In the split second permitted him, John had ducked and braced himself in the strongly built tubular steel turret seat and framework. He heard Greta scream and heard a peculiar, wounded cry from President Barr. Inside the van equipment and bodies—especially the dead-weight corpses of Albert and Walter—were flung wildly.

John's powerful muscles cracked with strain as a body slammed into him. His world spun, twisted, turned sickeningly, for several endless deadly seconds.

When the caved-in, battered van finally fell back from a half-completed roll and settled onto its right side, its wheels still spinning slowly, John relaxed his leg and arm-grips and shifted to the rumpled side of the van that was now the floor.

The van's engine, incredibly, was still turning over. Hans Lauter stirred feebly in the driver's compartment. He had been strapped in and the straps had held. But his hands were badly cut from glass from the laminated windshield. He swore with pain as he turned off the ignition.

Greta was alive, dazed, in a heap of loose equipment and supplies. Her legs were pinned by Walter's bloody, ruined corpse. She struggled for orientation. Her red hair was wet with blood from a scalp cut.

The radio had survived, too. The jubilant voice of the helicopter pilot cut the air: *"Base! I hit the van! It's crashed. It rolled like a square hoop!"*

Erica asked, *"Any sign of life? Is it burning?"*

"Negative. Negative."

"Land and investigate."

"Too dangerous. Clouds coming down. Fog. Won't see a bloody thing in a minute. Must return to base."

President Barr lay writhing in pain. A bent steel wall

rib had popped its welds during the long, rolling crash and he had been flung upon its jagged end. The metal had torn his belly open. A white, glistening, cut intestine showed in the six-inch-long wound exposed by a larger rip in his pants.

CHAPTER 24

It was complicated, but effective. The twin-lensed holocameras ranged like giant, glowering insects beyond the conference table, focused on President Julia Waggoner and, on her left, General Steiger and, on her right, Vice-President Roland Lewis.

Opposite them on the table were three large holopicture monitors showing, in perfect solidity, Senator Mark Douglas, Representative Tom Kinder, and CIA Director Edward Marin, who were all in a conference room in Washington, D.C.

Out of camera range were other senators and congressmen, with staff and administration officials. So, too, in the underground conference room, here were aides of Julia, military men, Dell Prentiss, Harvey Crenshaw, and a few others from Roland Lewis's staff.

Julia said, "You've all seen the satellite photo of Wilhelm Platz in Stuttgart." She felt nauseated. "John Norris's plane has been destroyed. We don't know why or by whom. We're monitoring every shortwave band possible, but there's nothing on the air about Norris, President Barr, or the New German People's Alliance.''

Senator Douglas took off his glasses and leaned forward. "Julia, I'm willing to go with this Lightning Force you propose to send into Germany, but I must insist on a personal guard force of my own, which I will handpick from the Illinois National Guard.''

General Steiger said, "Senator, there won't be much room. I personally will be commanding this Lightning Force and will guarantee your safety, and the safety of Representative Kinder, as well as that of the pool representatives from the news media.''

Douglas smiled coldly. He spoke directly to Julia. "I will be taking three staff and ten guardsmen. They will be subject to my orders, exclusively. Naturally, I'll cooperate with all reasonable and logical commands from General Steiger.''

"And I'll be taking ten men from the North Carolina Guard,'' Tom Kinder said forcefully. "Same conditions as stated by Senator Douglas. We have no intention of suffering the same fate as that of Jim Lang.''

"I understand your total lack of trust, gentlemen,'' Julia said coldly. "I am not going to argue with you. You may take the men you wish. My first and only intent is to get to the bottom of the situation in Germany. The first priority of this force will be to find and rescue President Barr and John Norris. The first landing will be in Stuttgart, to examine the VTO plane and rescue any of our marines who may still be alive. From there you will fly to Waldshut. After that . . . you'll have to decide jointly your moves and tactics.''

General Steiger shook his head in disgust. He didn't relish arguing with those two politicians. And having to take along five news hounds . . .

Julia turned to Vice President Roland Lewis. "Roland, are you sure you don't want to send a force of your own?'' she asked.

Lewis appeared startled, then wary. He sat up very straight. His silvery, bushy hair glowed in the strong holocamera lights. "I'm content," he said.

"Of course," Julia said acidly, "You have representation already in place in Germany."

The Vice President said stiffly, "What does that mean?"

Julia raked him with a caustic glance. "Why the Stoneman forces, who are pilaging the continent. Surely you support that effort? And surely Erica Stoneman is appreciative of that, as was her husband for forty years."

"I don't know what you mean." He glared at her. How dare she talk to him this way, on this occasion, with Douglas and Kinder and dozens of others listening and watching!

"Perhaps General Steiger and Senator Douglas and Representative Kinder and the news contingent will be able to find out what I mean."

CIA Director Edward Marin, the third-depth screen, had said nothing. Now he ventured, "The expeditions sent into the continent by the Stoneman companies in England were last reported in Paris. Recovering and preserving art treasures from that city alone will take months."

Julia looked sharply at his image. Marin seemed very nervous. Hadn't he had his usual pastry fix in time? She felt that his eating habits, in these times of starvation and austerity, were insulting and inappropriate.

She said to everyone, "I suggest we conclude this emergency conference as soon as possible. I must make my report to the country in an hour, and I want to include an announcement of this Lightning Force in my remarks." She turned to Steiger. "General, how soon can you and your men get into the air?"

"Depends on how fast Senator Douglas and Representative Kinder choose their guardsmen and get them to an airport. I have five VTO-15s on the way from Texas to Langley AFB, now, with fifty of my best men.

If everything falls into place, we could be on the way to Gander in six or seven hours."

Julia nodded. "Good. I trust everyone will coordinate and expedite to the limit. The quicker you all get over there and find out what is going on, the better for the country and for the world." She challenged Douglas and Kinder with her intense gaze. "Gentlemen? Are we agreed?"

The congressmen nodded.

Julia smiled. "Very well. I must go now. I'll leave it to our staffs and General Steiger to thrash out the logistics." She stood up. "Thank you all, gentlemen."

CHAPTER 25

PRESIDENT BARR LAY PANTING, WHITE-FACED, AWARE OF the extent of his wound. He whispered past pain-stressed lips, "I hope that does some good."

They were still in the crashed van. Lauter had just kicked the driver's door open and climbed out.

John Norris sprinkled antibiotic powder into the president's gaping, ragged wound. He didn't like the look of the exposed, bleeding intestine.

They heard the helicopters whispering close by, seeking the occasional look-in at the van, amid the lowering clouds and swirling mist. Another missile might strike any second, or a long barrage of cannon fire might sieve the van.

Greta delved into the medical kit they'd found. She handed John the largest press-on bandage she could find.

He shook his head. "Clips, first. Keep looking for painkillers. There should be something left."

But there wasn't. All the syringes were broken. The small sealed bottles were useless.

Lauter called from outside the van, "The helicopters are pulling out. The fog is too thick for them."

"Mr. President, I'm going to hurt you a lot," John said. "I'm going to clip the edges of your wound together, and then I'm going to loosely suture the edges. After that, we'll put a large bandage on it."

"I could have a torn kidney, or a torn liver," Barr said.

"Or maybe not. There's no way of knowing how deep that metal went. We'll get you to a Swiss hospital as soon as possible."

Barr grimaced. "Lots of luck. Do what you have to do." He jerked with agony as John did the job, and did not scream. John knew the greatest immediate danger to Barr was internal bleeding and peritonitis. He called to Lauter, "Hans! How much farther to Sackingen?"

"Eight or nine kilometers," Lauter answered. "Listen!"

John paused in his work. Greta held her breath. They heard the distant sounds of engines. But not helicopters.

"Hear that?" Lauter called. "That's Erica and her force catching up on us."

"We must get away," Greta said.

John nodded. He finished sewing the wound. "Mr. President, I'm going to have to get you out of here."

Barr nodded. He was sweating. "Whatever you think best. I'll help all I can."

John pressed the bandage in place with gentle, yet firm pressures.

The best exit from the overturned van was the gaping, shattered turret. The machine gun had been smashed out of the way. "Hans, help me with President Barr," John called. "Support him when I put him out through the turret."

"Yes, okay," Hans said.

It took all of John's strength to carefully, gently, lift

Barr out of the clutter of junk. He had to have Greta clear a place for him to step, and to laboriously drag Walter's gored corpse a few inches.

When Hans pulled Barr free of the jagged-edge turret he left bloody prints on the president's heavy jacket. In a moment, President Barr stood weakly, leaning against the van's now vertical roof.

The engine sounds were closer.

As John climbed out through the turret, Lauter said, "That woman will kill us all. I'm sorry, President and Norris, I must leave now. Greta?" She had emerged behind John and had her MAK-18. He pointed to a steep gorge that led upward into the mountains.

Greta appeared puzzled. "You won't help? You won't fight?"

Lauter spread his bloody hands. "It is hopeless. And one billion dollars I now have in Zurich. The game is over." He waited a second for her to move toward him, then turned away and walked into the tumbled-rock entrance to the gorge. He carried a heavy shoulder pack containing most of the gold coins from his earlier meeting with Erica Stoneman. He had pulled his pack from the driver's compartment of the van.

Greta watched Lauter disappear. "Scheisskopf!" she said. She seemed torn between leaving and staying. She asked John, "Where do you go now?"

"Down the road with the president for as long as we can. We can't climb."

The distant engine sounds had stopped. John guessed the exploded, burning truck and crashed helicopter had blocked Erica's progress. But for how long?

Greta looked toward Lauter, who was now in view again, climbing into a narrow defile. Her face twisted and she swore to herself. She pressed her lips together and glared at John. "What should I seek in the van, to help you? I will stay with you. Gott help me."

Five minutes later, John had Albert's sidearm belted

around his waist, and had wrapped President Barr in the big sheepskin coat worn by Walter. The huge, bloody rent in back didn't matter.

Greta carried a backpack containing the food and water that had survived the wild, rolling crash, the medical kit, and extra ammunition for her MAK-18.

President Barr had lost a lot of weight while in the hands of the terrorists, and had been allowed very little time for exercise. He was terribly out of condition.

The President said weakly, skeptically, "John, how far can I walk?"

"As far as you can," John answered. "After that, I'll carry you." He circled Barr's waist with a powerful arm and urged the president away from the van, down the road.

Greta followed, glancing over her shoulder occasionally. There were screeching metal sounds from beyond the two previous curves in the road. Either the truck or the downed helicopter was being moved out of the way.

Erica stepped down from the radio van and walked to the edge of the narrow road to peer down at the crumpled Mercedes on the rocks below. The car was lying, broken-backed, half in the swift-running river. Four of her mercenaries were working their way down the rocky cliff to check for life.

The truck held two cindery bodies. After an hour's delay in getting past the smashed helicopter, the exploded and burned Mercedes had yielded four blackened and segmented bodies, one a woman. But two other bodies—in strewn, cooked parts—had been unidentifiable. There was no way of telling for sure if Norris or Lauter was either of these.

She had just returned from examining the wrecked van. The radio was still there, and that proved Barr had been in the van. She suspected Lauter and Norris had been in the van, too, but the only two bodies found in it, both male, had not been the men she wanted dead.

Erica looked around at the damned low clouds which hovered on the road, creating a thick, damp, cold fog. She looked up at the mountain. Barr and Norris and Lauter could be anywhere up there. What kind of fantastic luck had allowed them to live?

She shouted down to her soldiers as they carefully picked their way down to the smashed, silent Mercedes, "Hurry up! Faster!" Their orders were to bring up all male bodies. Other soldiers were standing by with ropes.

Behind her, a soldier called, "Mrs. Stoneman! Radio wants you."

She returned to the radio van and climbed in. The technician said, "The special frequency light came on and a recorder kicked in . . ." There were a few things he didn't know about his console. He didn't need to be told to leave the van. This was very private Stoneman business.

Erica felt a tremor of fear. A secret part of the radio console had been designed and computerized to record a narrow-beam, shortwave, very fast digital signal from New York. The power involved was enormous and the signal time less than a second after a split-second initial contact to switch on the special recorder. Lane McDermott wouldn't have used this system except in a critical emergency situation.

The U.S. government was monitoring the entire shortwave band, but it was unlikely they would have the advanced detection devices and recorders on line to catch this compressed, coded transmission. To their regular monitors and recorders, it would be one second of intense white noise. It was very unlikely they could trace the carrier wave to the Stoneman Building.

Erica took a special booklet from her pocket and punched in the decoder program. She switched on the

CRT monitor and ran the tape. The screen came alive with the message.

WAGGONER SENDING LIGHTNING FORCE W/CONGRESS-
MEN & NEWSMEN TO STUTTGART, WALDSHUT. SEARCH
FOR BARR, NORRIS. FORCE ARRIVING AFB BIRMINGHAM
SIX HOURS. NO CONTROL.

Sickened, Erica stared at the screen. Then she convulsively stabbed a button and wiped out the message. Her hands became fists. The fear in her guts was bottomless, now.

She realized how terribly she had blundered. Lane had been right! She had not anticipated an expeditionary search force so soon. Not within a day!

Now, if Barr and Norris and Lauter survived long enough to be rescued, they would destroy the Stoneman empire within days, with Julia Waggoner's enthusiastic cooperation! None of her prostitute politicians—not even Roland Lewis—would have the courage to stand up against an enraged nation. Everything would be confiscated! She would be hunted down and put on trial for high treason! Even if she got away to South Africa, Barr might send a large military force after her.

Erica Stoneman experienced for the first time in her life the extreme gut-roiling knowledge of personal terror. She hugged herself and moaned softly. She closed her stricken blue eyes and tried to think. What could she do?

She realized that if even one of the three men survived, she and the Stoneman empire were doomed. And . . . oh, God! . . . if any of her mercenaries talked!

She had been so arrogant! So sure of herself! So full of power!

She had to make a deal. There had to be some kind of deal Barr would agree to! But maybe he was dead!

Erica bolted out of the van. She ran to the edge of the

road. Her soldiers were at the wrecked Mercedes, now. They were crawling into it, dragging out bodies. She snatched a pair of binoculars from a nearby sergeant. She had trouble focusing. Her hands shook. Two bodies —no, neither one was Barr or Lauter. A third body was pulled from the car. No.

A fourth. A fifth. No! The sixth was that of a chunky young woman.

President Barr, Norris, and Lauter were unaccounted for. They were alive somewhere! Somewhere close! She stared down the road, at the river, at the looming mountain.

Erica wanted to vomit. She fought the sour gorge rising in her throat. She walked quickly away, then knelt beside the road, facing the mountain, and let it come.

When she finally got to her feet and turned to face the world, her mind was clear, emotionless. She called to her commander, Miles Webster, and told him to begin a search for the three men. She posted a one-hundred-million-dollar bounty on each. And, she countermanded her previous "No survivors" order. She wanted them brought to her alive! A dead man could not tell where the others were. She doubted her men could capture all three together.

Erica cast a withering look at the low clouds, the intermittent fog. Her helicopters were back at the pumping station being refueled and re-armed. She guessed a three-hundred-million-dollar total bounty would make the pilots brave.

She hoped these low clouds would lift or burn away as the day progressed. "Webster!" she called. "Send a van all the way in to Sackingen! Get the helicopters into the air!"

John had carried President Barr two kilometers, but he knew he had reached his limit. His arms were trembling with fatigue and threatened to drop the severely wounded man.

His legs, too, quivered with exhaustion. He could not go another ten yards.

"Got to rest a few minutes," he said. He angled to the river side of the road and used the last of his strength to ease President Barr down on the gravelly shoulder.

Greta had said very little in the past twenty minutes, as she trudged along beside him. Now she sat on a flat rock a few feet down the slope and watched both men carefully. When John asked for a drink, she passed him the plastic canteen she'd taken from the van.

She regretted staying with John. Hans had done the correct thing. The game was over. Even now, if she should simply run away . . . but she didn't move.

Barr whispered, "Look at my stomach."

John opened the heavy sheepskin coat and saw that the big square bandage was bloodsoaked. The president's shirt, too, partially glistened with fresh blood.

Barr said, "Very bad, I think."

John nodded. "You need a transfusion."

"I have a lot of pain." Barr settled back onto his elbows, then onto his back. "When you hear Erica's men coming, leave me here. There's just a chance she won't have me killed. And even if her orders stand, I'd rather take a bullet in the brain than go on much longer like this."

John looked up at the boulder-strewn slope of the mountain. An ambush . . . "It depends on how many come," he said.

They all heard the engine sound. A powerful vehicle was coming fast from the area of the van's crash.

John signaled for Greta to move up onto the road. "We'll try an ambush from up there, to get whatever they're driving. Move!" To President Barr he said, "You'll have to be our bait, sir. When they stop for you—"

"I understand. Go on."

John barely had time to run across the road and climb up behind some fractured boulders to join Greta for an elevated shooting vantage, when an armored van, the same model they had used earlier, came growling around a curve.

John drew his gun, a Walther PPK, and handed it to Greta. "I want the MAK."

She almost refused, then wordlessly traded weapons. She thought he was probably better with the big automatic rifle than she. It had a pile-driving kick.

The van actually passed President Barr before skidding to a stop. There was a man in the turret. The machine gun swiveled to cover the mountain.

A long moment passed. Finally, one soldier left the van on the river side and ran back to examine the president. They exchanged words. The soldier called to the van, "The bugger's alive. He's the bloody president!"

Another soldier left the van and ran to the president. There was a short conversation.

John didn't like the situation. He didn't know how many men were left in the van. At least two: the driver and the turret man. He knew the turret bubble could withstand a high-velocity nine-millimeter MAK slug. And the door windows on the van were equally strong. Only special teflon-coated bullets were likely to penetrate the van's sides.

How to get all the men from the van? Kill the two soldiers with the president, then risk a run to the van and hope the door would still be open? He'd have to run through the machine gun's field of fire.

The soldiers with Barr had not killed him. In fact, one had taken off his jacket and folded it to provide a pillow for Barr's head.

Another van roared around the curve and stopped beside the president, protecting him and the soldiers from any fire from the mountainside.

"We can't attack now!" Greta whispered.

John nodded. He watched as new people left the second van to talk to Barr. He could see a hint of moving shadows cast under the van by a pale sun penetrating the thin, disintegrating clouds.

Suddenly a loudspeaker clicked on and a woman's voice blared in the silence. "JOHN NORRIS AND THE WOMAN. GIVE UP. LEAVE YOUR GUNS AND COME DOWN HERE WITH YOUR HANDS UP. YOU WILL NOT BE KILLED. THIS IS ERICA STONEMAN SPEAKING. I'M TAKING PRESIDENT BARR FOR MEDICAL TREATMENT."

John didn't respond. He waited.

"IF YOU DON'T SURRENDER, I'LL SEND MEN UP THERE AND THEY'LL KILL YOU. I DON'T REALLY WANT YOU, BUT PRESIDENT BARR WANTS YOU TO STAY ALIVE IF POSSIBLE."

After a short silence, "YOU HAVE ONE MINUTE."

"No win," John sighed. "Let's hope for the best." He put down the MAK-18 and stood up, hands high.

Greta muttered a German swear word and did the same.

They picked their way down the rocky slope toward the road.

CHAPTER 26

ERICA STILL WORE HER HEAVY, WARM DAY CLOTHES early that evening as she sat at her folding desk in the living room of her multiroom nylon tent.

The hum of the power generator and the whispers of air heaters, which made the tent a small oasis of luxury, didn't bother her. Those sounds were instead reassuring.

Her mind spiraled down to her main problem. She now had Barr and Norris, and a very pretty girl—Greta something—who had been Lauter's mistress. But where was Lauter?

It was now early evening, and bitingly cold, blustery weather had closed in. It would probably be freezing by midnight. Was Lauter in these difficult mountains? Making his way into Sackingen to cross the bridge into Switzerland? She had a van and half a dozen men at both the Waldshut and Sackingen bridges. Their orders were to shoot to kill anyone trying to get past them, and to keep the body.

Erica's earlier panic had melted away. Now she saw

clearly that she could salvage her position by framing Norris for Barr's murder.

She sat in her padded folding chair, toying with a pencil, and came out of her reverie to pay attention to the mercenaries' doctor who stood before her desk, reporting on President Barr's condition.

". . . kidney wasn't damaged. I managed to suture the torn small intestine."

"He'll live, then?"

"Yes, if the internal bleeding stops. It's still pooling in his lower abdomen. I'll have to open him up again and drain that blood in a few days, if he isn't in a hospital before then. I'll continue transfusing blood as needed, of course."

"Is he able to talk to me?"

"Yes, he's conscious. He's weak, but I've put three pints of whole blood in him now, and his color is back. He's still dopey from the anesthetic and drugs. I wouldn't advise seeing him before morning."

Erica snapped, "I'll see him when I please, and it pleases me to see him now!" She stood. "Accompany me," she ordered. She plucked her coat from a chair by the tent flap door and donned it as she emerged into menacing twilight. An icy wind ripped through the encampment.

"Damn weather!" she complained. But she knew this kind of late-spring extreme wasn't unusual, even in normal times. She led the way past vans, tents, and supply trucks.

When she and the doctor climbed into the fifty-foot-long motor home that had been converted to a tiny hospital, Erica said, "I will speak with Barr alone. After you've checked him for a minute, take that nurse outside." She indicated the young male nurse who sat at the medical station watching monitors while working on medical records.

Three minutes later, Erica entered the small, multibed

ward and saw Prsident Barr lying in the lowest of a triple
bunk bed. He was awake and turned his head to watch
her approach.

There were no other patients in the room.

She glanced distastefully at the telltale patches attached to his hairy chest and belly. Only his groin and
legs were covered by a white sheet. The bandage around
his belly was red at the lower edge where a thin, flexible
drain tube was taped. A bottle hanging near the floor
held his leaking blood. Another bottle fed new blood
into his hairy right arm, which had been shaved at that
spot.

She said maliciously, "I never knew you were an
ape."

He grimaced. "What do you want from me, Erica?
Thanks?"

"Yes. I'm saving your life."

He laughed painfully. "After you did your best to
have me killed."

"I've changed my mind, for the moment."

"What have you done with John Norris and Greta?"

Erica answered smoothly, "They will be killed tomorrow morning. Unless you agree to certain conditions, so
will you."

Barr didn't respond for a few seconds. "What do you
want?"

She took a deep breath. She unzipped her heavy coat.
"I want you to write an official thank-you to me for
rescuing you from the terrorists—the New German People's Alliance—and from John Norris, the assassin sent
by Julia Waggoner. And I want you to write and sign an
official presidential executive order requiring me to exe-
cute John Norris and Greta what's-her-name, as traitors,
as collaborators with Julia Waggoner in a plot to kill
you. I want you to write specifically that John Norris
tried to kill you by stabbing you with a piece of broken

glass in order to make your death appear an accident. He was acting—"

President Barr shook his head. "No, no, no—"

"He was acting under direct orders from Julia Waggoner so she could retain the presidency and continue to rule by decree as a dictator."

"I can't do that. That's monstrous."

Erica continued, ignoring his refusal. "And you must, of course, follow that line in word and deed in every respect after I bring you to a Swiss hospital and after you return to the United States and reclaim the presidency."

"No, no. That would involve . . . I can't."

"It would require that Julia Waggoner be arrested and put on trial for high treason and, if found guilty, either executed or imprisoned for life!" Erica spat the final words.

"You're insane." President Barr's lined, bearded face hardened. "You've gone over the edge."

"Have I? You will also sign an order authorizing my forces to hunt down and kill Hans Lauter, the leader of the terrorists who took you and held you prisoner at Waggoner's order."

"Even if I agreed . . ." Barr shook his head. "It doesn't make sense. Why would Julia want me held prisoner?"

"She doesn't! She employed Lauter and his gang to kill you! But he decided to double-cross her as the flare hit, and keep you alive. As soon as he could, he demanded ransom! She then had to send her special assistant, John Norris, a former CIA agent, a killer, to Germany to kill you himself. And he had to kill Representative James Lang to have a free hand. Lang's death is being painted as the result of an ambush by a few surviving renegade soldiers, and your death would be portrayed as an accident or, better, the result of an attack by my men. She could ruin me that way, because I have opposed her brutal dictatorship!''

Erica smiled and licked her lips. She was proud of that scenario. It fit together. It could be sold to the country. It would save the situation.

President Barr stared at her. "Why would I continue those lies once I was free of you?"

She chuckled. "Could you admit to the country, to the world, to Congress, that you are a stinking coward who was willing to sacrifice a loyal friend and a young woman who tried to help you, in order to save your own life? You'll be writing and signing those execution orders on-camera, you know. And your written commendation of me and my men and your accusations against Norris and Waggoner and Lauter will be on videotape. You'll smile at me and you'll shake my hand and thank me, and you'll thank my commander, and my doctor."

Erica laughed. "Those tapes will be broadcast and published in the United States before you're given to the Swiss. How could you renege after that?"

Barr said tightly, "Very elaborate, very neat. But I won't do it." He turned his face away.

Erica felt a terrifying chill. "If you don't, you'll die tomorrow! And Norris will die! And that pretty girl will die! Not by execution. Not quick and easy."

Erica squatted down beside the bed. Her beautiful face was warped by fear and anger. Her blue eyes were wide. She unconsciously disheveled her long blond hair with trembling fingers.

She said, "We'll take you back to the road and restage your injury. The Mercedes that crashed on the rocks—you'll have been in that, not my van. You and Norris and the girl were in that car, and as my men closed in, Norris stabbed you with broken glass. Your blood will be in the car. And when he and the girl tried to get away, my men shot them!"

Barr turned to look at her. His expression of intense loathing startled her. He said, "Fuck you."

Erica abruptly arose from her squatting position beside his low bunk bed, suddenly aware of his big arms. She backed away. This man had been an outdoorsman before his election. He could conceivably grab her.

She was disturbed at his reaction. He wasn't reacting correctly. Didn't he believe her? Was there a flaw in her plan? She elaborated, "Our doctor tried to save you, but your wound was too severe. You died on the way to a Swiss hospital."

Barr said skeptically, sarcastically, "And all of your men will obey you? All of your men will testify as you wish before a government court of inquiry?"

"Of course. They'll all be multimillionaires. They'll all be well coached, and they'll all know that a woman who is capable of killing the President of the United States is capable of making very sure of their death, if they say one wrong word. And besides, they'll be admitting their own guilt if they alter the story."

Barr frowned. "Then why keep me alive? Why take the risk of returning me to office? I could use my power to take revenge. I could—"

"No. I have agents—very loyal agents with a great deal to lose—in the United States government who could kill you if you even begin to think of going back on our arrangement."

She moved a bit closer to the bed. "Besides, Mr. President, you'd gain immensely from cooperating with me. I can make sure Congress and the states pass a constitutional amendment allowing you an extra term in office, if you like. Or you could simply continue to rule by executive order under the Emergency Powers Act, as Waggoner has. It doesn't matter to me, as long as certain pre-flare equity relationships are restored and the commodity and credit markets are freed."

Barr said nothing.

Erica tossed her hair and flashed a brilliant smile. "If I am your rescuer, I would return with you to the United States a heroine, a savior, and you would be justified in rewarding me and my enterprises with special favors and permissions. My worldwide looting, repopulation and colonization plans would become government sanctioned, even taxed, to help pay for the reconstruction of the United States."

She paused, gauging his reaction. She couldn't tell. She continued, "After you're tired of being president, I'll provide you with a suitable position in my structure, in the United States, or overseas if you like, and pay you any amount you care to name, for life." She felt she was convincing him. "We Stonemans have been taking care of our friends in high office for generations. Bonson, Rixon, Cord, Parker . . ."

"And of course you'd want exclusive rights to loot," Barr said. "The United States Navy and Air Force and Army would be used to enforce your monopoly. Rival looters would be killed or imprisoned."

Erica smiled sweetly. "Of course. What are governments for? That's the way it's always been for colonial powers."

Barr returned her smile grimly. "You're going after the whole world, aren't you?"

"Yes! Why not? If I don't take it and use it and manage it, more harm will come to it. In the short run and the long run, my stewardship of this planet will be best for everyone. I'll save millions of lives. We'll have the world government most people have always only dreamed about."

President Barr slowly shook his head. "Something's happened to you. You're insane." He looked away from her again. "Leave me alone. Give me a few hours of peace and quiet before you kill me."

Erica stared at him in amazement. "I can't believe you're such a fool!"

President Barr ignored her.

She raved at him for a while longer, but he would not react to anything she said. Finally, she calmed down. "Think it over, Mr. President. Either way, Norris and the girl will die. All you're deciding now is whether you will live or die." She moved to the door of the small room. "Think about it all night. You have until about seven tomorrow morning."

She stalked out of the hospital van and said to the doctor who was waiting, shivering, on the ramp. "I will be visiting President Barr tomorrow morning around seven. After that, I will have some special instructions for you."

Erica knew he could be trusted to do as she wished. He was a compulsive gambler who needed constant infusions of money to fuel his self-destructive mania. He had ruined his lucrative private practice in Exeter, stolen from his relatives, performed illegal operations, and had eagerly joined her plundering expedition.

But after this business of Barr and Norris and Lauter was finished, she would have all the members of this attack force of hers killed, one by one, discreetly, unobtrusively, "accidentally." She couldn't take any chances. Too much was at stake.

Erica zipped up her coat and walked regally back to her tent.

Her mind shifted to John Norris. She had observed him with shameless curiosity when he'd surrendered earlier—along with that German girl—and she felt a strange anger. He moved like a goddamned king! Like a tiger. A lion. There was something in his bearing, his demeanor, which asserted that he was somehow superior, no matter what the situation.

She wanted to test him. She wanted to humiliate him and crack that holy self-assurance.

Erica entered her warm, well-appointed tent apartment, shucked her coat, and walked into her bedroom.

She stripped and showered. She powdered herself and dabbed perfume in intimate places. She smiled frequently in the mirror as she worked with her hair.

Tonight. Tonight she would play with him. This mighty John Norris, this super man, this unkillable CIA agent. She would make him grovel and beg for life. She would let him hope, let him perform for her, and then. . .

Erica touched herself and laughed softly.

She put on an emerald-green silken lounging outfit that clung and rippled. She buzzed a wireless intercom to bring Hulda, her special cook, maid, and bodyguard.

When the stocky, brown-haired young woman entered the bedroom, Erica asked, "Are you interested in some vicious fun?"

"It depends."

"I'm thinking of having that big hunk of man, John Norris, brought in here for my amusement."

"I'll assist in any way I can, Mrs. Stoneman."

"Fine. You get him in here, but make sure he's been bathed, that he's eaten, and, Hulda, he's to be manacled."

After Hulda left the tent, Erica made herself a drink at the small, portable bar. She sipped the whiskey sour and idly looked around. It was amazing what could be done to provide creature comforts on a trip such as this, if one had the money and properly talented underlings. This four-room tent, with its heat and electricity, its water and air conditioning, was daily taken apart, folded, loaded into a large, specially designed truck, and in an hour, near the end of the day, reassembled, reconnected, in essence recreated, for her pleasures and comfort. A special three-man crew did the job.

Hulda led John Norris into the tent's warm bedroom an hour later. He was manacled at the ankles and wrists. Two feet of heavy chain permitted short steps. Behind his back, his wrists were linked by six inches of heavy chain.

John wore only jeans, a khaki shirt, and his boots. His dark blond hair was still damp from shampooing.

Erica had been reading, lounging in her bed. She put down her book on political history and examined John closely after Hulda brought him to the foot of the bed. God, he's big, she thought. Those shoulders . . . Her gaze drifted down his body and lingered at the large, sharply defined bulge at his loins.

She lifted her gaze to his compelling gray-green eyes. They were a shock to her; there was power there. This man was not afraid to die, and not afraid to win.

A shiver rippled down Erica's spine. She felt a ridiculous touch of fear in the pit of her stomach. She forced herself to smile. She said, "I wanted to meet the 'extraordinary' John Norris."

He said, "I've always wanted to meet Erica Stoneman." His eyes examined her as thoroughly as she him.

She felt a slow flush darken her cheeks. The arrogant bastard! She snapped to Hulda, "Strip him naked. Cut his clothes off." The manacles required that. She would not permit him to be freed for an instant. She asked, "Who has the key to those?"

"Sergeant Trent, ma'am. Hulda turned to John and began cutting his shirt away with a razor-sharp switchblade knife.

John said nothing.

Erica watched, blue eyes gleaming, as Hulda knelt, opened John's jeans and pulled them roughly down to his manacled ankles. Hulda cut the heavy denim cloth away, then brusquely pulled John's boots off. He had not been permitted, earlier, to put on socks.

Now he stood totally naked. He breathed easy. He kept his head high.

Erica commanded, "Face me!"

He turned. Again he examined her minutely, and seemed to delve into her mind.

She was disturbed by the many scars on his body. Talk about survivors! She asked, "Are you prepared to die?"

He shrugged. "It takes no preparation. It happens or it doesn't."

"You're not religious?"

"No."

"Aren't you afraid?"

"Sometimes."

Erica scowled. Her eyes drifted to his heavy genitals. She looked away. She said flatly, "I'll let you live if you'll do two things. I'll have you put into central Asia . . . let's say Mongolia . . . and you can survive as you can there, in that land of rotting corpses. Does that appeal to you?" She smiled and briefly met his gaze. "The other thing is your tongue. I love getting head. Give that to me tonight, and in the morning I'll make arrangements for your long trip."

John stared at her. One of the reasons for his string of successful missions and his surviving many life and death situations was his acute ability to judge people, to know when they were lying. He caught tiny body-language signals, tremors of voice, muscle tensions, weight shifts, breathing changes.

He knew Erica was lying. He asked, "Where is President Barr?"

"In our hospital van."

"How is he?"

"He'll stay alive as long as we keep putting blood into him."

John nodded. "Have you caught Lauter?"

Erica turned to reach for her third whiskey sour. "One of my road patrols shot him to death an hour ago." She sipped and watched John over the crystal rim. She felt warm and powerful. She smiled and cocked her head. "Well? Not a bad bargain for you, is it?" She slowly opened her green lounging top and exposed her pouting, large-nippled breasts. Then she inched down the silken pants. She wore no panties. She kicked the pants aside and opened her thighs. "Yes or no? I can have Hulda kill you on the spot, now. She used to be a detective on the New York City police force."

Hulda shifted her weight. The switchblade knife snicked open in her right hand. She watched John closely.

John finally smiled and said, "Why not?"

Erica laughed. "Yes, why not? Considering the alternative."

He sank to his knees at the foot of the bed. He leaned forward until his chest and chin rested on the satin, quilted comforter.

Erica was surprised at how fast and hard her heart was pounding. She edged lower on the bed. Closer . . . closer . . . She rose up on her elbows, blue eyes glittering, and watched him begin . . . felt him begin.

A thrill of sweet triumph filled her. Her eyes met Hulda's and they both laughed.

After a few moments, the pleasure began, as she watched his face buried between her soft white thighs. She gloated when John's eyes opened and locked to hers. But then he closed his eyes and she felt subtly cheated. Until the pleasures became strong and insistent, and she yielded her mind more and more to her body.

Erica discovered John's skills included this way of making love. He knew too much about a woman's intimate anatomy. He was too good at this! She resisted showing her arousal, her enjoyment. But her nipples hardened to thimbles and her breathing came faster, became erratic.

And then she didn't care, as the hot tide flowed from her loins to flood her body and mind with a glorious release of sparkling tension.

209

She wriggled away from his mouth and lay panting, quieting. She whispered, "Very nice. You surprise me."

John didn't reply.

She chuckled. "Ah, the strong, silent type. Very well, do it again." She shifted herself close.

After two hours, Erica lay gasping, quivering, her fingers clawed in John's hair, her loins jolting up at his clinging mouth. She emitted high-pitched moans. Her head whipped from side to side. Her belly constantly knotted and spasmed.

Finally, she croaked, "Enough!" She flung herself away on the bed and looked, dull-eyed, at Hulda, who was sitting in a bedside chair, bored, but still alert. She said, "Get me a drink. White wine, and get some fresh ice cubes from the other room."

Hulda looked at John, who had slumped tiredly off the bed from his kneeling position. He lay now on his side, wrists still manacled behind his back, ankles still chained. His eyes remained closed. He breathed deeply.

Erica caught the significance of Hulda's look. "Don't worry about Mr. Norris. Bring him a drink, too. I'm not through with him."

John heard and made a decision. He didn't move when Hulda left the room. He waited.

Erica laughed and got off the bed. "Do your jaws ache, Mr. Norris? Does your tongue feel raw at the root? Cheer up. I'll only require your wonderful services for another two or three hours."

She walked, naked, toward her bathroom. "Don't get any escape ideas. There are armed guards spaced around my tent tonight. I know your reputation."

John feigned exhaustion. He didn't respond.

Hulda reentered the bedroom as Erica disappeared into the bathroom. Hulda carried two glasses of wine and an insulated bucket, which hung from the crook of her arm. She put one glass on the bedside table, lowered the ice container to the floor, and carried the other glass to John. "Get up on your knees, asshole!" She held the open switchblade knife in her right hand, now, and the glass of wine in her left.

John struggled to his knees and masked slipping his manacled wrists under his buttocks. The six inches of heavy chain joining the manacles allowed his move. He whispered, "Thanks," as Hulda put the glass to his lips.

She sneered with contempt and poured the wine into his mouth.

John pretended to choke. He sprayed wine into her face.

Hulda recoiled, swearing, wiping at her eyes with the back of her knife-holding hand.

Even as he sprayed the wine at her, John was leaping into the air. He coiled, arms straining, and swiftly passed the manacle chain under his feet and forward over his knees, while in the air. He straightened, landed on his feet and stood now with his hands in front of him.

An astonished Hulda watched for an instant, before John's combined wrists smashed the heavy manacles into the bridge of her nose. So powerful was the blow that the front of her skull broke inward. Her eyes ruptured. Splinters of bone penetrated her prefrontal lobe. She fell like a stone.

John stooped to pick up the dropped knife. Now to use Erica as a hostage. He whirled to hobble to the bathroom—and froze.

Erica Stoneman stood naked in the bathroom doorway, a cocked .38 police special in her hands, braced, her beautiful face twisted with hate and satisfaction. "I thought you'd try something!"

He knew she was competent with that weapon. Fifteen feet separated them. He watched for a tightening of her finger on the trigger.

The instant held. She didn't shoot.

He relaxed slightly. She wanted him to die later, probably in a manner that would serve her better.

Erica said, "Drop that knife."

He dropped it.

She called the guards. She seemed not at all embarrassed to be seen by them, or by the apparent circumstances. One of the guards was Sergeant Trent. He was a big man, with blocky shoulders and thick arms.

"Put him where there's no possiblity of his getting free," she ordered.

"I can nail him into an empty ammunition crate, if that will suit ye," Trent said in a burred, surprisingly tenor voice.

"Good! Do that! Just so he's alive in the morning." Erica watched Trent and two soldiers hustle John away. She ignored the remaining three guards as they picked up Hulda's body and carried it out. She slipped a robe on and stalked furiously through the rooms of her tent. She poured herself more wine. She began to tremble and recognized delayed shock.

Erica drank deeply of her wine. She smiled grimly. "I was too smart for him." But she knew it had been a near thing. She'd previously hidden the gun in the hamper in the bathroom. In the time it had taken to get it out and return to the doorway, that astonishing man had killed Hulda and was picking up the knife. If she had fumbled finding the gun, delayed as little as three seconds . . .

Erica shivered. Her fear turned to anger. She went to her wireless intercom and buzzed for Miles Webster. When he came on the line, she said, "The girl we captured with Barr and Norris. Give her to the men tonight. Let them have some fun. Use her yourself, first, if you like."

Webster said, "They'll appreciate that Mrs. Stoneman. They've been talking about—"

A staccato burst of gunfire sounded from somewhere in the camp. There were faint shouts.

Erica demanded, "What's going on?"

Webster didn't answer.

CHAPTER 27

JOHN WAS TAKEN NAKED FROM THE BRIGHT WARMTH OF the big tent by two strong guards who gripped his arms, and Sergeant Trent, who followed with a drawn Colt .45. They entered the dark, icy wind and a pelting mixture of sleet and snow. Trent and the two guards were heavily dressed for cold. And they had AR-22 rifles slung over their shoulders.

"Where is this damned box you're going to put me in?" John asked.

"You'll find out." Trent prodded him with the muzzle of the .45. They walked fast, toward the pumping station. John had to take quick, short steps because of the two-foot chain which linked his manacled ankles.

When he and President Barr and Greta had been brought to this place earlier in the day, John had noted as much of the layout of trucks, vans, and tents as possible. He knew where the big hospital motor home was, and where Greta might be imprisoned.

John surmised the soldiers were using the ground level

of the pumping station as a warehouse of sorts. He let himself shiver violently in his captors' arms. "I'll freeze to death."

His hands were still manacled in front. He knew he could kill one or two of the guards. But Trent was a battle-wise case-hardened soldier-for-pay.

They entered the pumping station. A small gasoline-powered generator in a far corner roared softly to provide electricity. A few portable lights were on; one in the office, one near the instrument wall, and a few in the lower level where giant pumps sat, dead and cold. No other soldiers could be seen or heard.

A litter of crates crowded a dark corner near the stairwell. The concrete floor was very cold under John's bare feet. He continued to shiver violently. "I've got to have some clothes!"

Trent grunted. "Over there," he said. "The missiles."

John began to breathe deep and fast to oxygenate his tissues. He calculated positions, angles, tactics.

One of the guards holding his arms noted John's breathing. "Listen to him. The bastid's scared bloody shitless," he laughed.

"I'm freezing!" John whimpered. They had reached the dark area. A large wooden crate stenciled "*Warning— Handle With Care—HS-3 T57-J Missiles. This Side up,*" yawned empty before them. The distant light cast black shadows.

"Climb in," Trent ordered. The two guards let go of John's arms and stepped back.

"Listen, I'm President Waggoner's senior special assistant," John said. "I'm in a position to offer you more money and more privilege and a hell of a better life in the United States than you'll ever get from looting for Erica Stoneman."

"Into the box!" Trent yelled.

"I can offer you sanctuary, clemency, and a life of

luxury anywhere you want, in the States, or in Brazil, Argentina, Mexico . . ."

The two guards seemed interested. They looked at Trent.

Trent shook his head. "I've got a one percent share in this expedition, with special bonuses for just this kind of job. I'm a bloody millionaire already." His rough, high-pitched voice sounded content. "I've got diamonds in my box worth ten million. These men have a tenth share and diamonds and rubies and other gems by the fistful. And we've hardly touched this rotting land, yet. Every city is a treasure trove." He waved the .45. "Get in the fucking box!"

John slumped in apparent defeat. He began breathing fast again. His eyes darted from man to man in the dim light. He pleaded, "At least let me have a coat or a blanket. It's freezing in here. She told you to keep me alive till morning."

Trent said contemptuously, "Oh, Christ! Williams, give the bugger your coat for the night."

The soldier to John's left swore, but unslung his rifle, placed it on a closed crate beside him, and ran the zipper on his fancy, hooded, thick woolen coat. He had taken it from an exclusive ski shop in Luxembourg. As he pulled it down off his shoulders, John exploded into action.

Williams would be immobilized for at least a full second, probably more. The soldier to his right was too relaxed, lulled by John's begging, craven posture. His rifle was still slung on his shoulder. They both counted on Sergeant Trent.

Trent was John's primary target, the man most dangerous.

John had primed himself for an effort of extraordinary speed and strength. This was life or death. He moved so fast in the semidarkness, the second soldier didn't realize what had happened. In one instant John Norris was cringing, apparently shuddering with cold, and in the next, the bases of John's palms had smashed upward under the soldier's chin, cracking his jaw, stunning him.

John's manacled hands gripped the soldier's waist as they both fell into darkness. With supreme agility and power, John spun, used the soldier as a counterweight, and hurled the man into Trent with a hammer throw. Trent had fired once—the .45 slug tore through the thick wood of the empty crate.

Trent and the soldier went down into black shadows. John followed in a long, pantherlike leap.

Williams still fought his coat, his arms trapped in the sleeves.

John's martial-arts training took over instinctively. His eyes had adjusted to the darkness. He saw Trent's head come up, and his elbow buried itself in the man's thick throat, smashing the larynx and rupturing the trachea. He seized Trent's hand and tore the gun free. The Colt fired in that instant and the bullet ricocheted off the concrete and through a drum of diesel oil.

Williams had his rifle now. He turned to the melee, seeing only dark shapes.

John was surprised at how much time he had. He carefully shot Williams through the head. Then, without mercy, without pause, he sent bullets smashing into the brains of Trent and the other fallen, moaning guard.

Breathing fast, his mind in its all-out killing mode, John searched Trent's pockets for the key to the manacles. He found it and in seconds freed himself of the chains.

He listened for an alarm. There were some shouts outside, and he saw through the pumping station windows some bobbing of flashlights and lanterns. They seemed uncertain of the source of the shots.

John swiftly and efficiently stripped Williams of the rest of his uniform. The man had flung his bulky coat away to free his arms. Williams was almost as tall and wide-shouldered as John.

As he pulled on Williams's socks and low boots a minute later, a buzzing sound came alive in Trent's uniform, and a male voice called, *"Trent? What's that shooting?"*

John groped for the small packset on the body, and found a com set clipped on Trent's belt, near the right buttock.

"Trent?"

John pressed the mike's "send" button and made his voice as burry and tenor in pitch as he could, in imitation of the sergeant's voice. "Don't know. Wasn't here."

In the pause between transmissions, John laced up one of the boots.

"What's the matter with your voice?"

"Nothing. You sound queer, though. Must be weak batteries."

There was no further comment from Trent's superior. John had to assume the lieutenant or captain or commander was suspicious and would send a squad to check. He laced the other boot, took Trent's .45, a spare clip, Williams's automatic rifle, flipped up the big hood on Williams's heavy wool coat, and ran to the door of the pumping station.

He slipped out into the snowstorm, which had grown worse. A strong, blustery wind blew ice particles into his face as he made his way in the darkness toward the big motor home, which had been outfitted as a miniature hospital.

To his left, near the armored-van parking area, many lights bobbed. The force commander suspected an attempt to steal one of his assault vehicles.

He noticed two soldiers dashing away from Erica Stoneman's huge tent toward the pumping station. His time was limited, now.

John leaped up the metal ramp at the hospital's side door and barged in, AR-22 ready.

An odor of disinfectant permeated the air of the small room. A male nurse at a medical station looked up from studying a porno magazine. "What—?"

"Shut up!" John menaced him with the rifle. "Where's President Barr?"

The young man mutely pointed at a sliding door behind the station. On a wall, several monitors ticked and beeped with tracks showing Barr's heartbeat, blood pressure, breathing rate, temperature, and transfusion flow rate.

"You go in first," John said.

The nurse opened the door and led John into a narrow ward of stacked beds. President Barr was in the lowest bunk against the left wall, awake, surprised. He was festooned with devices. A tube fed blood into his arm; another tube drained blood from his belly wound.

"Bill, can you get up? Can you walk?" John asked.

William Barr took in the situation. "I think so," he said, "but if I do, I'll probably open my wound again, and . . ." He gestured at the drain tube and the transfusion needle in his arm.

"Do you want to leave?" John asked.

Barr nodded grimly. "She's going to have us all killed tomorrow in a frame-up of Julia."

"I guessed that." John turned to the nurse. "Disconnect him. Tape him up for travel."

The nurse protested, "He's still bleeding inside. He needs—"

"How long can I live without another transfusion?" Barr asked.

"God, I don't know! If you didn't move a lot—"

"Hemmings, lock the outer doors," a packset at his nursing station blared. It was Erica Stoneman's voice.

Barr insisted, "How long?"

"Maybe two days." The man jerked his eyes toward the other room.

"Talk to her. There's no problem here," John said.

"Hemmings?"

Hemmings ran to the nursing station and took the packset from its desk bracket. "Here. I was—"

John pressed the muzzle of the AR-22 against the man's ribs.

Erica said firmly. *"Listen to me! Lock the doors and don't let anyone in! No one! Not even the doctor. Not until I tell you to. Is that clear?"*

"Yes, Mrs. Stoneman."

"How is your patient?"

"No change. I was with him when you—"

"All right. Now lock those doors." She clicked off.

John nodded. "Good idea." He went to the side door and bolted the locks. He went with the nurse back through the multibed ward, through the door to the driver compartment. Those doors were locked, too.

The surgery room at the rear of the hospital did not have an outer door.

Then John said, "Now get him ready to travel."

Eight minutes later, Barr was dressed in the nurse's uniform and shoes, and slowly, carefully, he pulled on the man's parka, taken from a small locker under the nursing station.

John had locked the nearly naked nurse into the surgery room. The man was bound and gagged.

President Barr found gloves in the coat's pockets. "Good." He looked quizzically at John. "Now what?"

John pulled an armload of woolen blankets from a supply closet. He handed Barr two blankets and a roll of tape. "Tape these tightly around my waist. I'll do the same for you. We're going to need the warmth tonight and tomorrow."

As Barr worked slowly, moving as little as possible, John explained further. "By now, all the helicopters, vans, and diesels are under triple guard, and God knows where the ignition keys are. I wouldn't have time to hot-wire one of them. So we'll have to—"

The door rattled as somebody tried the knob. A voice called, "Okay in there?"

John called back casually, "Yeah, fine. What's going on?"

"That Norris bastard got away. He was fucking bloody naked in Stoneman's tent with her!" The man cursed. "Then he fucking killed her woman and Sergeant Trent and Williams and Stockman. He's out somewhere, now, running around in Williams's uniform."

John called, "Bloody hell!"

"Gotta go. Keep locked up!"

"I will!"

Barr gave John an odd look. He whispered, "Naked?"

Heavy boots climbed down the ramp and away. John said, "It's a long story. It wasn't my choice."

Barr had finished taping the blankets around John's middle. "Tell me later. What about getting out of here?" He handed the tape to John.

John worked quickly. "We'll have to take one of the boats tied up at the pumping station dock," he said, "I noticed them earlier, when they brought us here."

"Won't they be guarded, too?" Barr asked.

"Maybe. But not as heavily as the motorized stuff. We'll have to take what they least want to protect." He handed Barr the Colt .45 automatic. "Don't use this unless absolutely necessary."

A moment later, John unlocked the door and looked out into a blizzard. He motioned to President Barr. The two men left the hospital and disappeared into the black night.

They had covered only a few yards before President Barr began grunting with pain. John had to ignore it as he led the way down the slope toward the river.

There were some moving lights, upstream, near Erica's tent and the pumping station, where the helicopters wobbled and pulled against their ties. In the freezing

220

wind they heard shouting. Any false alarm or equipment breakdown would be a godsend.

Barr tugged at John's coat. "Can't go much farther."

John peered through the snowy blackness. "It shouldn't be far to the water." He looped Barr's right arm over his shoulders and helped him, as they picked their way into increasingly treacherous, rocky, steep terrain. The ground was black; the snow was not sticking.

Finally, they heard the rush of fast-moving water against rocks. John said, "Stay here, sir. I'm going to get a boat." He pulled the blankets free of his coat and wrapped them around the president. He checked his AR-22, then said, "I'll be back as quickly as I can," and melted into the white-speckled darkness.

He remembered that the boat dock was near the huge intake pipe that extended out into the river.

John stopped every few seconds to listen and peer ahead. He worked slowly downstream, knowing he would come upon the dock sooner or later. If there was a guard where would he be?

He found a stone stairway leading down. He stepped down boldly. He called, "Archy? Where the bloody hell are ye? I've got some hot coffee for ye!"

A voice called, "Here! I'm Michael."

John stepped onto wood planking. He saw a soldier huddled under an upturned rowboat on the dock. He walked toward him. "What happened to Archy?"

"I don't know! I've been here for two hours. Hey, give me some of that coffee!" He squinted against the stinging snow. "Who're you?" The soldier started to bring up his rifle.

John clubbed him in the head with the steel butt of the AR-22.

The soldier fell sideways and lay still.

John stripped him of his coat and dragged the body to the edge of the dock and shoved it into the icy black water. He threw the man's rifle far out into the river.

Chained to the dock were two boats with outboard motors. John was positive their tanks were dry. Survivors would have siphoned the fuel long ago.

He found a set of oars under the rowboat, and had no other choice. He put the boat into the water and laboriously towed it upstream, often slipping on rocks and parts of trees. His boots were sopping wet, as were his pants to his knees, when he found President Barr and helped him into the boat.

A moment later, John pushed off from the rocks. The rowboat was swept, turning, into the current. John and President Barr used the oars as poles to keep the boat off the shore rocks. It was impossible to see far enough in the snowy night to row safely.

A curve in the river blacked out the dim lights of the Stoneman camp.

CHAPTER 28

Erica led Miles Webster into her tent after a fruitless search of the camp. She brushed melting snow from her heavy jacket and stamped mud on the carpet in the entranceway.

Then she turned on him in a seething fury. "What a great commander you are! You picked this rabble of soldiers! You swore up and down they were the best! Real professional fighters!"

"And they are." He smarted under the whiplash of her tongue. By God, he'd never sign on to serve a woman again. They didn't understand—

"They sure are! Three of them take a naked, chained man away and he kills all three, gets out of his chains, dresses in one of their uniforms, takes their guns, and waltzes into an *unguarded* motor hospital, takes my most important prisoner, the key to all my plans, and they vanish!"

"Mrs. Stoneman—"

"That is marvelously professional, isn't it? Like shit!

It's so fucking incompetent—'' She couldn't think of a phrase that would fully express her contempt. Her hands knotted to small, white fists.

Webster said quickly, ''They didn't get away in a van or a helicopter. And Barr is seriously wounded. He won't last a day if he has to climb around in this storm all night. The doctor said—''

''I know what the damned doctor said!'' Erica screamed. ''And I know John Norris knows Barr's condition as well as we do! Now, they're either holed up somewhere—maybe in our goddamned camp—or he's found a way—What about the river?''

Webster snapped, ''The two boats at the dock were still chained there.''

''Why wasn't there a guard at the dock?''

''There should have been. Sergeant Trent was in charge of posting—''

''He's dead,'' Erica said irritably.

''He probably pulled that man to help—''

''Oh, shut up! I'm tired of your excuses.'' Erica paced the tent room. Her long blond hair was wet and wildly askew from the wind. She wondered if Hans Lauter could possibly have hiked back to Waldshut, slipped into the camp, rescued Norris . . .

She snapped, ''Where is that girl? Greta.''

''Still locked in the equipment room in the lower level of the pumping station, where you told me to put her.''

''I also told you to give her to the men for fun and games,'' Erica said.

''There wasn't time for that. The shots were heard, and—''

''Yes, I know. Get her. I want to talk to her.''

Webster half-saluted. ''Right away.''

When he turned to leave, Erica screamed at him, ''At dawn! Damn you, before dawn! I want an all-out, total, life-or-death search for Norris and Barr! Forget Lauter! Your life and your fortune depend on finding those two!''

He nodded, tight-lipped. He turned again to leave the tent.

Erica watched him leave, hands on her hips. She whispered to herself, "Idiot!" She went into her bedroom to fix her hair.

It was ten minutes before a soldier brought Greta to the tent.

Erica hadn't really looked closely at Greta when she and Norris surrendered on the road. She hadn't seemed important. Now, she could be crucial.

Greta stood sullen and defiant, green eyes squinting against the bright light in the tent. Her short red hair sparkled with melted snow. Her hands were bound tightly behind her back with heavy-gauge wire.

The two beautiful women stared at each other.

Erica held the .38 police special she had used during her confrontation with John Norris. She had been thoroughly frightened several times during this expedition, and she would never again take a needless risk. She valued her life too much.

Erica motioned for the soldier to stay. She sat at her desk and studied Greta. "I presume you speak English."

"Yes.

"What is your feeling toward John Norris?"

Greta was no fool. She said, "I do not like him. He is cold, a monster who kills like a machine. He thinks only of his duty to his president and to his corrupt government."

Erica nodded. "How true. Did you have sex with him?"

Greta flushed and nodded.

Erica rose and moved closer, like an angry cat. "Did you enjoy it?"

Greta shrugged. "I was ordered to make him happy."

"Did you hear the shooting in the pump station?"

"Yes."

"Do you know what happened?"

225

"No." Greta showed pain. "My hands are hurting. There is no circulation."

"In a moment." Erica walked around Greta. "Do you know where Hans Lauter might be?"

"No. He abandoned us to save himself and his precious billion dollars!"

"I'll tell you what happened tonight. Because of the incompetence and stupidity of some of my men, John Norris has escaped and has managed to take President Barr with him."

Greta's green eyes widened but she said nothing.

Erica stopped pacing and paused before the younger woman. "I can offer you a great deal in exchange for your cooperation in finding Norris, Barr, and Lauter. I could hide you from the American authorities and make you rich." She met Greta's puzzled gaze. "Or I can give you to my soldiers for as long as you last, and then have you shot."

"I would not like to be raped and shot."

"Naturally. Will you act as my agent? Are you willing to help find and kill these men?"

Greta said positively, "Yes. They used me and rejected me! They don't want me. I owe them nothing but my revenge."

Erica chuckled grimly. "A woman scorned. Good!" She motioned to the soldier. "Free her hands." To Greta, she said, "Stay with me."

CHAPTER 29

THE SUN WAS BRILLIANT IN A BLUE SKY, FOLLOWING THE previous day and night of snow and icy wind. Three armored personnel carriers rumbled along Freudenstrasse as they approached Wilhelm Platz, in Stuttgart. They were led and followed by jeeps, armed with machine guns. A Hornet reconcopter buzzed overhead. Where the jeeps could not find a way among the rusting, dead cars and trucks, one of the powerful carriers bulldozed a lane.

They originated from Stuttgart's International Airport, where five VTO-15 planes had landed. Two SF-2 heavy cargo planes had landed after special jeepscrapers, from a cargo VTO, had cleared a runway of debris.

The convoy reached Wilhelm Platz. John Norris's destroyed VTO lay where it had exploded and burned.

Lightning Force soldiers and Guardsmen piled out of the two lead carriers. They spent half an hour securing the blocks surrounding the Platz. Lightning Force cameramen recorded everything.

Finally, the VIPs and the newspeople emerged from the third carrier.

Senator Douglas, ashen-faced and wearing dark sunglasses, avoided looking at the putrescent bodies in the streets and Platz. He had to force himself to approach the ruptured and burned VTO.

He and Representative Tom Kinder were surrounded by the media people with their holocameramen and aides, and a few military people.

General Steiger and his Lightning Force investigators had been examining the destroyed plane since the security operation had begun. LF engineers, directed by expert investigators, were cutting parts of the burned and damaged fuselage apart, seeking bodies and physical clues.

After several hours of work and the politicians had posed with the charred, days-old corpses of the marines, and after interviews and preliminary commentary, a press conference was held by Steiger and his investigators, while Douglas on hand as prompted, cued inquisitors.

Senator Douglas nodded as an aide whispered in his ear. Camera lights flared on, cameras zoomed. Douglas asked Steiger, "General, what happened here? How was our plane destroyed?"

Steiger glared at the staring lenses. He hated being on camera. "Senator, the VTO was struck by microdelay HS air-to-target missiles. The warheads penetrated the skin and exploded. One wing took a missile and exploded, showering the plane with burning fuel. The belly tanks were hit, too, and the ordinance went up."

Tom Kinder signaled he would speak next. Cameras swiveled toward him. "Were there any survivors?"

"No, sir. We've found seven bodies, as near as we can tell. From melted metal—dog tags and parts of metal on their uniforms—we've established seven American marines died here."

Kinder asked a follow-up question: "No sign that

Julia Waggoner's special assistant, John Norris, was in the plane?"

"No, sir."

"No evidence that President Barr was in the plane, or nearby?"

"No, sir. President Barr was not in or near this plane when it was attacked. We've checked every corpse in this square and in the surrounding areas.

Senator Douglas took the spotlight again. "General, I noticed a lot of what looked like bullet holes in the fuselage. Am I correct in thinking this plane took ground fire, as well as missiles?"

"You are, sir. Special nine-millimeter APT machine-gun rounds went through the armor like an ice pick goes through cheese. Our men didn't have a chance."

Douglas continued, "So they took an air attack—missiles—and armor-piercing machine-gun fire. Local survivors couldn't have mounted an attack like that, could they?"

General Steiger's face hardened even more. "No, sir. Not unless they had a military helicopter armed with the latest American missiles, and at least two NATO nine-millimeter machine-guns firing teflon-coated rounds."

Douglas barked, "Are you saying an American force attacked this plane?"

The reporters were galvanized. They broke protocol and began yelling questions.

Steiger bellowed angrily, "I'm saying a military force, under our ordinance, did the job!"

"Who?" the reporter bellowed.

"You tell me!" replied the general.

Representative Kinder danced in front of a camera. "You want me to guess? I think we'd better ask Julia Waggoner, who!"

CHAPTER 30

PRESIDENT BARR GROANED AWAKE AT DAWN. HE WAS lying in the bottom of the rowboat, wrapped in three woolen blankets, with a fourth blanket tented over him by an oar to keep out rain and snow as much as possible. An automatic rifle lay beside him.

He opened his eyes and took in the still boat, the tent, the gun. The rowboat was apparently grounded on the shore somewhere.

He felt hot and chilled at the same time. His bandaged belly ached severely and felt wet. He was afraid to touch it. He called hoarsely, "John?"

He heard a scrambling on rocks nearby. John Norris lifted part of the overhead blanket and looked in. "How do you feel, sir?"

"Lousy. Weak as hell. Where are we?"

"About ten miles downriver from Waldshut, where we started," John said.

"Only ten?" the president asked.

"We were going blind last night. We foundered a

couple times on the rocks. The boat was taking some bad hits. I had to get us stopped." John showed badly scraped hands. His clothes were wet. "And you passed out."

President Barr felt helpless. "What do we do now?"

"I was about to start out again," John said. "I think we should try for Basel, about forty miles further downriver. It's a Swiss city, and they'll have a hospital."

John didn't know how much of that city had been destroyed by the flare or by winds and firestorms that followed. It might be as dead as Stuttgart.

Barr nodded. "Let's do it, then. I'm bleeding to death."

Erica hadn't slept all night. She'd had a long talk with Greta, in between negative reports from Webster and others. She saw in Greta a woman self-victimized, a brainwashed fool. She saw Greta's socialist rhetoric and love for the masses as a psychological mechanism, a structure adopted to ease severe emotional pressures.

She thought most liberal, bleeding-heart, help-the-disadvantaged, altruistic impulses in America were born out of similar character conflicts. There had to be a lot of guilt and anxiety involved.

Now, at dawn, the weather was clearing, and she anxiously awaited reports from her helicopters which were already in the air, searching for Norris and Barr.

One of her mercenary soldiers was missing, not counting the three Norris has killed. It was already established that there had been a guard at the pumping-station dock. Several other men, who had previously stood guard down there, swore there had been an overturned rowboat propped up on the dock. It wasn't there now.

Erica paced beside the radio van. Greta remained silent, nearby.

Erica was obsessed with catching Norris. He had made a fool of her! Her mind raced like a computer, her body felt jerky and manic, while in her bones a deep weariness lay like a black fog.

She sent Greta to get her something to eat.

A muffled reception sounded in the van. "Anything?" she snapped.

"No, ma'am. Routine ten-minute position report."

"Well, tell those pilots to make a position report every five minutes!" She stalked around the radio van. She could not stay still, could not sit down, could not rest!

The radioman called, "Mrs. Stoneman!" She ran to the van's side door.

"Special-frequency beamed message," he said and climbed down out of the van. A narrow-beam digital squirt had kicked on the special recorder once before. He knew he wasn't wanted.

Erica climbed in and slammed the door shut. She consulted her booklet of private codes, which was always either on her person or under lock and key.

She punched in the program, switched on the monitor, and ran the tape. The small screen filled with the message.

LIGHTNING FORCE FOUND NORRIS VTO, EVIDENCE OF MISSILE ATTACK, SOPHISTICATED ARMS. SUSPECT WAGGONER. ON WAY DOWN TO WALDSHUT. ETA 6:30 A.M. YOUR TIME.

Erica looked at her watch. It was five-fifty. She whispered, "Jesus Christ!" She wiped the message tape and switched over to the short-range radio frequency. She switched into the beginning of a report from one of her helicopters.

"—*boat, seventeen klicks downriver. About eight klicks to Sackingen. S-1 over.*"

She felt a wild thrill. She broadcast, "S-1, repeat that! What about a boat?"

"*Ah . . . a rowboat. A man rowing fast. Looks like a*

long black bundle in the boat between his feet. He's about eight klicks upriver from Sackingen. S-1 over.''

Erica broadcast, "S-2, where are you?"

"S-2 over Rheinfelden. Over."

S-2 was her largest, most heavily armed, and fastest helicopter. Rheinfelden was 25 kilometers beyond Sackingen. She ordered, "S-2, return to base at top speed. Return to base at top speed. Do you read?"

"S-2. Will return to base max. Out."

She called, "S-1. S-1. Keep the rowboat in sight. Do not yet attack. Do not yet attack. Acknowledge."

"S-1 will observe, not attack."

Erica said, "Correct, S-1 Out." She burst out of the radio van. She told the radio technician, "Get ready to move!" She unclipped her packset from her belt and said into the mike, "Webster! Webster!"

Mike Webster replied, *"Yes, Mrs. Stoneman."*

"Break camp instantly!" Erica shouted. "I mean, NOW! And listen, I want your whole force here on the road to Sackingen within thirty minutes. Everything must be gone from here. No traces that we've been here! Understand? No evidence linking me to this place!"

"Yes, I under—"

"No garbage left behind, no gas cans, no drums, no litter, no outhouses, no bodies, no tent stakes, nothing! This is absolutely vital! Clear?"

"Clear, Mrs. Stoneman."

"And if you have the time and the men, I want any local survivors who know us, who have seen us . . . I want them killed, and their bodies thrown into the Rhine. Understood?"

"Understood."

"And Webster, when you get to the truck and van and the two cars on the road—and the helicopter—get that van and the helicopter into the river deep enough to be covered. The German cars will be thought to have been wrecked during the flare. But get those bodies into the river!"

Webster said, *"I will, Mrs. Stoneman. May I ask why this emergency—"*

"There is an American government investigation force on its way to Waldshut, now! Now!"

"Understood!"

"I'm going to fly ahead to Sackingen with a few men. Send one van full of men to Sackingen, now, at full speed. I want to be able to intercept Norris and Barr if they get that far. Out."

Erica clipped her packset and walked to the helicopter landing area. Behind her, the camp became a beehive. Her large tent was already coming down. Truck and van engines coughed to life.

Greta caught up to her with a box of sandwiches and a big thermos of coffee.

Erica's largest helicopter appeared in the western sky.

CHAPTER 31

JOHN WAS WORRIED BY THE STONEMAN HELICOPTER THAT had obviously spotted them ten minutes earlier. He wondered why it didn't attack. The other helicopter had *thrummed* by overhead—on its way back to Waldshut, he presumed.

"Sir, I'm going to row closer to the Swiss side of the river," he said. "We might have to hide in the rocks pretty soon."

The morning clouds were lifting. The sun was looming hot and bright.

The helicopter hovered out of range of John's AR-22. But it had a nose cannon and could stand away and pound their little rowboat to kindling if the pilot so wished—or had orders to do so. Why was Erica delaying? Did she want to be in on the kill? Was she still committed to the frame-up scenario she had outlined the day before?

President Barr had not responded to John's words.

John shipped the oars and lifted the tented woolen blanket covering Barr's head. "Bill?"

Barr twitched in his cocoon of blankets. His pale, bearded face was beaded with sweat. His eyes were half-lidded, dull. His breathing was fast and shallow.

John dipped a piece of cloth into the swift, cold Rhine and dripped water into the president's parted lips. He placed the cool cloth on Barr's forehead.

John unshipped the oars and began pulling hard for the Swiss side. He wasn't going to make Basel. He gritted his teeth in weariness and anger. President William Barr was dying.

An approaching *thrumm*ing alerted him to the flight of another helicopter. The big chopper that had flown back upriver minutes ago now headed toward the boat, low, mean-looking.

John leaned into the oars. There were some huge, protective boulders in shallow water at the shore.

The engine noise grew louder. John glanced over his shoulder and saw flashes from its nose-mounted gun. He spun the rowboat around and pulled momentarily upstream, as a vicious series of eruptions in the water tracked the boat on the right, while the terrifying sound of the cannon blasted the air.

The copter swept past, and a powerful draft of wind rocked the boat. John knew he had only a few seconds before it wheeled around for another attack, or the other chopper came down to attack.

He swerved the boat between two big rocks an instant before the granite shuddered from the explosive impact of armor-piercing cannon shells.

He leaped from the boat and hauled it onto some smaller rocks. As he gathered President Barr into his arms, he looked up to see the larger chopper maneuvering into position to send a missile into the gap between the boulders.

He grunted with huge effort as he lurched quickly

away from the boat. President Barr came to consciousness with a scream of pain as John unavoidably manhandled him into a crevice.

The rowboat erupted into a million killing splinters accompanied by shattered rock. But John and Barr were sheltered, though deafened.

John had only the Colt .45 for a weapon; the AR-22 had gone up with the rowboat. He pushed President Barr farther into the narrow, L-shaped crevice. His ears were ringing and popping, and he felt dizzy.

President Barr groaned in agony. "John . . . what happened?"

"Erica's helicopters are throwing everything they've got. We—"

Another missile shattered rock a few yards away. The ground shook.

More missiles struck nearby during the next few minutes, and sporadic cannon fire fractured the rock in a wide area along the river bank. There seemed to be a desperate, all-out quality to the fruitless attacks.

But the missiles stopped coming after six had been fired, and the cannon fire stopped, too. John guessed the pilots were out of missiles and probably very close to having exhausted their cannon feeds.

Barr said weakly, "I'm cold. I'm still bleeding."

John had nothing to say. There was very little hope left. He heard one helicopter fly away, but the other stayed. It hovered above the river, and its pilot watched . . . waited. . . .

John expected that the next move would involve the other chopper's landing some soldiers as close as possible, and a search—rock by rock—would begin.

Then from above, higher up on the shattered mountainside, came the thudding of a machine gun.

John squirmed out of the crevice and looked up at the hovering chopper.

The helicopter veered away abruptly, with a roar of its

engine. It climbed, turned, and hovered near the far shore, out of range.

John could imagine its radio reports. Who had been shooting at it? A Swiss army patrol?

John's eyes searched the mountainside for a clue.

A familiar voice shouted, "John Norris! You are down there?"

John yelled, "Yes! What are you doing up there, Lauter?"

"Protecting my second payment, I hope. President Barr is with you?"

"Yes! But he can't walk. I need help!"

"Coming down!"

Hans Lauter and two men came into view and began carefully working their way down. John didn't recognize the other two. One of them carried what appeared to be the wrecked van's turret gun. The other supported a heavy backpack. Lauter, too, moved carefully due to a heavy pack.

John crawled back to President Barr. "There's a chance, Bill. Hans Lauter has found us."

Barr whispered, "My legs are cold."

The helicopter stayed out of range, observing.

Lauter scrambled and slid down the last few yards to the boulder-strewn river's edge. His wire-rimmed glasses were askew, he was unshaven, and his clothes were dirty. But his brown eyes gleamed through his weariness, and he smiled. He said, in quick explanation, "These men are Swiss survivors. I hired them last night when I took refuge in their cabin. We crossed over on a portable boat they have, and we stripped the van. I got the radio out, too."

"How did you first get across to this side?" John asked.

"The bridge at Sackingen. I ran across before the bitch Stoneman placed a van there. I've been following her transmissions for hours. Those helicopter pilots gossip a lot, you know? I knew you'd gotten away with Barr. How is he?'' Lauter squatted and looked into the crevice at President Barr, who appeared unconscious again.

John told what had been done for Barr, but that now the president was undoubtedly bleeding to death.

Lauter gritted his teeth. ''Verdamnt!'' He looked at the hovering chopper half a mile away. ''The other one will be back soon, with more rockets. We must move him up to the car.''

One of the silent Swiss climbed up to where their car was hidden and returned with the canvas rear seat.

They tied Barr to the seat. His legs dangled off the end.

On the way up, as all four men carefully maneuvered the groaning, semi-conscious Barr up the rocky slope, Lauter asked, ''What has happened to Greta?''

''I don't know. I didn't have time last night to hunt for her. I don't know where she was kept.''

''Well . . . she will survive. She has beauty and a mind. Perhaps I will seek her, later.''

The road on the Swiss side of the Rhine was little more than a precarious dirt track that snaked along the side of the mountain into gorges, then climbed steeply, then nosed into muddy slides, across tumbling freshets. . . .

The car was an ancient gray Citroën with a noisy three-banger engine. It had been designed to be a ''people's'' car—cheap, reliable, ugly.

President Barr mumbled incoherently as he lay in the rear canvas seat. When putting him into the car, after reinstalling the seat, John and Hans noted that the underside of Barr's blanket wrappings was wet with blood.

One of the Swiss drove. Lauter sat beside him, his heavy pack on the floorboards between his legs. John and the Swiss, bearing a machine gun, rode the running boards.

The helicopter edged closer.

Lauter said, "There's a small village on the Swiss side of the Sackingen bridge, called Stein. A much better road leads from there to Basel."

"Quiet!" John said. Over the straining, coughing, gasping Citroën engine, they heard the van's radio, which was tied to the shelf beside the minimal dashboard. It had been wired to the car's electrical system.

The radio had been on all the time, hissing white noise. Now its small speaker cleared with a squelching peak of static and a man spoke over the drumming of an engine. *"S-1 to S-2. They're in a gray car. Coming into view from a draw."*

Erica Stoneman's voice blared, *"S-1, attack them! Attack them!"*

"I'm low on ammunition. Fifty rounds left."

"I don't care! Use it! I'm sending S-2 to help."

The Citroën passed between the mountainside and a bulky outcropping of striated granite. The Swiss driver slowed and stopped. "We are protected here," he said in English.

John instantly knew the man's thinking. He said, "We can't wait for them to run low on fuel. We have to get President Barr to a hospital. He needs a blood transfusion."

Lauter nodded. "Go ahead! Stein is only one kilometer away!"

The Swiss with the machine gun said in a low, dark voice, "It will cost more gold, the risk."

Lauter showed exasperation. "All right! Ten more krugerands."

"Twenty."

"Yes, twenty! Go!"

The driver revved the rackety engine and plunged the old car into a stretch of naked, rutted track on crushed rock. A sheer face of granite reared a foot from the left side of the car. A fall of loose, shattered rock nibbled and teased the car's right side tires.

The Swiss gunman had to hug the car to avoid being brushed off by the rock wall. John seemed to hang on a runningboard poised over nothingness. President Barr, lying in the rear seat, groaned weakly from the jolting and jouncing.

They were spotted by the waiting helicopter. The pilot radioed, *"They're bloody naked now. I'm going in."* He swooped low, gathering speed as he arrowed toward the crawling car outlined against the smooth granite wall. The sound of his cannon echoed in the river gorge. *Pum-pum-pum-pum-pum-pum . . .*

Erica paused before climbing out of the big helicopter which had carried her, Greta, and five of her soldiers to a charred field beside the bridge across the Rhine at Stein. She had changed her mind after learning that Norris and Barr had gotten help after landing on the Swiss side.

On the bridge sat the van she had dispatched the day before to prevent Lauter from crossing into Switzerland. Its three-man crew was standing at the railing, watching upriver. They could see the helicopter swooping over the river as it attacked the car on the Swiss side.

She unclipped her packset from her belt and broadcast, "You men on the bridge! Get in that van and—"

The men didn't move.

She checked the packset. The battery monitor registered in the red. She viciously threw away the walkie-talkie and went back into the helicopter cockpit and told the copilot to move his ass. She used the helicopter radio. "The van on the bridge! This is Erica Stoneman! I can see you! Go to your radio!"

One of the soldiers scrambled into the van. He replied, *"Yes, Mrs. Stoneman."*

"Drive over here into Stein and block the road that leads to Basel."

"Will do. Out."

Then S-1 reported: *"The bastards still have belts for that heavy machine gun. Don't dare get too close. Couldn't hit them on my first run. Down to twenty rounds."*

Erica was infuriated. "You damn coward! You've got a cannon! A million more in gold if you wipe out that car!"

"They're around the curve now, into boulders again. I won't be able to get a clear shot."

Erica almost screamed her frustration. Why wouldn't these stupid men do as she ordered?

She climbed down out of the helicopter and gestured to the five soldiers who had left the chopper a minute before. They were led by a Corporal Burns. "Get into the village and stop that damned car! It's almost here!"

As the men trotted off toward the cluster of burned houses a hundred yards away, Erica called Greta to her. "Did Lauter have any men in Switzerland? Any friends who would help him?"

Greta shook her head. "I do not think so. We were very few. All he had left were the gold coins you paid him for your visit with the President Barr."

Erica gnawed a knuckle. Yes, of course. Lauter must have gotten across the bridge before the van arrived to cut him off, or he had sneaked past the van in the snowstorm. Naturally, her well-paid men had stayed in the van to keep warm! And Lauter must have paid a couple of the survivors in or near Stein to help him. Somehow he had known Norris and Barr had escaped.

The son of a bitch had somehow crossed back to the German side and promised his—his mercenaries—they could keep everything taken from the van—the turret machine gun, the ammunition, the emergency food stores, and— She asked Greta, "Was the van radio still working when we captured you?"

Greta said, "I think so."

Erica slapped Greta hard, rocking her off balance. "You bitch! Why didn't you say so before? You heard they have a machine gun. They just happened to be following the rowboat after my helicopter spotted it and reported its location on the river! He's got that radio!"

Erica climbed back into the big helicopter and ordered the copilot out of his seat again. She snatched up the radio microphone. "Hans Lauter! Can you hear me?"

CHAPTER 32

THE SWISS GUNMAN WHO HAD BEEN FIRING THE HEAVY, awkward machine gun wasn't hit by a cannon shell as the chopper made its attack, but by deadly shards of splintered granite. His hand was severely gashed and he fell back against the rock wall and was brushed away from the side of the Citroën. The machine gun clattered off the roof.

The old car had been smashed by broken granite ripped by the cannon shells that burst pot-sized craters in the dense stone.

John had ducked low, clinging to the car's door post, unable to do anything but hope the pilot was too nervous and scared to hang in for the two or three seconds of straight-on flight necessary to aim true. The Swiss gunner had fed a belt of tracer ammo into his gun and was expertly firing into the helicopter's cabin. The pilot had seen those deadly bright streaks arcing toward him and had peeled away too soon. He wanted to live long enough to spend the millions he was making. Look what

244

had happened to Cyril yesterday! To hell with dying for Mrs. Stoneman!

The Swiss driver wanted to stop and help his friend. The radio blared with the exchange between Erica and the attacking helicopter pilot.

Hans Lauter pressed a pistol into the right side of the driver. "You will keep going! We must not stop!"

The man's lips tightened. He kept the old car crawling through the rough track along the side of the mountain. They had negotiated the naked curve along the face of the granite wall and were now in a warren of huge, jagged boulders.

Somewhere in the sky, the chopper buzzed in frustration.

John kept his ear cocked for the radio transmissions. He heard Erica order the van on the Sackingen bridge to proceed into Stein to block the road to Basel.

Now he and Lauter heard Erica broadcast angrily, *"Hans Lauter! Can you hear me?"*

They emerged from the boulder area and entered a burned forest of stark, blackened trees. Stein was only a few hundred yards ahead. They could see some of the gutted houses. A firestorm had swept south after roaring through the Black Forest, then consumed Sackingen, leaped the Rhine, and seared the Stein area before raging on into the Alps.

Lauter pulled the radio's mike from its slot and pressed the transmit button. He shouted over the coughing, straining racket of the engine, "I hear you, bitch!"

"Give me Norris and Barr, and I'll let you live."

"You lie! Please do not insult me with lies!" Lauter shouted. "Do not be concerned with us. We will simply disappear into the mountains. You will never see us again."

John listened, but was opening the backseat door from his precarious perch on the right-side runningboard. He slipped in and knelt on the floor to check on President Barr, whose groans were becoming much weaker.

The car continued to bounce and jolt over rocks and fallen limbs. Only the fact that the rear seat was a canvas trough kept the president from being thrown to the floor.

John braced him as well as he could. Blood had stained the canvas, as well as the blankets enfolding Barr.

Erica broadcast, "*I have your woman, Lauter. I have Greta. If you want her back, give me Norris and Barr!*"

Lauter contemptuously slammed the mike into its slot without answering.

John said, "We'd better be ready for an ambush."

"*Lauter!*"

Lauter addressed the Swiss driver, "Is there any way for us around Stein? Any way to get to the Basel road without going through Stein?"

"No. There is only a road to Frick and on to Zurich from there. It is from the bridge."

The Citroën slid down a short slope and out of a thick tangle of blackened, limbless trees, into full view of a roofless stone cottage.

"*You're all dead men!*"

John asked the driver, "Are there any boats we could use?"

The Swiss stopped the car. The cottage ahead was on the fringe of the village and was a good place for an ambush. The gaping stone windows appeared ominous. He answered John as he examined the road ahead and the cottage. "No, no boats. They all burned or were taken by the people still alive to help those only partly . . . partly roasted . . . to Basel. There is no doctor in Stein. The survivors in Sackingen would not let us cross the bridge." He studied the cottage, scowling. "Then the fire came. . . ."

Lauter said, "Go ahead."

"I think we should leave the car here. We can climb into the burned forest and skirt the village."

"President Barr cannot walk. Even carrying him would be too much for him." Lauter poked the driver with his gun. "Forward at top speed. It is his only hope."

The Swiss became grim.

John glanced at President Barr as the driver put the car in gear and revved for a lunge forward. Barr's bearded, sweaty face was shockingly pale. Drained. But he still breathed.

The radio blared again as Erica ordered the airborne, cannon-armed helicopter to land beside her larger copter in the black-stubbled field on the Swiss side of the bridge.

John noted that the car's gas gauge showed nearly empty. He doubted they could make it to Basel even if they had a free run. He raised his voice as the car gathered speed. "If we want to have any chance at saving Barr, we'll have to take the van that's blocking the Basel road."

Hans twisted around to look at him. "What do we have? I have a pistol. You have a pistol."

No firing came from the cottage. They passed it and entered a paved lane bracketed by burned houses. Ahead, a larger street showed a gutted, concrete-walled store which had collapsed in on itself. The street wall still stood, and boasted a wide, fancy, doorless entrance.

John saw the helicopter that had attacked them earlier sinking to a landing farther to the right, near the river. A charred ruin blocked further view.

The radio blared, *"Webster, where the hell are you? What's keeping you?"*

After a few seconds, Webster radioed, *"We're having trouble getting the helicopter far enough into the river to cover it."*

"Hurry it up! I need you! Send some men forward to me, now! I'm in Stein, beside the bridge ramp."

"Will do. But I must report on another matter. I was not able to find all the survivors in Waldshut who—"

"All right! Get some men to me!"

Lauter said to John, "The only way we—"

Stutterings of rifle fire ripped at them from the cottage behind them and from the left-side shell of a house. Slugs whipped and whined by the fast-moving old car. Its sides of heavy-gauge steel dented inward from occasional hits.

John ducked below the window line, as did Lauter. The Swiss driver cursed and steered for the gaping doorway in the fallen building ahead. There was no other escape.

The car crunched through the opening and jounced up heavily against fallen rubble. It tilted perilously to the left and stalled.

John threw the rear door open and roughly pulled President Barr out of the teetering car. Lauter and the driver also scrambled out. Lauter salvaged his heavy pack.

Barr whimpered as he was manhandled and carried to a kind of fortress among the fallen inner walls to the rear of the building.

The Swiss kept on going. Lauter called, "Stop! Coward!"

The man looked back, white-faced. "I have no gun. I have no part of your fight." He crawled between two blocks of concrete and was gone.

Lauter looked at Barr, and then at John. "I should follow him."

John cocked his .45 and watched the tumbled perimeter of the building. A flash of movement caught his eye. He said, "There's one chance. We fight our way to Erica and take one of her helicopters." He watched a soldier's head rise slowly from behind a ragged pile of brick. Erica's mercenaries didn't wear helmets. John shot the man almost precisely between the eyes.

A spray of rifle slugs ricocheted from their broken concrete fortress. It came from behind the still-wobbling Citroën, only about thirty feet away.

Lauter smiled sourly. He pulled a silver flask from the rear pocket of his jeans and unscrewed the cap. "That will be difficult." He took a swig of schnapps and passed the flask to John. "Do you fly them?"

John nodded and put the flask to President Barr's slack mouth and poured in some liquor. "Bill! Drink this!" he insisted.

Barr coughed and swallowed convulsively several times. His eyes flickered open. He swallowed more. He stirred. He whispered, "I'm dead. I hurt like hell." He reached for the flask.

John said, "I'm going to get one of those assault rifles." The man he had just shot should have had one. "Lauter, get over there and draw some fire."

Lauter looked at him, then obeyed. He crawled out of the small, accidentally formed bunker, through the gap used by the Swiss.

A moment later, he fired three times at the car.

John peered through a narrow crevice in the wall of broken concrete, his automatic ready. When the mercenaries exposed themselves to fire at Lauter's position, the .45 leaped three times in John's big, strong hand, and two men died.

One bullet tore through a blond youth's throat, causing him to flail, strangling, away from the car's dented hood.

The other, older man took a heavy slug in the shoulder and was spun around, showing for a second the gaping hole in his back where the flattened slug had exited. He fell away from the protection of the car's bulging, odd-shaped trunk and in that split second John's third shot shattered his chest and pulped his heart.

Someone shouted, "They got Burns!"

Through a ringing in his ears, John heard frantic movement away from the car. He caught a glimpse of two mercenaries fleeing through the ornate doorway. His fourth shot chipped plaster an inch from one man's head.

Lauter fired at them, but missed. He crawled back into the rough fortress. His brown eyes, behind dusty, wire-rimmed glasses, showed admiration. You are very good with that."

President Barr had emptied the flask. He threw it away. He seemed to have been partially revitalized by the liquor. He said, "John, pull me up. I want to sit up."

John said, "Bill, I'm going to pick you up now and carry you toward Erica's position about a hundred yards away. We're going to try to take one of her helicopters. We could have you in Basel in minutes."

Barr shook his head. "Bullshit. I wouldn't make it. You're not carrying me anywhere. I'm not going through that torture again. I'm in agony just lying here." He wiped his sweaty face with part of a blanket. "I've bled so much. . . . John, pull me up into a sitting position. I have to write something. Get me a piece of paper . . . a pen."

John looked to Lauter, who nodded and rummaged around in his backpack.

John eased President Barr into a position so that his back was braced against a tilted slab of sooty concrete. Barr showed a grimace of pain, but didn't cry out. The layered woolen blankets enclosing his torso and legs were wet with blood.

Barr accepted the black ball-point pen and legal-sized sheet of paper handed to him. The paper was printed on one side; it was a copy of Swiss banking laws provided to large depositors. He smiled wanly when he saw it, and whispered, "Irony."

John handed him a small, thin sheet of slightly warped, dirty metal—part of a sign—to use as a writing support.

John watched Barr write slowly and carefully, and felt desperately helpless. He took the opportunity to climb out of the rough fort and check the bodies of the mercenaries.

The blond youth still twitched, but was unconscious. Blood poured from his throat. He would be dead in a minute or less. John took the youth's AR-22 and pack of 50-shot clips. He moved on and took the assault rifle of the older man whose uniform indicated he had been a corporal.

When he returned to the fort, John handed Lauter one of the rifles and a pack of ammunition. Lauter nodded his thanks. He was watching President Barr.

The president was failing. The shot of energy and lucidity provided by the flask of liquor was wearing off. He labored to complete each word.

John said, "Bill, I could write for you, and—"

Barr shook his head. He whispered, "This is my last will and testament. I'll write it . . . and . . . sign . . . it."

John and Hans waited in anguished silence as Barr scribbled slowly, painfully. He squinted and blinked. His breathing became faster and more shallow. He was panting when he finally, with agonizing slowness, signed his name.

Barr let the pen slip from trembling fingers. He whispered, "I can't . . . see . . . anymore." He seemed to settle into the concrete, to shrink subtly, to diminish, as his life ebbed.

He sought John with vague eyes. "John . . . try to get my body back. I don't want . . . Erica . . . to . . ."

His breathing faded. He smiled. His voice was so faint John could barely hear it. "Amazing . . . the . . . pain . . . is . . . gone. . . ."

And then President William T. Barr's breathing stopped and he stared at John with dead eyes.

John looked away.

Hans Lauter sighed.

John took President Barr's last testament and read it.

I, William Terrence Barr, of sound mind, make this last will and testament of my own free will. I give all my worldly possessions to my daughter, Marcia. I testify that I was mortally wounded by order of Erica Stoneman.
William Terrence Barr

John read it aloud to Lauter.

Lauter nodded. He asked, "Do you think anyone will believe that?"

John shrugged. "What are you going to do now?"

Lauter pulled on his backpack, still heavy with gold coins. "I'm going to disappear. I have one billion dollars deposited in Zurich. I have this money. I'll survive." He smiled. "I may even reconstruct the New German People's Alliance." He picked up the AR-22 and stood up. "What will you do now?"

John said sarcastically, "You really care about people, don't you?"

"Yes, I am idealistic."

"But you won't risk anything for Greta."

"No. She was never that important to me."

John folded Barr's will and testament and slipped it into a shirt pocket. "I've got a few minutes before Erica's reinforcements arrive," he said. He drew one of the dark woolen blankets over President Barr's head. He gently hoisted the body onto his left shoulder and stood up, the AR-22 in his right hand.

"I'm going to try for one of her choppers," John said. He turned away, then looked back to Lauter. His gray-green eyes were like ice. "And if I have a chance, I'm going to kill her."

CHAPTER 33

JOHN PLACED BARR'S WRAPPED BODY IN A CLUSTER OF dead, sticklike bushes near the smaller of the two helicopters in the field near the Sackingen bridge. The charcoal-gray woolen blankets matched the color of the burned ground. From a few yards away, the bundle was virtually invisible.

He had approached the large field carefully, keeping the empty, smaller helicopter between himself and the more distant, larger chopper, which was a locus of activity.

A copse of charred trees stood thick and stark, fifty yards farther to the right. To the left, the long ramp to the bridge rose from the village.

The big helicopter was not anchored and showed a man in the pilot's seat. The passenger door gaped open. On the ground beside the larger machine, Erica Stoneman stood talking to three of her soldiers. She wore a blue jumpsuit, a gun holstered at her right hip. Her long blond hair moved in the fairly stiff breeze.

Greta stood apart, near the tail rotor, staring at the black-stubbled ground. Her hands were not bound.

John considered spraying the group with his AR-22, but from this angle, Greta would be in extreme danger. He wanted to move closer. He was still wearing the uniform he had taken from a dead mercenary the night before.

John didn't see a mercenary rise from a squatting position in the thick cluster of trees on the right. The man pulled up his pants and froze when he saw John creeping toward the empty, tied-down helicopter.

John reached the chopper seconds later and stepped up in a foothold to peer into the cabin. He studied the instrument panels. The ignition key wasn't slotted. He hadn't expected it to be. The door was locked, as well.

The pilot of the bigger helicopter keyed the starter of his engine. The machine whined, coughed, and snarled into a smooth roar of power. The vanes began swishing around.

John saw Erica climb into the helicopter and settle into the copilot's seat. But neither Greta nor the three soldiers standing close to the copter moved. Erica was using the radio, but she might be about ready to leave.

John was easing back to the ground when he heard a footfall close behind him in spite of the engine noise from the other helicopter. He had begun a twisting dive to bring his gun into play, when a steel rifle stock cracked the right side of his head.

In the split-second explosion of pain and disorientation before warping darkness claimed his mind, John instinctively tore the mercenary's guts to shreds with a burst from his AR-22.

John's awareness swam through sickening pain to the light of day. His head felt split open. He was lying on the burnt ground, his face in the black dust and charcoal stubble. His hands had been tied behind him very professionally with strong, smooth twine. A part of his mind guessed: nylon.

He stirred slightly and realized a loop of the twine was around his neck and linked to his bound wrists. It would be impossible for him to slide his hands under his rump and forward under his feet. Erica wasn't risking that again.

Erica spoke from above him. "Is he awake already? Are you awake, Norris? You bastard! Open your eyes and look at me!"

He slitted his eyes enough to see her standing a few feet away, legs apart, hands on hips. Beside her, a mercenary soldier glared down at him, too. Immediately behind them loomed the big helicopter, engine idling, vanes turning slowly.

John moved his head slightly and groaned at the sudden pain. He saw Greta staring hopelessly at him.

He rolled slowly and saw another soldier, on his other side, pointing an AR-22 down at him.

Erica raged, "You're only alive because Smythe didn't want to damage the helicopter if he used his rifle. But you got him, didn't you?"

John felt blood trickling down past his ear to his neck, and onto the ground. The right side of his head felt cracked, and paroxysms of fiery pain exploded in his temple.

Erica shouted, "Do you know how many of my men you've killed? Where are Barr and Lauter?"

John moved again and grimaced from the blinding head pain. Nevertheless, he struggled to a kneeling position. The left side of his face and most of his uniform were smudged black, and the right side dripped blood. He had apparently been dragged fifty yards or so to this spot.

Erica demanded, "Did you hear me? Where is Barr?"

John managed to say, "I don't know." The question told him she hadn't had him searched. Bill Barr's will and testament would have told her the president was dead.

John made a supreme effort and lurched to his feet.

Erica backed away a few steps, as did the soldier at her side. They were afraid of him, even though he was wounded and bound. A shoulder patch indicated the soldier was the pilot of the other, smaller helicopter.

Erica drew her pistol. "You don't know! Is Lauter—does he have another car?"

Greta made a small movement to attract John's attention. John hung his head to mask a glance at her. She flashed a paring knife at her side, then covered it with her hand.

She had stolen it from the kitchen van earlier in the morning.

The helicopter pilot called out, "Mrs. Stoneman, Commander Webster has a report for you."

Erica glanced at John, who was swaying as if about to fall. She holstered her pistol and said to the soldier with the AR-22, "Watch him!" She climbed into the helicopter.

The other pilot stood aside. He unsnapped the flap of his holster uneasily. He fingered the butt of his sidearm.

John let himself sway off balance. He lurched forward and staggered three paces to the side of the helicopter, near Greta. His dirty, bloody head hit the laminated armor-skin and he screamed through his teeth. He turned so his tied wrists were facing Greta. An instant after his scream, she put a bracing right hand on his arm—and at the same time pressed the knife into his hands with her left.

The guard said angrily, "Get the bloody hell away from him!"

Greta backed away. "I was only—"

John sank to his knees, head low, his back angled against the helicopter, hiding his hands from the guard and from the nervous pilot.

Greta had sense enough to create a diversion while

John used the small knife awkwardly to cut the nylon twine. She said to the guard while walking toward him, diverting his attention, "I don't care what happens to that man! That American pig!" She cleverly circled behind the guard to obviously not interfere with his line of fire if he had to shoot at Norris. Actually, by continuing to talk, she caused his head to turn. "I want to find a man who will take care of me and love me."

She headed for the helicopter pilot, smiling. "I think Norris has done you both a favor by killing so many of the other soldiers. Now you'll be getting a far bigger share."

She stopped a few feet from the pilot. She toyed with the buttons of her shirt. She smoothed the material down over her firm, braless breasts, causing the nipples to become notable. Both men eyed her body.

John remained outwardly still, head down, but behind his back he sawed away at the high-test twine. Finally his wrists came free and the loop around his neck went slack. He didn't move. He waited to see what opportunity Greta might create. His vision blurred and his head pulsed with agony. Yet, in spite of that, he also listened to hear what Erica was saying inside the helicopter. He heard her voice rise above the engine and vane noise. "They're in Waldshut now?"

Greta had unbuttoned the top three buttons of her shirt. She hip-swayed close to the pilot. "Do you want a good, hot woman to take care of you?" She pressed against him. He automatically put an arm around her and grinned cynically at the guard who was supposed to be watching John.

Erica appeared in the helicopter doorway. "What the hell is going on here?" She glared at her other pilot and Greta. She drew her pistol. She glanced down and saw that John's hands were free.

Greta said loudly, "An immoral decision, hündin! The lesser of two evils!" She snatched the pilot's gun from his opened holster. It was a French 7.63mm automatic he had acquired in Paris. She knew the gun and knew how to use it.

Greta spun away from the astonished man. In a split second, she had released the safety and cocked the gun. She shot three times at the soldier with the AR-22.

He went down screaming, clawing at his groin. His rifle clattered a few feet toward John.

White-faced, terrified, Erica began panic shooting at Greta. Had Greta remained in one place, she would have lived. Erica was emptying her .38, shooting wildly. But Greta dodged to the left, further away from the pilot, who was only now beginning to dive to his right.

A slug clipped a chunk of flesh on the inside of Greta's upper left arm, almost in the armpit. Half an inch higher, half an inch lower . . . but this small gobbet of muscle contained the major artery feeding the arm.

Greta fell and rolled, unaware of her wound. She came up on one knee and aimed at Erica. Her armpit began jetting hot red blood in her shirt sleeve.

Erica howled with terror and dodged back into the helicopter. She screamed to the pilot, "Get up! Take it up!" She scrambled to keep low and slid the door shut. "Take off! Take off!"

Greta had squeezed off two shots at the small, armored glass windows of the helicopter before she became aware of the pain in her armpit and the pulsing fountain of blood. She lifted her arm and stared stupidly at the flow of blood in her soaked sleeve.

The instant Greta grabbed the pilot's gun, John staggered to his feet and reeled toward the guard with the AR-22. But the abrupt movement caused a terrible dizziness and nausea, and John went down, the paring knife still clutched in his right hand.

The swirling, sickening vertigo claimed him for endless, precious seconds. He heard shooting, screaming, roaring. . . . When his vision cleared, he saw Greta sitting on her heels watching blood spurt down her side, soaking her shirt and the left side of her jeans. The automatic lay loose in her blood-wet left hand, on the ground.

The guard lay writhing in pain a few feet away. The helicopter was throttling up, the vanes speeding. The other pilot was getting up from the black ground, staring at the tableau. The AR-22 lay only four feet from John's outstretched arms.

The pilot yelled and ran to prevent John from getting the assault rifle.

John gathered himself forever and lunged for the gun. The disorienting giddiness took him again, but he had a hand on the weapon. The pilot kicked the rifle from John's closing fingers.

John instinctively grabbed one of the man's ankles, bringing him down heavily. Through swimming, warping vision, through blinding pain, John clung and stabbed with the paring knife.

The pilot grunted with pain and clubbed John's bloody head with a fist.

John almost passed out. Despite great hammer blows of excruciating agony, he could only cling and stab, again and again.

Sobbing for breath, almost senseless, John gradually realized the man wasn't struggling or hitting anymore. John lay gasping, letting some strength accumulate. His vision stopped spinning and he was able to see that he had mortally wounded the pilot. Blood welled from dozens of stab wounds.

The big helicopter lifted. For a moment the air was a maelstrom of buffeting, black-dusted, choking wind. Then, as the chopper swept away in a climbing turn, John saw Erica staring down at what she had left, her face clenched with hate.

Then the helicopter was gone, over the bridge, heading north and west into Germany.

John made it up to his hands and knees. He had to worry about that three-man van Erica had positioned to block the road to Basel. Those men might be ordered to make sure he and Greta were dead, and to pick up the pilot and the soldiers' bodies in Stein and here, and to blow up, hide, or possibly fly out the smaller helicopter, which still sat fifty yards away.

John slowly hung the AR-22 on his back, and took spare magazines from the groin-shot guard. The man wasn't yet dead, nor was the stabbed pilot. Both men twitched and groaned and watched him with fading eyes.

John searched the pilot's uniform and found the door and ignition keys to the smaller chopper. Only then did he go on hands and knees to Greta.

She had toppled forward and to her right. Blood still flowed from her armpit, but in a tiny, pulsing trickle. She barely breathed.

John couldn't tell if she was conscious. Her eyes were closed. He said, "Thank you."

Her eyelids flickered open and her green eyes saw him. For a few seconds she did not respond, then her mouth twitched and she whispered, "It . . . was . . . not . . . worth . . . it."

He said, "It rarely is." He kissed her.

Greta died two minutes later.

During those minutes of silence and sadness, John's strength returned and his dizziness abated. His head continued to be a throbbing agony, but most of his bleeding stopped.

He was able to carry President Barr's body to the remaining helicopter. There was room for Greta's body, too. He strapped them in.

As he started the engine, he saw three turreted vans speeding toward him across the bridge. And above—the big helicopter was coming back.

John's gaze flicked across his instrument panel. Enough

fuel for about ten minutes of flying. Twenty rounds left in the nose cannon's magazine.

His machine trembled as the vanes moved and power surged. He eased the throttle forward.

Bullets tracked past his chopper in the burnt field, kicking up spurts of black dust. The van that had been blocking the road to Basel had just turned into view from Stein's main street. The turret gun was hammering at him.

John lifted off the ground, spun his machine, and quickly compensated for drift. His fingers switched on the cannon and tightened on the firing button. The chopper shuddered as he sent a short burst of shells slamming into the approaching van.

The van seemed to have a heart attack. It jerked and veered wildly to the left. It smashed head-on into a thick, charred tree trunk, leaped, turned, and crunched onto a fire bubbled-and-cooled blacktop parking lot. It skidded into cars long since burned, and burst into orange flames.

Even as the van was hit, John lifted higher and swooped around to approach the bridge. Through a haze of thudding head pain he flew low, keeping the other helicopter in view. He had to know when a missile was launched. He pushed his throttle fully forward.

A flare and curving rocket track told him the time was now.

John felt a new wave of dizziness overwhelming his sight and balance. But he had to risk flying alongside the steel bridge.

The missile flashed toward him.

Fighting nausea and vertigo, John dove his chopper below the bridge-ramp level and arrowed for the water.

Because of its speed, the turn was too sharp for the missile. Suddenly its target—the smaller chopper's exhaust—was gone behind concrete and steel. The missile exploded against a girder and sent shrapnel whizzing down onto the road. The approaching trio of vans braked and skidded.

John gritted his teeth from sickening pain. His disorientation increased. The first bridge pylon rushed toward him. The Rhine sparkled in the sunshine a few feet below his helicopter's runners. The road deck slid over his chopper's clawing vanes.

He banked and turned sharply left. The pylon disappeared to his right. He flashed into bright sunlight from under the bridge and climbed in a swooping vertical lift that brought the big attacking helicopter into his sight.

His instincts and reflexes acted to trigger all the cannon shells remaining in the magazine. The copter shook from the recoil. John had a warped, rippled glimpse of three ragged holes blossoming in the other helicopter's belly.

Then his own chopper hung, shaking, in a precarious, deadly stall, barely three hundred feet above the river.

It fell away and plummeted toward the dark, rushing water.

Next to John, President Barr's dead body flopped forward against its straps and an arm seemed to reach for the throttle.

John couldn't keep his stomach under control. He spewed vomit over sections of the instrument panel. He closed his eyes to keep the world from spinning out of control. Was he spinning? Had he lost his tail rotor?

He managed to right the copter, but it still sank, unable to overcome its inertia. The engine roared, shaking the frame violently. He brought the vanes to maximum pitch.

For a heart-stopping moment, the helicopter bellied down into the water . . . and then slowly lifted free.

John opened his eyes and scanned the skies through swimming vision. The other helicopter was nowhere in sight. He climbed and turned, seeking, and finding a huge orange fireball on the mountain fringe of Stein. The van he had shelled was still burning, as well.

John spat to clear his mouth of ugly-tasting vomit. He remembered something and flipped on the radio. He should have had it on from the beginning!

Erica Stoneman's strident voice pierced his mind. *"—you want? Who is it? Norris? It has to be you! Can't you be killed? Damn you! I'll pay you anything! A billion dollars! Norris? Answer me!"*

He'd hoped she'd still been in the other helicopter. But she must have joined Webster on the ground and sent back the big chopper to finish everyone in the field. The vans had been ordered to make sure.

John didn't reply to her radioed pleas. He remembered her saying, back at the field when she was on the radio to Webster, "They're in Waldshut now?" There had been panic and terror in her voice. Who were "they"?

Erica's voice blared, *"Do you have Barr? Who is in that helicopter!"*

John felt in his shirt pocket. He still had President Barr's last will and testament. He lowered his head as more nauseating waves of pain made him almost lose consciousness. The chopper lurched and dove.

He regained precarious control and turned toward Waldshut, upriver. He thought he could make it. There should be enough fuel. He throttled back to cruising speed.

He was sure an American search force was now in Waldshut. When he landed with President Barr's corpse and testament . . .

John Norris managed a smile. He was resigned to living in very interesting times.